Not James

Torion Oey

For Merlin and Piper.

Chapter 1: **Not**

I awake to the screaming of men. My grogginess fades as I realize the shouts are right in my ears, and the same people are holding me up. They are dragging me somewhere, my feet scraping uselessly on the stone floor. Bits of memory fall into place in my mind: a warm, dimly lit room, the smell of alcohol, and people screaming. So much screaming.

"Wake the hell up, you good-for-nothing drunk!"

My eyes flutter, then clear as the people on either side of me continue to drag me along. Huh. That doesn't sound right. I shake my head and focus on the jagged stone pavement slowly passing under me. My head is throbbing, but it couldn't be from alcohol. I never drank any of that stuff in my life. And their hands, they're painfully digging into the skin of my arms and shoulders...

"HEY!"

The man's voice resounds in my ear, pulling me out of my stupor enough for my vision to sharpen. His sudden shout doesn't help clear my head, though. I feel the spray of his saliva on my neck. I try unsuccessfully to pull my arms out of my captors' tight grip while tilting my head to get a look at them.

"About time. We'll let the guards handle you from here," the man who spat on me says. I manage to get a look at his bearded, roundish, and generally ugly face; his oversized mouth frowns with the effort of heaving me, and his nostrils flare under a semi-bent nose.

Just as I register his face, I'm thrown onto the floor and there's the sound of metal clanging behind me. Adrenaline pumps through me as I get up just as fast, all remnants of my grogginess vanishing. I twirl to see that I'm in a cage. The two men smirk and walk away without another word. On the bearded man's back is a sword. My sword. "Hey, that's mine!" I shout, only to hear him belt out a gruff laugh as he exits the hall through a door. So far I haven't been recognized, but if the guards come in...

Grimacing not in pain but anger, I close my eyes, picture his face in my mind, and memorize it. Then I examine my prison. The long metal bars keeping me in are placed far enough apart for a small child to get through, but not a grown man. There's a little padlock that is looped through two holes: one on the cell door, one on the cell itself. It is rusted, but most likely won't be coming off with brute force. Beyond the cell bars is a single cobbled hall dividing lines of more cells on either side, an unlit sconce in each. At the far end is a prison registry, bindings closed, lying atop a sandpapered teak desk. I can barely make it out in the low light allowed by barred windows only some of the other cells have. It looks like they've taken me to a guardhouse. Not only that, one that can't afford magician fire or even electricity.

I let out a sigh of annoyance and reach into my pants pocket for some wire the pilferers hadn't, well, pilfered when the door at the end of the dingy prison hall clangs open. Blast. Two more men, these dressed in standard guard uniforms unlike the other two, walk toward me. I hold the wire behind my back and wait as they approach. For some reason they do that silly outthrust leg kick typical of the Royal Guard march every other step they take, even though there's no one here to witness them besides me. For crying out loud, they are in unison as well! I suppress another sigh as I wait. "Excuse me," I say when they're finally close enough that I don't have to shout, "but why am I in here?"

"You caused a scene at The Salted Lamb last night that upset several people," one of the guards says in a completely monotone voice.

"Huh," I mumble, fingering the wire behind my back as I recall what really happened. A grungy, dismal tavern scene. The unbearable smell of sweaty men playing at some gambling game. One of them—the bearded man who took my sword—rowdily nudging his friends and calling attention to my friend. And a rude comment on my friend's size. "Ohhh, I remember now. That bearded guy was making a ton of noise, so I told him he was smelly."

The same guard looks at me closely. I tilt my head down and to the side, hoping it's enough to obscure traces of resemblance to the king. "He told me you punched him in the face."

"Well, yes, but that was after he insulted my friend's appearance." I glance at the guard who is sharing a look with the other guard. "Hey, aren't you forgetting something? They punched me back, obviously," I say, bringing one of my hands out from behind my back and passing it lightly over a spot on my face that ached. "So that makes it even. Let me out."

"No," the guards say in unison.

"But that guy took my sword! You can't just let someone steal something because the victim did something wrong!"

"Isn't that ironic?" A deep woman's voice echoes from the other end of the hall. She ducks her head to clear the door. Silently shutting it behind her, she rises to her full height and casually walks toward us. The bottom of her face is dimly illuminated by the light filtering through the windows along the wall that would normally be at eye-level to any other man. Her build is bulkier than the bearded man's—or any given man's.

One guard gasps. "Is that... a Giant?"

Ignoring him, I call, "Oh, shut up, Idrid. I wouldn't be in here if I didn't care about your honor."

"You two know each other?" the other guard asks, finally turning and taking a step back toward my cage when he registers the half-Giantess. I debate reaching for him through the bars while he's distracted.

"Yes," Idrid says lazily, coming to a stop in front of the guards. She ignores them and watches me coolly. "I'm his mother."

The guards look her up and down, frowning, the first expression they've made thus far. I roll my eyes. "You're really big," the same guard states. Idrid's mocking eyes fill with rage, and the next second the two guards are lying unconscious on the floor.

My claps resound thinly along the jailhouse. "Impressive! You know, when someone says you're big it isn't always an insult." I pull the wire through the bars and wiggle them into the padlock.

"Yeah, whatever," she mumbles as I fiddle with the lock. "You didn't have to get in a fight in the first place."

"That was not actually my intention." I pause my lockpicking to undo the flap of one of three leather pouches I wear around my hip and flash Idrid its glimmering contents. "Not nearly enough to pay off Stalvan and return south, but it's something."

Idrid's eyes narrow. "I thought you said it was about my honor?"

"It was. It was an honorable theft. So, did you get my sword back?" I ask, trying to make conversation while I work. I feel resistance against both nubs of the wires and adjust their angle.

A quiet raking sound emits from the lock as the ridged end works its way deeper.

"No. The guy had a group of friends waiting for him outside and they left together."

"Do you know where they went?"

"You're not seriously thinking of confronting them again, are you?" Idrid folds her arms over her chest and glances down at the unconscious guards. "They could recognize you."

"Idrid, they stole my sword."

"So what?"

"It's mine."

She sighs. "They were talking loudly about going back to the same tavern, the idiots."

My hands slip and I let out a curse.

"We don't have time for this," Idrid says impatiently, and slams her fist into the lock. It crumples and the piece of the metal looping through the holes breaks off. She grabs the entire lock and rips it off the cage door. It swings open, and I walk out tentatively.

"Thanks." I stretch my arms and legs a bit, my head still filled with a dull pounding from the blow received the night before. "Do you mind if I go get it alone? It's kind of personal." I leave it unsaid that her size would attract more attention. "I promise not to get into any more trouble."

Idrid only shrugs, then steps aside.

"Meet me outside town, eastside." I pass her by, biting my bottom lip to stifle a smile and comment. Mommy. Ironic, considering the circumstances that brought us together. Orphaned, she'd been taken in by an acquaintance in the kingdom capital Telnas. The extra cost of food for harboring a growing Giant in addition to already ridiculous property taxes put him in a bind so I took her in. Well, out, actually, since I couldn't afford a place myself. But we each had our talents and could hold our own; me with swordplay and thievery, and her with brute strength and knowledge. Both of us were orphans without a place to belong, so we got along in more than one sense. Both spurned by our home country. Thinking back on it, she was 10 and I 15. Crazy how I've been traveling with her for half her life.

A quick turn back tells me Idrid is searching the guards for money. I taught her so well. No other guards are stationed inside the guardhouse, leaving me in the clear until the two guards wake up. I slip out the door at the end of the hall and look around. The Salted Lamb is at the edge of town, thankfully, giving me a lot of room to get in and get out without any more disruptions. I don't wait for Idrid and instead scurry off, taking the quickest way to the tavern from the jailhouse.

I do my best not to be seen. I skirt between buildings, using their shadows and alleyways to make my way. Weird how seeing the town in early daylight is so different than at night. We had only arrived yesterday and everything looked bigger, cleaner. Now it just looks like a dump. Dirty brown bags and rusted bottles that I hadn't noticed before litter the streets. Seemingly every other side alley I pass by is inhabited by unrecognizable old men sleeping on the kicked up dirt. Probably the origin of the foul smell from last night, though now all I can smell is my own sweat due to the scorching sun slowly rising in the east.

I turn the corner of a battered and frighteningly scorched brick building. My eyes lock onto the bearded man only just arriving outside the tavern with a group of friends. Sometimes I wish I was more careful. This is one of those times.

"Hey, you!" the bearded man shouts, pointing a bulky finger my way. "What're you doing here?"

"You have my sword, you buzzard." All his friends grimace and roll back their shoulders. "Gonna have one of your lackeys hit me while I'm not looking again? You're a brave soul."

The man waves at them dismissively, then reaches up and draws my sword. "Nah, I think I'll cleave ya in two!"

I bite back several curses as the big bad bearded man narrows the gap between us in several large strides. His charge loses momentum as recognition washes over his face, and his feet trail into a walk, then stop altogether within several feet of me.

"Wait a sec. You're— No, it can't be— You're King James?" His stuttering amuses me, only for a moment, then the incredible anger returns. Anger for being stolen from. More than that, anger for being recognized. I only just got back, and I happen to run into one of James's friends? I don't want guards hounding me.

"No, I'm Not James," I retort, springing from my position and deftly landing a swing of my right fist into his jaw. The blow rocks the man back, though it isn't enough to put him down. In slow motion I watch his awestruck face turn to stunned. Not one to stop and wait for his turn, I use the momentum I have while leaping to jump with one foot and spin, swinging the back of my left hand directly into his nose. Not the best spot to hit someone.

My hand throbs, though I continue my attack, dropping my hands to the ground and using them to prop myself up as I kick back with one of my feet into the bearded man's side. That finally causes him to buckle over, gasping for air, giving me the chance to entangle myself on top of him, yanking the sword strap off his back. Something snags it, and I realize the bearded guy's thick neck is preventing me from taking it off. "Let it go!" I snarl, dodging the man's wild swipes of my sword. He makes furious grunts and aims the sword directly at me.

Before he can take the stab, I flip my body over him and yank the sword strap toward me, which then unintentionally yanks the big guy closer to me. Taking advantage of his staggering, I kick one of the man's feet out from under him and he topples over. My sword leaves his grasp when he hits the ground with a big thud, a cloud of dirt erupting from under his body.

I bend down and pick up my sword and remove the strap. Angry shouts and curses are thrown at me by the bearded guy's friends. One with an overbite stomps toward me, readying a fist. My shoulder digs into his gut as I straighten up, causing him to stumble back and rattle a long, murky window of the tavern. I place my sword against the back of the bearded man's head who is still lying face-down. "Don't take my stuff," I tell them and jog away. The sounds of jeering accompany me until I round the corner of the town's final building. I take a quick glance behind me to make sure I'm not being followed. The scattered thatched, curving rooves are alight while the dirt-and-cobble streets are only starting to pack with early risers. Once satisfied that I'm not, I trudge up the low incline toward the top of a hill that stretches away from the town's outskirts. There Idrid waits.

"What took you so long?" Idrid asks at the top of the hill overlooking the town. I see that she's brought her belongings: a brown, baggy traveler's pouch befitting her size whose strap loops her torso from shoulder to waist. At its base I see the weighty outline of several thick books causing the fabric to protrude. Somewhere in there is another bag with survivalist essentials I'd bought for her, including a leather flask and matchsticks, though she somehow makes more use of her books.

I give her a look.

"Hey, I just want to be fun and quippy like you," she says. I can see the effort she puts into forcing the corners of her mouth upward in what she must think is a mischievous grin.

"Stop trying to be like me. Only I can do that."

"All right, fine."

We trudge away, both wanting to put as much distance as possible between ourselves and the town.

"Where are we going?" Idrid asks.

"No idea."

Silence.

"How did it get to be so late in the day?" I ask while shielding my eyes. It's still only midmorning, though the heat foretells a grueling day if we remain in direct sunlight.

"You were out of it for a while and I found it amusing. I don't think I've ever seen you inebriated."

I tut, annoyed. "That's the last time I try to defend you." What annoys me more is my memory of the night is getting clearer. I was not really inebriated nor was the blow to my head what knocked me unconscious, but I had been taken off guard by my own narcotic drug. The bearded guy had pushed me, displacing the liquid in my mug intended for someone else. Some spilled and got in my mouth. I curse my clumsiness and pat one of the brown pouches strung along the hip of my waist that holds my self-made ingredients.

"I don't need defending," she replies, unnoticing my gesture and furrowed brow. She isn't aware that I mix chemicals with alcohol, one of the many secrets I've kept to myself. She continues, saying, "We were also in there long into the early morning and you probably lost track of time."

"Taverns aren't open past midnight save for holidays."

"It just so happens today is one of the biannual solstices, which is why the sun is already so high," she explains. "Don't you know this?"

I shrug, keeping my eyes low to the ground. She doesn't need to know I'm uneducated.

"Can we go somewhere so that the sun won't shine directly in our eyes?"

I look up and am blinded, though not before my trained eye cements the image of the landscape. Ankle-high corn grass sprawls endlessly either way before low trees that get progressively clustered until forming a nigh impenetrable thicket. Immediately I avert my eyes back to the ground. "That's a good idea." Simultaneously we turn slightly to our left and continue walking, my heart quickening at the familiar sight of the long fields. I question the excitement of being back in the country where I was born, after so long spent in the deserts in the south. This place had done nothing for me. Wrong, it'd forced me to live a life of solitude from which I'd fled; the one time I returned I met Idrid, and, because of the kingdom's war on Giants, we had to leave again. Perhaps, I think hopefully, now it is a different time. Things will be better.

"Did you kill him?" Idrid interrupts my thoughts.

"No," I say, a little regretfully.

Idrid blows out a long whistle. "And he didn't think you were—?"

"He did, but I politely told him I wasn't." I frown at the thought of the man's relation to the king. Whatever the case, that's another town I'll have to steer clear of for a while.

"'Politely.' Pbth," she snorts out, her large arms swinging freely beside her as she walks. I appraise her, not for the first time, taking in her whole body. Her oak-colored hair falls around her flat face, blanketing her cheeks and shoulders. She must've grown a bit since the last time I've really looked at her, because when I go to look at her eyes I have to tilt my head up. She has been growing ever since we first met, at which point she was roughly the same height as me. Now she is the size of a mini Giantess, a solid few inches past my six feet. Her eyes narrow and cut to me, though she says nothing. Thankfully her tolerance of me has grown as well. If anyone else had been ogling her, she would've bashed their brains out.

"Have you ever… thought about… settling… down?" I ask slowly, drawing out the words with the steps I take.

"Finally confessing your love, are you? Well, being ousted from Lynnor because of your debt won't make that very easy."

"It was just one gamble!"

"And ten-thousand gold. That's why I hate magic—it ruins everything."

"It wasn't magic," I say, pinching my nostrils together out of habit whenever magic came up. "It was honest sleight-of-hand, which was what made it so appealing."

"Whatever. You don't have to pay it back, you know."

"I will," I say confidently. "And I kind of do. Lynnor treats their bets more seriously than their laws."

She shrugs. "You and your twisted sense of honor and honesty." We lapse into a brief silence. Then: "Weird you'd bring up settling down now. We've traveled together for so long."

True, we had made an unspoken rule to not bring up our pasts that's lasted all this time. It's nothing we've needed to discuss. But… "I'm just wondering what your long-term plans are, that's all. You still haven't told me much about your past."

"Neither have you," she remarks.

"I don't need to tell you about that." That was sort of a lie, though the truth can wait. I guess being back in the country we met is making me wonder. Facing her, I say, "Anyone can see it clearly by my face. You know who I am, but I don't know who you are."

A small gust of wind blows back her hair, relieving her of having to push it aggressively out of her face. "Does knowing someone only require the knowing of their name?"

The small incline we are heading down levels out onto a small stretch of dry grass that progressively gets greener as it reaches the tree line of the forest ahead. Stepping over one of the many small boulders strewn about the field of grass, I say, "No, but at least mine has some indication of who I am."

Idrid takes some time to think about this. "Yes and no," she finally says as we pass under the overhanging branches of the first trees. "It's an indication of who you're not."

"Sure, but I don't have any indication of who you're not."

"Imagine everyone you've ever met."

"What?"

"Think about them. Not me or you, everyone else."

"What does this have to do with anything?"

"I'm not like any of them," she says simply. "Just like you aren't James. You're Not James." The leaves slowly filter out the sun directly overhead, only letting slivers of light fall onto the wild roots that dig in and out of the earth.

I nimbly take small leaps and find footholds to continue on our self-made path while Idrid walks easily over the wildlife. "Fine, but that doesn't explain exactly why you're not like any of them."

Her deep sea-green eyes find mine. "Why are you not like James?"

Seeing her point, I refuse to say anything.

"Will you ever tell me?"

At first I don't answer, continuing to jump and land lightly among the tree roots. The reason I'm me... I know she's really asking about my relation to the king. Thanks to him I'd been constantly traveling most of my life. There is no relation between us. Several moments later, when I'm breathing slightly heavily, I say, "Hopefully I won't need to." But I know I will have to someday.

Chapter 2: **James**

Word travels fast. People talk, tell stories, sometimes changing bits here and there, and it spreads. Most often it isn't recognizable from where it first began, but now and then the truth in it remains intact enough to actually be informative to the listener. This is how James, King of Lanmar, learned about the rumors of someone who wasn't him.

He first heard talk in the grand dining hall of Telnas's palace among his associates about some man who was wandering the countryside. James questioned the slightly tipsy woman, one of the many royal guests whose title he had forgotten and who had been talking nonstop the entire meal about this man.

"Well," she started, pausing to hold in what James assumed to be a hiccup, "he looked like you, my lord."

"How so?" he asked. By that point everyone else at the table had dropped their conversations to listen to what the king and woman were discussing. It was rare for King James to entertain gossip.

"He— uh— looked exactly like you, in fact... h-hic. The spitting image of you. With your sssilver hair... only slightly unkempt. Heheh... and dirtier clothesss... A dirty wittle James..." She swayed a bit in her chair before her husband placed a hand on her shoulder to steady her. He whispered in her ear and her eyes became sharper momentarily. "Uh... I went to greet him, but then he told me he wasn't you... and walked away. Quite strange, really."

"Did he?" James pondered. Putting his elbows on the table and steepling his fingers, he turned his attention inward, now ignoring the woman who had started to hiccup uncontrollably. "Odd indeed."

At this moment, only a second after James made this remark, the man sitting at James's left who was his advisor spoke up, saying in a light rolling accent, "I, too, experience times when I mistake one person for another." His name was Filento Listophofol, for his ancestors came from the small island Oala off the west coast of Lanmar where names were quite extravagant. His warm brown and bushy mustache rose with his smile.

"Yes, indeed, the other day I thought you," Filento gestured one arm briskly at a man with a large beard, "Burk, were you," he gestured his other arm across the table at the tipsy woman's husband, who had a similar beard, "Seph." That got laughs out of both men, and Filento chuckled with them.

James remained deep in thought even as conversations picked back up all around the table.

Several nights later, during yet another dinner, it was Burk who mentioned another instance of meeting someone who wasn't James. "Er, well, I didn't meet him myself, per se, but a good friend of mine met him. He couldn't stop going on about how much he looked like you, my lord, down to the light grey hair and grey eyes."

"Interesting," James said to himself, again leaning on the table to steeple his fingers in front of his face. "I think I'd like to meet this person."

And like that, searches for the man who wasn't James ensued. Though they didn't amount to much. Guards throughout the land were given instructions to bring in a man who fit James's description. Most of them scoffed at the idea (quietly, to themselves) of looking for someone who looked like James because, frankly, they didn't care. Most of them only became guards so that James's original guards, most now part of the Royal Guard, couldn't further oppress people. This brought spirit to the people, though it didn't help them in distinguishing which guard was decent and which one was loyal to James.

But then one man, claiming to have been assaulted by the king himself, was let in to the palace dining room to tell James of the person who wasn't him. The news brightened James's day considerably, and at once he rounded up the Royal Guard to go after this man. They were to also enlist the dispersed guards throughout Lanmar to help in the search, and if the other guards declined to help, they were to be dishonorably removed from the guard. To be dishonorably removed is, simply, to be removed from the guard in a manner that is not honorable. Dishonorably removed guards were never allowed to get a job anywhere ever again, though this had little effect, because no one that wasn't loyal to King James listened. The truth was most people didn't like King James and his despotism, from his high taxes to his high work quotas. They simply tolerated him.

Despite such obvious disloyalty to King James, it was dangerous to outright rebel. He had powerful friends both inside Lanmar and outside, such as Filento, who was rumored to be one of the most powerful magicians on the continent. This was intimidating to the people of Lanmar, to think that a tiny independent isle off their coast could produce someone of such prominence.

Filento was only one among many others who were rumored to be powerful in their own ways. If the people so much as began an uprising, James could call on almost any bordering country to roll in and stamp it out before it gained momentum. With these friends, and an extremely elite and powerful Royal Guard, there was little the people of Lanmar could do. But the little they could do they did, and that was enough for them.

"This man you seek," Filento said to James on their way toward the north palace balustrade overlooking a courtyard, "is he dangerous?"

James smirked, his extravagant green-and-white garments flapping in the otherwise quiet hall. "Dangerous? Hardly." They reached the balcony and halted. Below them stood dozens of rows of guards armored head-to-toe in the nation's pale colors. Each row consisted of twenty, both men and women, both trained in magic and weaponry.

"Attention!" James's voice rolled over their heads and across the courtyard. "There is a man who looks like me—an impostor—who is using my looks, my identity, for his own gain. He cannot be allowed to continue opportunistically going between towns of Lanmar and doing whatever he likes." Raising his hand, he pointed at the center of the army. "This is an order by your king: bring him in by any means necessary. If that means killing him, so be it. For Lanmar!"

"For Lanmar!" the guards chorused.

Turning, James saw Filento's raised eyebrows.

"Not dangerous, you said?" Filento folded his arms and walked back inside.

"While an advisor, he's still young," James muttered to himself. *Too many have already grasped the implication of my doppelganger, though they feign ignorance and hide it with pleasantries.* His hands clenched atop the stone railing, his well-kept fingernails digging up loose minerals. It is a king's duty to model stability. No one can disrupt this balance. Not even…. With a shake of his head, he withdrew as well. He would play the games of royalty. He would make nice. Meanwhile, the guards would hunt.

And so it truly began, the search for a man who was not James.

Chapter 3: **Not**

The trees clump closer together but I stick to my instinct and continue forward. At times like this I like to pride myself for my knack of finding my way through places. It is true, because Idrid told me so after I navigated us out of a barren tundra. Seems easy enough when you can get a clear view of your surroundings, but when there's nothing on the horizon, it is difficult to tell which way to go.

Idrid walks beside me, taking at most three steps to avoid trees that begin to separate us, while I acrobatically hop, step, and leap my way across the ever-growing roots. It is especially dim under the canopy of leaves, and I notice Idrid throwing curious glances my way which I ignore, already too busy exhausting myself to get over the uneven footing. I can no longer see the ground, only a carpet of roots.

Rustling leaves and branches sound from overhead, either from wind or wildlife. It isn't until I hear the groans of the trees that I pause to think about where we're heading. Idrid ducks under a low-hanging branch and stops in front of me. "Something's off," I tell her, clambering to lean against the nearest tree and listen some more. "Yeah, something's definitely off. There's no sound of birds chirping when I distinctly recall there being birds chirping not five minutes ago."

To my astonishment, the woods get even darker. I can barely make out Idrid's slightly worried face. I look up to see branches… melding together and blocking out the remaining sunlight. "Uh," I say as all light vanishes, leaving us totally blind.

"You're right, something's off," I hear Idrid comment, followed by the sound of her heavy body's impact with the ground.

"This is no time to be resting," I hiss.

"I don't want to get lost, so I figure if I sit down there can't possibly be a way for that to happen."

"Fine." That leaves me to figure out a way to get out of here. A faint chorus of voices lull out a pleasant melody somewhere to my right, which is rarely ever a good omen. Soft luminous lights that echo the singing appear and seemingly float in the distance, too far off to see exactly what is making them. The sudden appearance of the unearthly light startles me, but not as much as the tunnel that now surrounds us and is going the direction we were headed. The glowing lights twitch far at the end of it, from where the singing is undoubtedly coming.

"Is this a tunnel of roots?" Idrid asks warily, getting off the ground. I look away and see that there is a wall of wood surrounding us.

"Looks like it. Let's go." I push off the tree and can walk easily now that the larger roots are no longer obstacles.

"Isn't this concerning?"

"Yeah, which is why I'm going to go see what it is so that we can alleviate our concerns."

"But the trees moved."

"So?"

"It means magic is being used. I don't like magic."

"Don't worry, I have a sword."

"There are probably forest-dwelling Elementalists waiting to pick us off."

"And I have a sword." The singing isn't getting any closer, but the tunnel ends in what looks like the end of the forest. "Aha, we're almost out. Is it night already? We must have been in there longer than I thought." Idrid keeps silent, her fists clenched. We reach the end of the tunnel and it takes me a full ten seconds to understand what I see.

Still far off are the mysterious lights, but that isn't what's bothering me. The tunnel of roots opens and drops off into a low valley of grass that spans at least the length of the grand city Telnas, which is said to be thirty square miles. At the far reaches where the lights glow are even more trees. Trees the size of buildings. I follow their progress upward and almost fall over from dizziness. About twenty stories above us are branches—no, bridges—bridges made out of branches, stretching all the way over and across the whole expanse of the valley. That is a lot of wood. In between the branch bridges, set upon the largest branches, are wooden structures. Each structure stands upright like the trees they're built on; they rise up steadily, truncating slowly before ending at flat circular rooves. Each tree-like structure has diagonally carved windows, bright with sparkling light. Even farther above these structures (much more than twenty stories) are the tops of the trees, creating a roof.

Millions of lights float everywhere like stars, illuminating a city made out of trees. The singing wafts down to meet my ears, sending tingles throughout my body. I shiver, and gaze back down at the clearing that I thought to be the end of the forest. One massive tree standing alone at its center stretches up into the city above, and I make out large stairs encircling the tree all the way up. Windows carved at intervals glow with light, though it is impossible to see what's inside at this distance.

All at once my thoughts pull me out of my marveling. I hear Idrid muttering several statements of awe over and over. "In all my life, never have I seen or heard of anything like this," she whispers.

I grab her wrist and pull her down the slope toward the lone tree.

"What makes you think we're allowed to go up there?" Idrid asks, brushing my hand off her but continuing to follow.

"Whatever magical creatures live here, they made a tunnel that led us here. Might as well oblige them and see why." It is difficult walking, my eyes straying upward to take in the beautiful lights and houses, and I trip several times when I forget to look down to see where I'm going. Minutes drag by, the sheer distance between the end of the tunnel and the tree giving me a rough estimate of how massive this place is. Finally we make it to the foot of the wood stairs encircling the tree, and we pause to catch our breath.

Before either of us can start climbing, a section of the tree springs outward. I jump back, reflexively pulling out my sword. It is just a door, a very tree-like door, fitted so perfectly it was impossible to notice its fine outline. Several normal-looking people with slightly hunched backs step out and close the door behind them. The way they move appears like an agonizing ordeal, as if they themselves are made of wood. They turn to look at us. Idrid and I look back at them. No one speaks.

In this awkward time I take the chance to appraise what they look like more closely. Most wear clothes like drapes, made out of leaves. I finally notice their skin is not just pale but off-colored. At first their vaguely teal skin looked opaque, though now I can see a light ripple with their slow breathing, similar to the multitudes shimmering from the canopy far above and across the expanse.

"Hi," I say when the silence has gone on too long.

"Hello," one replies in a deep voice. He steps forward and offers his hand. I take it, and we stand there for a moment. The others look at each other and nod approvingly. Idrid waits behind me, her hands bunched into nervous fists.

"Where are we?" I ask finally, since no one else looks like they are going to say anything.

"Flwihhndg," says the same man, or something like that. It's hard to tell with so many consonants.

"Can you tell us why we're here?"

"Yes." A long pause. I glance over my shoulder at Idrid. She shifts her legs uneasily, shrugging.

"Why are we here?" I ask, beginning to realize they need prompting.

"We are aware that the king of Lanmar is after you."

I blink. "James?" My hands clench and unclench around the hilt of my sword while my mind feels like it's been put in hot water. "Why—" Anger cuts my word short. I've only been back a few days.

In response to this, the others nod some more. "You should know what that means. So we wanted to tell you about that." The man nods, clearly pleased with this, then turns around and opens the tree door again.

I stare in disbelief at the way it opens; his hand melds to the front of the door only for a moment and he simply pulls. The others begin filing back inside. "Wait, who are you? Why did you want to tell me this?"

The man turns back, his eyes unfocused for a moment. They clear, and he smiles warmly. "You can call us Woodlanders. It's a simple word that you can understand." He pauses to take a breath before continuing. "And we wanted you to know this because we don't like the king. He keeps expanding, pushing into our home." Again, his soft brown eyes glaze over. "Oh, and he sends his guards after you. Welcome home," the man adds, then steps back inside the tree. Before I can speak, the door shuts and I'm left staring at the tree.

"WAIT A MINUTE!" I yell, shoving my hands against the miniscule imprints of the door. I dig my fingernails between the cracks and yank them back open to find the man and his companions staring wide-eyed at me. "You expect me to do something about James cutting down your forest?"

"We know who you are," another Woodlander speaks, this one female with a lilting voice in tune with the singing going on in the branches above.

I'm about to shout, but stop myself at the last moment. The temperature in my head starts to cool as I begin to analyze the situation presented. Twice now I've been forced to run. Will I allow it to happen again? An image flashes into my mind and I recall a memory: wide and tall windows whose multicolored panes tint the sunlight streaming through and upon long carpets; I'm squinting through one of the panes at a cityscape in the distance beyond walls that have me enclosed; a hand grips my shoulder, whirling me around, and then I'm on the floor holding my face where sudden pain lances my cheek. I blink away the memory and look at Idrid. Her sea-green eyes look the same as when I first saw her. Even then they'd lacked the innocence of a child. Guessing what she'd been through, it was expected. Back then she and Giants were being hunted, and now according to these creatures I'm being hunted. It all comes back to the royal family. "How, do you think, I am supposed to stop James?" I ask evenly, only slight irritation dripping into my voice.

"Are you serious?" Idrid says.

The Woodlanders look at each other, their smiles more annoying than friendly now. "His entire Royal Guard has been sent out in search for you," the same female says.

I sense another long break of silence coming. "And?"

"James and the rest of his court are still there."

Understanding washes over me. "How long will the Guard be out looking for me?"

The man with glazed eyes says, "As long as it takes to find you."

I nod, ideas proliferating. "All right," I finally say. "What's in it for me?"

"You'll find your fair share of treasure by going into the palace," the woman says, her voice pinched.

"I meant from you."

Her eyes sharpen and seem to emanate a faint ivy glow. "Safe passage out of this forest."

I note the subliminal threat. "By the way," I say lightly, turning to the male Woodlander. "You say you know me, but this isn't my home. Never was."

"Yet you keep returning. Have you another name for such a place?"

Several remarks roll across my mind. "A detour."

"Business?"

My eyes cut to the female who has a meager smile framed on her face, her gaze steady with mine. Her question confirms half of my suspicions. They know of me, more than most, though it all seems second-hand, typical of pawnbrokers' shady information network spanning across the nations. How they got it while hiding in this sea of trees I can guess has to do with the type of magic the male one is using. "I've indeed been contracted."

"Conscripted," Idrid murmurs under her breath before hunching over and breaking out into a series of false coughs. "Gambling debt," she splutters.

"Let's just say," I talk over her, "there's more to it than simple work or play." Idrid composes herself and there's a brief silence where I imagine if the Woodlanders had eyebrows they would've been raised. "A sense of fulfillment, for one."

"We hope you find this… fulfillment, then," the female Woodlander says.

"Yes… Thanks for the information."

The Woodlanders return my thanks with a nod, then shut the door silently. I turn to look at Idrid, who has loosened up a bit. "I think we have ourselves a little adventure cut out for us. Come on—" I beckon, making for the side of the grove opposite from the way we had come in.

"Are you seriously thinking of infiltrating the palace?" Idrid's voice calls from behind me. Looking over my shoulder, I see she's still standing in the same spot.

"Darn right. You coming?" I say, stopping in my haste to wait for her answer.

Idrid looks up, and I think I see something close to disappointment in her frown, but she turns and takes several steps to eliminate the distance between us. "It'll be tricky getting in. There'll doubtless be a private force guarding the palace, not to mention all the guests he has over almost every night. Plus, the guards are already out looking for you. I really don't see how—"

I wave my hand to cut her off, then smile at her. "I'm glad you don't need convincing."

Her mouth lilts downward along with her eyebrows. "Did you really think I of all people would?"

I shake my head. "How do you know he has guests over almost every night?"

"Uh," Idrid pauses, thinking. "People talking, really. Just gossip. But I don't see how this is any different than before, especially when they're looking for you."

"True," I say with a smile, for once knowing something she doesn't. "They'll be combing the streets around the palace frequently, but what'll happen when they don't find me? After a while, they'll extend their search, sending more and more guards out to different cities, spreading out, thinning, getting weaker and more—"

"Okay, I get it."

"Good."

"But why do you care all of a sudden? It can't be you're an environmentalist."

"I care because he cares," I say too quickly. Idrid frowns but doesn't press it. "James, that is. And that changes everything. Before I was just an elusive specter. Now that he's certain I'm around, I'm a wanted man. And he won't stop looking, even if we leave the country."

I turn to continue the trek to the edge of the grove but am stopped when Idrid interjects. "It's still two against…" she pauses to do a tally in her head, "…about one hundred. Servants, mostly. Cooks, maids, all trained in combat as well. Probably James's most trusted will be by his side to defend him. Most wielding magic."

I pat her arm gently, reassuringly. "I have a sword."

Chapter 4: **James**

It was curious to anyone who didn't personally know James as to why he would care so much about bringing in someone who looked like him but wasn't him. All anyone thought at first was that this man who wasn't James was using his similar looks, or James-liness, to take advantage of others. Some of the Royal Court who weren't close to James only thought he was fascinated by a doppelganger. But as the king predicted, rumor started spreading throughout the land that this man was the true heir to the throne, though only a handful of people truly believed it. More simply wished for it without hope.

Fools. The fervent sound of pen on paper swirled in the quiet of the bedchamber. The odious scent of ink mingled with the waxing candle atop the desk. The ache in his hand grew the longer he gripped the pen, but he wrote on. This last rumor spread simply by chance was true; James could not let that hope catch. He knew better than anyone the danger a blip of truth held. It turned the nation against a people, almost saw them to a bloody extinction. I did nothing to stop it.

The final scribble left the page he wrote on with an emphatic scratch. He scanned the new decree carefully. Yes, this would do. Tensions between magicians and non-magicians were longstanding in Lanmar and it was all he could do to ease the tension with frequent, nigh unmeetable agricultural work orders to turn their frustration on him. Whether they met it or not was of no concern; defying the quotas would sate their resentment and punishments wouldn't be so severe to warrant rebellion. Resentment was a much better tool than fear. Fear bred chaos. His thoughts returned to the all-too recent genocide and he gritted his teeth. *My parents were fools for using Giants as a scapegoat.*

Bundling the paper into a breast pocket of his overcoat, he stood, the legs of his chair moaning along the floor. He swept out of his chamber and into the main hall, the attending servant awaiting him already fussing with his hair. Who would've thought prolonged peace would be so difficult to manage? He grimaced and the servant who'd been tucking strands behind his left ear momentarily faltered. The truth of a magician heir could be the spark to tip the nation into civil war. He needed his not-self found quickly.

"The guards really are good for nothing, aren't they?" James notes, walking along one of the many long hallways beneath the palace.

"I'm afraid so," Filento replies, keeping pace several feet behind the king. "But the Royal Guard is loyal to you, and so is the Magic Guild." He glances at the servant leading the way.

"You don't need to keep secrets down here," James says coolly. "Strange to say, my servants are the most loyal people I have." He notices the servant's shoulders rise slightly.

"Sir, don't forget that I am loyal to you as well."

James laughs, nodding his head. "Of course."

They lapse into silence as the hallway juts sharply to the side. Torchlight continues to illuminate their way until finally they arrive at their destination. The servant fiddles with a key chain before finding the right key and sticks it into the door lock. The lock unlatches, and the door swings open. The sound of rushing water as loud as a waterfall meets their ears, and they all step inside with James in the lead.

The prior hallway, while absent of furnishings due to it previously operating as Telnas's prison network, has a single regal carpet running lengthwise. This room is absolutely barren, for good reason. Concrete as dark as pitch is carved in neat squares beneath their feet. The air is thick and moist, pressurized by the tons of stonework far above the low ceiling. Walkways line a chasm in the center of the room that runs parallel to the door. A single metal bridge five feet in length spans the gap.

James steps over to the railing beside the bridge and looks down at the rushing water below, following its progression toward the left wall and then out of sight. Its surface is an unnatural luminescent blue. "It amazes me how much work this must be for the Guild," James murmurs, his eyes following the water back to the opposite wall from where it rushes into the room.

"The Concilium, you mean?" Filento ventures.

"Concilium, Guild, they're basically the same thing now," James says. He turns around and looks at the servant. "Would you mind entertaining our guests when they arrive? I think I'll be down here quite a while."

The servant nods and leaves, shutting the door behind him.

"Still, it won't be quick enough," James says, looking back down over the railing. "If only the water was ready, we'd be unstoppable... this really is the worst time."

Filento sighs, though the sound is lost in the crescendoing echoes of the water. "I'd assume this process would take a while."

"That's not what I mean," James says, crossing his arms and tapping his fingers against his sides. "I fear the worst on two fronts. If the northland gets wind of this, Lanmar will be annexed within weeks. And, my... doppelganger is coming."

"We are well prepared for the invasion of an army, let alone a man," Filento says, squinting curiously. "How do you know he actually is coming?"

James looks at him, dark grey eyes glimmering with the reflection of the water below. "I would," he says. The way he was treated...

Filento nods as if understanding the king's thoughts, then looks down. "I don't believe I've seen the titration process."

"You want to?" James says, his mood shifting from foreboding to business once more. "The guests should be arriving soon, and I hate to involve foreigners in state affairs. I—" He pauses, thinking. "I suppose you've been loyal enough. Come on, then. The tower should be right above us."

Nodding once more, Filento says, "I'll follow behind you."

The two cross the bridge in single-file over the flowing azure water and exit the room through a narrow door at the other side.

Chapter 5: **Jasmine**

Despite the road between Picaroon Port and Chalman running so close to a magician's tower, the path is always fraught with danger. None of the magicians ever come down from the tower, which makes Jasmine assume that the magicians simply enjoy the show of frequent muggings.

Blasted nobles, she thinks as she passes by the tower, its tall blue roof curving sharply into a treacherous point. The tower lies in a valley along the northern border of Telnas, though it is tall enough to poke far over the valley's edges and cast a shadow over the road.

As her horse rears up, Jasmine shifts her attention back to the road and sees that a traveler stands in her way. She can also see the traveler holding up a dead sea bass by its tail. Calming the horse, she says, "Get that thing away from my horse, you rat."

Defying her words, the traveler tosses the bass to land several feet in front of her horse.

Cursing, Jasmine gracefully dismounts before the horse completely panics. She smacks the horse on its rear to let it run free. "That wasn't very nice," she says as her horse races off over the Palan Fields to the north. It was one of the better horses the swindlers at Picaroon had somehow scrounged up, one they had yet to assess the value of then double the price. At the least, now it wouldn't have to live stabled in that rathole. "Now I'll have to walk all the way to Chalman."

"You might not make it that far, darlin'," the traveler says, a stupid grin spreading across his face. He pulls out a knife with a blade no longer than a finger.

"You're planning on robbing me with a butter knife?" Jasmine asks. "Do you know who I am?"

"I know you came from Picaroon, so I know you'da done the same."

She looks him up and down with a frown, from his shabby undersized pants to his dirt-blond mop of hair. "I doubt it."

The traveler advances, knife pointed outward at her. Jasmine waves her hand, and a gust of wind carries the fish off the packed trail and into the man's face with a satisfying smack.

Slowly, the fish sags off the man's face and falls back to the ground. Before he registers what just happened, a chorus of shouts draws both of their attention to the fields where a group of people on horses are charging toward them.

"Bugger this, I'm outta here," he says, turning and running.

Jasmine, for her part, plays it cool and waits while the group draws closer. She counts seven of them, though one wearing a deep red cloak gives her concern. The leader, she surmises from the way the riders encircle her.

Just when Jasmine thinks the group are simply going to run her over with their horses, they let up and begin to circle around her on the road. It is a classic intimidation tactic, though it's effective since she can't monitor every one of them.

The horses are outfitted with custom saddles that you could not get anywhere in Picaroon, indicating that these people are much more than any common thieves.

"What do you want?" Jasmine asks, still staring at the one wearing the cloak.

"This is a toll point," the woman says through a black facemask stitched into her cloak. "Travelers must pay to travel between Picaroon and Chalman."

Absurd, Jasmine thinks. Tolls between countries make sense since they also serve as checkpoints. Though this… is definitely a scam. "Who, may I ask, is the beneficiary of this point?"

"By decree of King James, proceeds go to the Royal Court."

James and the Court? Jasmine freezes, looking more closely at the cloak. "That's… You're part of the Magic Guild."

"I'm impressed," the woman says. "Not many know about the formal wear of greater magicians." She halts her horse within the circle and leans over its wild brown mane.

"Have you, by any chance, seen a man that shares the appearance of the king?"

The circling horses begin to make Jasmine dizzy, so she stops turning in place and focuses on the leader. "What do you mean, like a doppelganger?"

The woman nods encouragingly.

"Depends. What does the king look like?"

"Grey hair, grey eyes, slender form, about this tall." The woman puts a hand up to show the height.

"I'd remember someone that peculiar."

The woman straightens back up, her light smile of eagerness gone. "That's a shame."

"I don't have anything of value," Jasmine says modestly, cowering slightly to give the impression of being a nonthreat.

"Everyone has something of value," the woman says. Her gaze falls to Jasmine's hand, where a bright ruby ring sits on the middle finger.

"What's your name?" Jasmine's voice quivers convincingly, letting her body communicate a frail façade while her thoughts churned. She could believe Guild mages would strongarm anyone so long as it didn't disrupt the peace between them and non-magicians too much. It seemed one of the few issues the king cared for whenever he deemed it time to step away from his luxury meals, anyway. By his ordain, only

Court-sanctioned magicians could perform magic in public; it is the reason students were sequestered to the Occult Towers that functioned as schools. Not that Court sanctions meant much when the magician is corrupt. Or the Court.

"Faye," Faye says. "That's a nice ring you have. I'll take that, along with your money."

So it is a scam. What a rotten country. Jasmine pats the outside of the purse she carries on her left shoulder, the sound of gold coins clinking against each other. "Won't you spare me and allow me to keep some money?" she says sorrowfully.

"No," Faye states, emotionless.

"Fine." Jasmine raises a hand in surrender, then suddenly makes a fist and slams it into the road. The ground buckles, sending several riders off their horses while other horses fall over on top of their riders, ending their intimidating circling.

Faye's horse stays on its feet, and she rides away as if in retreat.

Knowing all too well that causing the ground to move is too easy to beat a greater magician, Jasmine gets into a low stance and watches as Faye circles back around and begins charging her. The sound of a pop alerts Jasmine, and her lips curl up into a smile. A Conjuror, huh?

In Faye's hand is now a javelin, which she throws with surprising speed.

Jasmine puts her hands up in front of her, hardening the air. The javelin bounces off the invisible wall and clatters to the ground.

Faye doesn't break away from the charge.

Jasmine hears another pop above her head. Instinctively she dives out of the way. Spinning around, she sees a wickedly curved axe embedded in the dirt where she stood. She can conjure things at a distance?

Hoofbeats thunder upon Jasmine. A glance back reveals Faye to be now holding a sword that is mid-swing. Her reflexes kick in. Arcing her back in a half-turn, she holds her hand out as if she will catch the sword. Instead the sword ricochets off a pocket of hard air just before cutting into her hand. Faye presses the sword down as she rides by. Jasmine brings her hand around in a crescent over her head, following the sword as it scrapes along the hardened air she creates. The horse carries Faye away, and the sword disappears with a little pop.

Now some of the riders who do not have horses on top of them are getting to their feet. They hold out their empty hands as Faye rides by and with several pops each hand is suddenly occupied by a crossbow.

Gritting her teeth, Jasmine makes another wall of air just in time for the arrows to bounce back harmlessly. She needs to take them all out fast.

Before Faye can come back around on her horse, Jasmine pushes her wall of air to encircle the thieves. Having done this many times, she now forms a bubble around them and allows the oxygen to escape.

While she waits for the thieves to go unconscious, Jasmine notices that Faye has another javelin in her hand and is poised to let it fly. Jasmine also notices Faye is riding dangerously close to the bubble she has the other thieves trapped in.

In an instant, Jasmine breaks the air bubble and extends it out so that it entraps Faye just as she rides by. Faye is knocked off her horse, and the horse veers away, running off back across the fields.

Now Jasmine has them all trapped, and all she has to do is wait. Faye gets up, though immediately falls back down when she finds it hard to breathe. Jasmine watches as Faye's eyes flit to meet hers. Just when Jasmine thinks Faye is about to go unconscious, she hears another pop.

Once again she dives out of the way, another axe barely missing her. She looks back triumphantly at Faye, whose eyes are now closed. The rest of the thieves are motionless. Releasing the air, there's a loud fwoomp as the oxygen rushes back into place.

She walks casually over to Faye's body and kneels down, checking for breathing. Her stomach rises minutely.

Jasmine mentally congratulates herself for managing to not kill anyone, and begins relieving Faye of her gorgeous red cloak. She threads her fingers over its folds, feeling the meticulously subtle imprints of its cross weave. The Royal finery leaves trepidation constricting her stomach. She and the others aimed to kill. *Is it because they knew I was a magician? Or are they so bold as to kill citizens?*

Her eyes creep across the scene. Moans come from beneath the horses still struggling to get up off their sides. The thieves beneath will probably not be following her anytime soon. A glint catches in the sun and her hands clench. There peeking beneath a fallen man's rust-colored lapel is a silver sword-and-tree pin. Not thieves. Guards. She didn't want to believe it. But there it is. They all really are working with the Royal Court. Looking at the magicians' tower, she realizes she will be in even more trouble if anyone else sees her steal one of their fancy cloaks.

Faye's body flinches, a sign she's moments from waking. *No more thinking. Do what you do best: run.*

Throwing the cloak around her shoulders and immediately loving its feel (it's a great fit, too!), she manipulates the air to propel her along the road, her feet dangling just inches from the ground.

She makes good progress gliding like this, and in minutes has caught up to the traveler who first tried to rob her.

In a moment she passes him by, and he lets out a disgruntled yelp when the force of the rushing air knocks him off his feet.

Smiling, her cloak wrapped snugly around her, she looks ahead toward the next town.

Chapter 6: **Not**

"I wanted to see what was up there," Idrid says as we step out of the tunnel of roots that had formed for us at the other end of the massive clearing beneath the canopy, making a straightforward path out of the woods.

"Me too," I agree. "That was some pretty singing. But I'd like to stay away from magic users. Did you see that Woodlander's eyes glaze over? That had to have been enhanced sight. There's no other way they could know that James was looking for me, given their skin looked like it hadn't seen sunlight in years."

"Eegh." Idrid shudders. She gazes down the grassy incline. At the bottom, a dirt road travels all the way to an inscrutable point in the distance beside hills that segregate the coast from the mainland. "Convenient that Telnas is only about a three day's ride away, judging by the Dagger Hills on the horizon. It'll take us a week to walk, probably."

I smile. "I'm glad you're so smart, Idrid. I have no idea what I'd do without you."

"Probably be smart, yourself…" Her words trail off when I begin to trot off down the hill to the road. "Where're you going?"

"Where there's a road, there's sure to be travelers." Grinning now, I extend an arm off northward. In the distance, a carriage trundles toward us. My sheathed sword bounces off my back as I make my way down. I stop and search for the best spot to hide. Idrid's lumbering steps tell me she's coming, which brings me to a predicament. There are no bushes large enough for her to hide in. It's all mostly grass. "I suppose we should be straightforward with them," I say when Idrid makes it down. I can see four horses, their fur a monochromatic shade of dark brown, pulling the carriage swiftly behind them.

"We could just take two of the horses," Idrid suggests, though I know it's just idle chit-chat to pass the time. Being in the business of nomadic thievery, we rarely give up the opportunity to take something, especially when it aids travel.

"No way, that's a very fancy looking carriage they have. See how its outline shines? Those are gold trimmings. We could very well ride straight up to the palace in that thing."

Idrid nods and crosses her arms, drumming her fingers on them. "That'll save us a lot of work. How about after we exit the carriage? You could probably act like James, because you're you, but I'll be a bit of a problem."

I look at her, surprised. "Are you actually admitting to your size being out of the ordinary? Not that that's a bad thing," I quickly add. "You know what'd be great? If you put on a blanket or cloak or something to make you look even more threatening—" I stop in the middle of my suggestion when she gives me a glare.

"Who were they?" Idrid asks, hooking a thumb back over her shoulder at the forest's edge. "They dressed like plants. I assume they opened that tunnel for us to find them for a reason. Do they watch over the forest?"

I bark out a laugh. "If only the spanses had such protectors. They did sound concerned with James cutting into the forest, though."

"Didn't they refer to it as their home?"

"They did."

We stand silently for a while, waiting for the carriage, which is still rumbling along some ways down the road. Continuing her line of thought, Idrid asks, "They live there, right?"

"They do."

Idrid gives me a withering look, knowing now that I was playing the prompt game. "Is it not their home?"

I flash her one of my many practiced smiles, aiming for a look that's half-amused and half-condescending, since it's rare I get a chance to explain things to a book-reader. "They may look like plants, they may live in plants, and heck, they may even live like plants, though I don't trust anyone or thing that calls a forest as large as the Talwood theirs."

Idrid gapes at me. "That is the Talwood? No way."

"It is," I assure her.

Unassured, she states more than asks, "Then how did we go through it so quickly? Every book that mentions the Talwood says it's a hundred miles long at its thinnest. And that's east-to-west. Anyone that didn't get bored or die while traveling its length and recording their findings reported it stretching over five hundred miles, with more yet unexplored. That's not a forest you casually travel through in a few days, much less a few hours."

"You're quite right," I say, dropping the goofy smile for a straighter face. "Though this is the Talwood, given the Dagger Hills in the west that you already noticed, since you noted the time it would take for us to get to Telnas. Where did you think we were, anyway?"

"Well, obviously somewhere other than the Talwood," Idrid says gruffly. "Given we've been primarily walking north and east, the town we were in had to have been along the southern border of Lanmar, since that was where we were traveling. Wait a minute…"

"I think the town's name was Ferry, which is a stupid name for a town with no rivers," I say, ignoring her pause. "In which case, we were walking along the southern border of Lanmar. I believe we've somehow gotten to the northern border."

"You're telling me we went into the Talwood in a semicircle only to come back five hundred miles north, the same length anyone's ever recorded the Talwood being?"

"Well, yeah, what other forest marks the entire north and east border of Lanmar? I'm sure whatever books you've read are very old and from the same time people believed the world was created from Dunlon's hat box, which, as spacious as a grand magician's containers may be, hardly could hold over five hundred square miles of forest. Besides, this road here has to be the Tiller that runs all the way to Telnas."

"Okay," Idrid relents, raising her hands, which are each the size of my face. "I'm assuming those Woodlanders must've used some magic to leap us to the closest convenient place to get to Telnas."

"Yes," I say, frowning at the fact Idrid is aware of such magic. "Though that kind of magic has to be very powerful. That's kind of a problem…"

"How?" she asks, raising her eyebrows. "If we didn't get teleported it'd be weeks before we get back to Telnas."

I shake my head. "Nothing. I just don't like magic being used on me."

"That we can agree on. Speaking of Telnas, you don't seem too worried about going back. Who knows how much the palace has changed?"

54

Giving her a shrewd look, I tut. "What makes you think I've been there before?"

Idrid doesn't answer, though any answer would be unnecessary. Just her look is enough to indicate what she's thinking. You obviously share physical traits with the king, your whole persona revolves around not being the king, so you must be related. Of course, that is what any outsider could deduce. We have long known one another and our clandestine knowledge of each others' pasts, however selectively disclosed between ourselves, made the fact I'd lived in Telnas more than obvious. I was simply giving her a hard time.

The loudening rattles of the carriage wheels catches my attention. In unison we drop the topic and stroll casually toward the oncoming carriage. The man driving it no doubt has seen us by now. He pulls back on the reins, bringing the carriage to a stop, and I can fully admire the decorative structure. The roof has long, solid gold corners, each corner ending with a swooshing swirl like a brush mid-stroke on a canvas. Leaning both ways, I can see the painted symbol of Lanmar on either side of the carriage: a blue sword hilt with an upside-down silver blade, and a contrasting brown tree set just behind, its leaves and branches sprouting from the very tip of the sword's hilt, evoking an unusual feeling of life and death.

"What do you want?" the driver asks in a high squeaky voice.

"Why is it royals always sound annoying?" I mutter under my breath for Idrid to hear, then louder to the driver: "We want your carriage. Give it to us."

The driver bursts into giggles, taking several moments to quell his laughter. "Really? Not a chance, peasants." Something about the way he enunciates the word "peasants" gives me the feeling he was the kind of chap you'd want to hang around with at parties.

"Hey, we'll make it worth your while."

"What could you possibly offer us?" the driver scoffs, gesturing behind him at the regal carriage.

"We could, you know, not kill you, or something."

"You can't be serious!"

I am getting annoyed by his voice. A shame, he's probably a nice guy if I could get past the way he talks. "I've got a sword," I say informatively, tapping the hilt protruding over my left shoulder with two fingers.

"This is absurd! Get out of—"

I leap suddenly, using the horses' backs as stepping stones, my sword, firm and steady, pressing into the front of the driver's purple velvet coat all in an instant. "Please," I say, "shut up." The driver's laryngeal prominence bobs as he swallows, and his arms lift up in surrender. "Do you mind," I pause to cough, "telling whoever's in there to get out?"

The driver nods quickly several times, his semi-long blond hair flopping up and down comically, and knocks delicately on the smooth wood. "Come on out," he calls. "We've got trouble." This last statement scares him, and he turns back to look at me with pleading eyes.

I shrug my shoulders and nod at him, indifferent to whatever he says as long as it gets those inside to come out.

The carriage door opens wide, slamming hard, and two foreign men with pale skin, dressed much more extravagantly than the driver, appear around the front. I size them up, calculating their size, strength, and speed.

"Paikoff! What the hell is this!?" exclaims the one wearing a royal blue waistcoat covered smartly with a black cloak reaching just below his knees.

"A stick-up. We're taking your carriage."

"No you bloody aren't!" the other man says.

My eyes flick back and forth between the driver and the two men. "I have a sword." I give it a flick to prove my point which gives the driver's coat a small cut.

The two men's faces light up with anger. They roll their shoulders as if they are getting ready for a fight. "You'll have to kill us first!" the blue-coated one replies.

I look over my shoulder at Idrid, who hasn't moved yet. "Does anyone understand what I'm saying when I say I have a sword?"

She tilts her head. "Sometimes even I don't understand."

I look back at the driver, who raises his hands again, afraid of what I'll do. Rolling my eyes, I pull my sword away from him and drop down off the driver's seat. The men instantly go for me, arms outstretched.

I could cut them off. Or maybe just the fingers.

I make small, quick flourishing swirls with my sword, light and careful, nicking several points on both men's arms. They recoil, looking down to see that their sleeves are in tatters.

"If you two continue to fight, my next swings will draw blood," I warn.

The blue-coated man spits on the ground. "Let me get my own sword, then we can have a true fight!"

I stop to consider this. The man interprets my pause as me agreeing and goes to get his sword out of the carriage. "I admire your heart," I admit, walking around the other man so that I have some open space to fight. His snarling face relaxes and is replaced with a thoughtful curiosity. I raise an elbow to cover my mouth as I cough again. "Though you are pretty stubborn."

The blue-coated man reappears holding an ornate short sword. The metal hilt extends upward around the blade itself, thinning in individual spirals fancily. The blade extends a meager couple feet. Though the sword is very fine, it is the same type you'd find hanging on a wall behind the imposing desk of some rich snob. It is aesthetically pleasing but impractical in use.

These fools will pretty up anything, even if it isn't beneficial. I appraise my own sword, noting its advantages over the short sword.

Before I can ask how we do this, the man lunges, his sword pointed at my heart.

I nimbly take a small leap backward just out of reach.

When the full extent of his lunge is met, when his blade is barely poking my own cotton shirt, I slip the tip of my blade in the space between the man's hand and hilt, and twist.

My blade cuts him; his palm bleeds and causes him to release his grip on the sword with a cry. I go to pick it up when the other man suddenly shouts, "YOU'RE JAMES!"

At this, the blue-coated man's reddened face pales. "Great Dunlon, I cannot believe my arrogance," he says in a hushed voice, kneeling.

"You're James?" the driver shrieks, clambering off his seat to kiss the ground.

"No, no-no-no-no, stop," I say, now holding a sword in either hand, pointing them at each man. "I am Not James, and I'd appreciate it if you remember that."

"But— My lord, do you not want anyone knowing that you're here?" the blue-coated man asks.

I sigh, swinging both swords down in frustration, cutting the air. "I am not your lord, and yes, I don't want anyone knowing I'm here. Now, I'm commandeering this carriage."

"Of course," the other man says, bowing his head in reverence.

"Great. Come on, Idrid, get in. Oh, and you," I point a sword at the driver's shivering form, "It'd be great if you drove us to Telnas."

"Oh, James, we were going there to dine with you! Let us come," the blue-coated man says.

"I'm Not James," I say as Idrid squeezes inside the carriage. I sheathe my own sword and lift myself onto the folding step. "Sorry, but we need to go alone."

"Of course," the other man repeats. "We shall find another way. Farewell, Ja— I mean, not James." He looks up to give me a conspiratorial wink, and I force myself not to roll my eyes again.

Idrid fills the entire cushioned left side, so I take a seat on the right. Knocking on the wall, I call, "We're ready to go!" A few moments pass before we feel the carriage begin to roll forward. At the same time I hunch forward and cough uncontrollably.

"Not!"

I feel Idrid's hand on my back as my body heaves. She's asking if I'm hurt, though I can't respond. My lungs burn and I quickly gasp in a breath before I succumb to another fit of coughing. Finally, when I no longer feel as if I'd inhaled spice, I sit up straight. Idrid's hand falls away in surprise at my quick recovery.

"Are you all right? What was that?"

"It's nothing," I lie, my voice weak. I clear my throat and nod to assure her I'm fine.

"I've never seen you allergic. Or sick."

I knew I'd have to tell her sooner or later. "Fine." I lift up my shirt by the hem. She starts to protest, but stops when she sees my chest. I already know there are some scars from mishaps in swordplay; she'll see them now for the first time. I search her face and am thankful she appears more thoughtful than worried.

She tentatively reaches out and places her palm at the hollow of my chest. "You're still convulsing, though it's minimal."

I nod again, letting go of my shirt when she pulls her hand away. "The Woodlanders' magic affected me."

Idrid's face blanches in anger and she moves to shove open the carriage door before I stop her.

"What they did wasn't harmful. I—my body just reacts poorly to magic, no matter what kind it is. It's why I dislike magicians." I watch her as she sits back opposite me. I wait for the questions that are sure to follow. But she doesn't ask any. Instead, she laughs.

"And here I thought you held a simple prejudice like most non-magicians."

I open my mouth. "You think I'm that petty?" I feel the beginning of a judgmental silence and quickly move on. "What about you, then?"

She quirks her head. "Why do I dislike magicians? It's personal. So, what are you going to do with that?" Idrid asks, referring to the short sword still in my hand.

So she's avoiding telling me. It's just as well, since I didn't tell her the whole truth. "Hm." I admire the decorative hilt. I strike it forcefully against the inside of the carriage and break off the ornamental pieces that spiral around the blade. "That's better," I say with a smile. Turning it over, I notice there's the same symbol of Lanmar engraved on the bottom of the hilt.

"I could've used some of your persuasion skills out there," I say.

"You handled it," she replies.

I look up and see her watching the world pass by outside the window. "We still need a plan for getting both of us into the palace."

"I'm still unsure why you want to go."

I sigh. "Ceasing an endless hunt for your head not good enough reason for you?"

She shrugs. "How do you know it's for your head and that it'll be endless?"

"Fine. Let's just say it's personal. And, since we're thieves, we can make it lucrative. It is a palace, after all."

She gives another shrug, satisfied enough with my answer. "What do you suggest we do to get in?" She looks me in the eye. I look away, off onto the horizon at the Dagger Hills. The luscious red drapes beside the window catch my eye and my lips quirk upward. "What?" she asks cautiously.

"This looks like it'll fit you." I take the drapes in a hand and feel the smooth fabric. "Comfortable, too." I rip them from the carriage and throw them over Idrid. She doesn't move, letting them land and envelop her.

"They are big enough," her voice emanates from within the curtains.

"They only need some holes for you." I pull them off her and use the short sword to carefully slice some rough arm holes and a larger slit for the head. "There, try it on."

She takes them and pulls them over her head, easily slipping into them. "They're good, though, tell me again, why do I need to wear this?"

"Because it covers your dull peasant clothes," I say in a nasally voice similar to that of the driver. My thoughts return to the two men and their relation to James. They clearly would have skewered me without a second thought. Just about everyone treats us as disposable, especially royalty, until they mistake my identity. I press my hands against my cheeks to feel the fleshy contours of my face. If I was different, would I have it any better?

She raises the curtains back off herself and folds them up. My eyes widen momentarily when she draws out the survivalist kit from her traveler's pouch instead of one of her books, though narrow again when she stuffs the curtains inside. She smirks at me. "What about you?"

"Although I hate it, I'll have to not be Not James. I'm surprised those men haven't heard of me yet, especially since they were going to meet James."

"Probably came from outside Lanmar," Idrid suggests. "They said something in some other language… Paikoff."

The carriage rattles, filling the silence that follows, neither of us having anything to say.

"Not, if we get in… what are we going to do?"

I think for a moment. "I'm not entirely sure. It seemed pretty clear when we were with those Woodlanders, but now I have no idea."

Idrid sighs and crosses her arms over her chest.

"Sometimes the best plan is not to have one," I say, mimicking her by crossing my own arms. "It makes life truly genuine, that way."

"What the heck does 'genuine' mean?"

"The way I see it, planning isn't the same as living. When you plan, everything is set up and goes exactly the way you want it to go. Or it doesn't, but that's bad planning. People spend so much time doing it that they forget that there's the present moment where they can do anything. There is no spontaneity, no fun in planning. It's basically a set of rules about how you are going to live and that's it. I don't want to live by rules, made by me, or anyone else…" I trail off when I notice Idrid is staring hard at me.

"What?"

"Nothing, you just seemed… Nothing. I'm going to take a nap." And then Idrid falls asleep, leaving me to my thoughts as I watch the sunlight fade on the passing fields outside.

Chapter 7: **Maia**

Far to the southwest, past Telnas, past the Abador Fields, and far enough away from the infrequently unstable Sundering Coast and Expanding Wetlands to be considered safely habitable, is one of the three Occult Towers of Lanmar. It rests, not on any visible land, but on a rock bed thirty-some meters below sea level and roughly half that length from the coast. The distance has decreased considerably in the past several years, due to the nearby Sundering Sea pushing the coastline ever closer to the tower, though the residents don't worry, for they can move the rock bed at a moment's notice. The tower retains a luminescent yellow-white sheen in the sun, rivaling that of the coast when it is alight at high noon, and is sixty meters in height, though its majority is below sea level. If its full majesty were to be seen from the shore, it would reach an impressive eighteen stories high and stand out like a beacon for ships at sea. Since it does not, much to the displeasure of the olden Royal Court's construction advisor who wanted the tower to serve multiple purposes, resources had to be allocated further south of the tower to build a real lighthouse. In the end all worked out ergonomically, and the land south of the tower was ripe for a harborage which in turn broadened the growing borders of Lanmar while benefiting the desert people of Halet whom received an interminable removal of tariffs for parting with the land.

From that harbor one adolescent girl routinely walks to go to the Tower of Bel. Maia, a young apprentice Elementalist to an older student named Greg, leaves the prevalently brick-and-mortar harbor through its rambunctiously imposing northern gate. Maia has always wondered why such a large sea-green gate with a multitude of colorful banners waving at intervals, carefully measured from their foundation tubes up the sides, was necessary, given the entire north and east sides of town lacked any form of a perimeter. She thinks this again now, raising an arm up to lightly brush one banner with the image of Lanmar's crest that is low enough for a five-foot thirteen-year-old like herself to reach as she passes under it.

The thought subsides as she sets her mind on placing either foot in front of the other on the lengthy trek to the Tower of Bel. Most days she would be seen by travelers, sailors, deckhands, porters, guardsmen, or the few people who actually live at the harbor. Very often she'd pass by these same people with a firm and bright "Hi!" Today the north gate path is vacant. It is a haul day, and all hands would be carrying glorious troves dredged from the sea between the ships and setting them up and down the docks. On the way out of the house she'd seen tradesmen setting up stalls between the docks and storehouses. Already on display were charcoal-and-clay pottery brought from the southern country Lynnor, long, two-toned bird feathers from a species of avian local to the Lynnor highlands, and, the hallmark of any busy day in the port, sparkling trinkets advertised to aid buyers in discerning the better hauls. Eeuw. Fish smell rotten and taste rotten. Better or worse, fish are all the same to her. Good thing for her it's also a training day.

Easing her shoulders back so that she walks in the healthy, upright position most teens find uncomfortable, she lets the peculiar feeling of being alone go with a sigh. It isn't that she minds being alone; it's that she rarely ever can be in a bustling harbor town. She glances back at the base of the archway. It's unusual for not even a guard to be stationed there, even with the uptick in light-hands making off with wares on haul days. Come to think of it, her father said last night some new order from Telnas's officials would have the guard tightening its focus on thieves. There was something about a search for someone before she lost interest in the politics.

The steps she takes become rhythmic, changing with whatever mood or melody passes through her mind, and soon enough she has reached the end of the trail where the dirt drops off and gives way to an incline of smooth earth, replaced by sand toward the incline's base, which then stretches off into the wide beach.

Maia moves into a light jog down the hill, picking up speed, until she's racing along the sand leading to the shoreline. She slows when the unsupportive footing of the sand becomes too cumbersome to continue at a run. I'll have to learn some day to form solid ground from more than water, she thinks, then becomes excited as she nears the water's edge.

Sinking to her knees, she moves her hand along a small subsiding wave, feeling its ebb and flow. Maia focuses, keeping the water's slow nature in the back of her mind as she stands back up, then goes still. Moments pass in which nothing seems to happen. A minute goes by until, finally, the flow of the water is interrupted.

Maia can see it, the surface of the water hardening to a crystallized state that slowly spreads. It continues, faster now, and the hard surface that was once the size of an ice cube is now a thin makeshift raft of ice. Not done, Maia places her foot firmly on the ice, sending out more tendrils, cementing it in place so that there is now a sturdy column beneath the surface. She does it again, putting her left foot down in front of her right so that she's now totally on the ice, and it lands firmly, causing the ice to extend further out.

Getting a rhythm while concentrating the water in front of her to harden, she begins walking forward slowly without stopping. The depth the ice has to travel to support her feet increases, though Maia's discipline causes the water to crystallize faster without fail.

Maia eyes the tower rising from the waves ahead of her. She has formed her own path along the water many times alone. Just last year, Greg approved her to be capable of doing so, though many of the younger students required the presence of a more practiced Elementalist to reach the tower. However, the control she needs is always draining. Only recently has she begun trying to do different things while using her magic, and like now she could only ever think of mundane things like Oh, there's the tower ahead of me and I'm hungry.

Finally, she reaches the tower and stands at its gleaming wall, appraising its simple beauty. The sandstone reaches straight up, then sharply angles out of sight to form what Maia knows is the dome. The current master of the tower has an office just below it, though Maia has never seen him nor the office, which leads her to think that this was only a story Greg told her when she was first learning Elementalism.

She glances back. The water has mostly returned to its liquid state, and shrinking chunks of ice are floating away on the surrounding currents. Turning back to the solid wall separating her from the inside, Maia shoves her hand against it, her fingers extended. For any normal person the motion would cause broken fingers, but the sandstone slides away at her touch with a mushy sound like a footfall on sand. An inch into the wall, a chunk of sandstone the shape of a small bar meshes firmly, meeting her palm.

Gripping the hold, Maia yanks it out like anyone would pull at a door. A section of the tower around her hand peels open where there previously wasn't an opening, its dimensions generous enough for her to walk inside.

She flees inside out of the beating sun, and admires the bend of the inner wall where she pulled it outward. She doesn't know how, but the tower somehow knows to seal itself after every entrance. As she watches, the opening swings closed, the sandstone reconnecting itself to form a smooth surface once more. From the inside, the tower, totally enclosed, would seemingly be pitch black, though in here it impossibly reflects the bright light reflecting off it from the outside, albeit somewhat muted.

She knows the Tower of Bel was constructed out of sand taken from the nearby gleaming yellow-white coast. The Elementalist constructors bound the sand grains together to make a hard, rubbery, yet oddly pleasant-to-touch surface, insoluble to the occasional heat wave, and non-erodible to the crashing waves surrounding it. Such a comfortable surface to touch causes many of its residents to walk barefoot while within the tower. Some, such as Maia's guide Greg, make excuses like, "Freeing my body allows me to connect better with the world around me," even though one's clothes don't matter in the least when conducting magic.

"Maia." She turns and sees Greg walking across the barren floor toward her, barefoot. He stops in front of her. "Always so punctilious. Are you ready for today's lessons?"

Unsure of what his first sentence meant (she theorizes his use of big words around her is a way to signify his superior station), she nods. "Mmmhmm."

"Great," Greg says. He beckons for her to follow, the sleeves of his worn blue tunic billowing around his biceps as he gestures. Maia does. She sees that he wears his usual pair of tan pants kept up by a simple length of rope with no tie or buckle. Such a substitution for a belt is strange, even to Elementalists, though Greg says the casual everyday magic he uses to connect and tighten the rope is good practice. The look is minimalist and compliments his broad frame, often making Maia feel uncomfortable whenever she dares to look for too long.

She looks down at herself. She wears a light-green jacket fitted over an airy plain-grey shirt and travel pants. Only on special occasions does she wear anything remotely girly, which to her constitutes a blouse and never a skirt or dress. She likes the snugness of just plain pants rather than largely open-ended legwear, which in her coastal environment is convenient given the weather is typically windy with many updrafts.

Before the opposite wall of the tower, the floor gives way to a line of stairs following the inner wall, traveling both up and down in a spiral. It is the downward stair that Greg takes, Maia following three steps behind. The entrance floor is always empty and isn't used for anything other than welcomes and goodbyes, and each of the lower levels has particular themes in which Elementalists train and practice. Coming to the first floor below the entrance, Maia finds three other apprentices with their guides moving the air in various directions. One of the apprentices, Renauld, is moving his arms in big motions as if pulling back a mass of theater curtains. She feels the kicking wind he creates circling around the floor, causing everyone's clothes and hair to be whipped up.

He pauses when he sees her and the wind subsides, his curly ginger hair blowing softly. Maia waves to him and he waves back, then he continues to create wind currents around the room. The last she hears before proceeding down to the next floor is one of the apprentice's guides scolding Renauld for interfering with their training.

The next floor down is Maia's favorite, and, from what she's explored of the tower, the largest space. A massive tree sits squarely in the middle far below, its branches touching the ceiling above. The tree has no leaves, though no leaves are necessary for the peculiar plant's survival, and anyone could see its vibrant and healthy shade of brown.

It takes three full rounds around the perimeter stairs for Maia and Greg to reach the bottom, and Greg walks to where one large root stretches across the length of the floor from the massive trunk and meets the outer wall at an abrupt stop. Maia stands beside Greg, who is mouthing words silently to himself, obviously thinking of his lesson plan.

From around the tree there is one other person's voice saying words of instruction, another guide advising her apprentice no doubt.

"All right, Maia," Greg says, drawing her attention away from the tree. "Let's start with something simple." He glides a hand across the tower wall a few feet above the root, and a neat rectangular hole opens, allowing in a rush of sea water. Greg, his hand motionless in front of the hole, moves it back and the hole quickly closes. "Quick, now, catch the water before it drains downstairs and gets everyone down there wet," he says, shaking his hand once to remove the droplets from his skin.

Maia obeys, in her mind's eye encapsulating the water with her will, physically holding both her hands in o-shapes. The water freezes on the floor around them. A few drops hang in the air around the tree root in an unnatural formation. She notes, with a pang of jealousy, the casual motion Greg used was simple but still caused the wall to do what he wanted, unlike the effortful motions she and Renauld have to make when manipulating objects.

"Good," he says, "Now, make a bubble. Hold it… here." He points to a space in the air between them over the root.

The water, aligning with her thoughts, recedes into itself, packing together into a close space on the floor. Then, as she mimics the motion she wants by lifting her hands up to her stomach, the water rises in a neat bubble between them. She watches the bubble bob slightly, points of it undulating, but with a fraction more of her concentration, the movement ceases, creating a perfect sphere.

"Excellent." Greg moves away, walking along the root to a spot halfway between her and the trunk. "This next part will require some focus, and I want you to do it slowly. And follow the steps. I want you to create a continuous, single-drop stream down from the bubble to the surface of the root. For this, first you must concentrate on allowing the smallest amount of water to leave the bubble. Then, you will have to guide the water, defiant of gravity, in whatever velocity you deem fit, as long as it reaches the top of the root. Nod if you understand this first part."

Maia nods, knowing Greg is saving her from having to speak so she can keep her concentration, though she is very capable of talking while manipulating things as easy as a little water. It naturally flows to her will.

"Then, I want you to continue moving that stream up the root to where I am. Once you have the first part, this part should be easy. Okay? Start when you're ready."

Maia begins instantly when he tells her, allowing the tiniest infraction in the bubble. It is slow, very slow, but a droplet moves from the bubble's base, extending longer and longer until it's clear she has created a miniscule stream running through the air down from the bubble in slow motion. She keeps the flow steady and slow. The slowness of the stream seems like she is taking it carefully, but the process of having the water fall quicker would be much easier with the help of gravity, and lengthening the duration of any magic can quickly drain any magician.

After two minutes, the end of the stream finally touches the top of the tree root, and then it continues to lengthen along and upward, climbing the root ever closer toward Greg. Maia knows this is a flexibility test, meant to strain how wide her concentration could go and what actions she could take. She shows no strain as the stream gets longer, and even she is amazed with herself for simultaneously holding a bubble midair, creating an escaping stream from that bubble to fall unnatural to gravity in one direction, and continuing that stream in a completely new direction.

No, Maia realizes, she's giving herself too much credit. She is only guiding the second leg of the stream along the surface of the root. If she did this same exercise without a surface for support, she might have more trouble. It is true, such a small, simple help could be all the difference between a good performance and failing miserably.

The thought almost causes her to lose concentration, the end of her stream stopping momentarily before she gathers her thoughts and urges it forward at the same slow speed. The stream has made it halfway between her and Greg. Giving only a cursory glance to see his reaction, she is pleased that he is smiling slightly. He rarely shows approval.

Maia has a deep urge to try and impress him some more, and though she can feel the strain on her will, she knows she can do more. Clamping down on the desire to show off, she continues the process until there is a continuous stream from the midair bubble to the root in front of Greg several feet away.

"All right," Greg says, taking a step back and sitting down. "That's it for the practice lessons, though I will stay for as long as you hold the water as it is so that I can measure your endurance."

Disappointment flashes over Maia's face, though she hides it the moment after. The concealment is unnecessary since Greg is still fixated on the shape of the stream, eyeing the stream and bubble's shape for any interruptions. At this point Maia is ready to give in and wait for her control to break when her desire to do more becomes insatiable.

Without thinking, she urges the thin stream to travel further up the root toward the tree, the current obeying, now travelling the same speed as a toddler learning to walk.

"Maia, what are you doing?" She can hear the frown in Greg's voice, though ignores him.

She concentrates on quickening the current, and soon enough the stream reaches where the root extends out from the tree's trunk. She doesn't stop there, instead forcing the stream to continue up the trunk toward the branches.

Midway up the tree the current freezes, Maia contemplating what she wants to do next.

"Maia…"

As soon as the thought comes into her head she acts. The stream travels lengthwise around the tree to encircle it. The current is fast now, and she can see the effect it has on the bubble floating beside her. Already it's shrunk down to half its original size, the water draining rapidly to join the thin stream travelling up the root and trunk. All of a sudden there is no more bubble, only a stream of water quickly receding up the tree to join the rest.

Maia has encased the midsection of the tree in a layer of water. Pleased, Maia then attempts something she's never done: manipulate a living thing.

Greg is silently gazing up at the tree along with Maia, a look of consternation plain on his face. Slowly settling the water closer to the bark, Maia attempts to push the water in.

Her will is met with an iron-like defiance, as if she is pressing up against a wall. Testing the strange force with her mind while the layer of water flows gently along the surface of the bark, she tries again with greater force. The wall remains firm, though at the most basic level of matter she senses, by chance of her paying attention to something so small, some of her water entering the tree before being pushed out. The pushback is stranger than the wall, but she doesn't know what's doing it.

Wait, no. It does not matter what is preventing her from giving the tree energy—it's why. The realization dawns on her, and slowly she brings both of her hands up in front of her, palms out, as if she's resting them on a surface. All thoughts of forcing the water inside the tree disappear, replaced by simply offering the water and only the water. As soon as she thinks this, she feels a strange tingling sensation as the wall-like force that surrounds the tree ignores the water and intermingles with her own will. She never knew someone's will could be touched by something as if it were partly physical, though this must be what happens when using magic with something alive. Putting all her focus into the basic water molecules, she pushes again, with both her metaphysical will and her physical hands.

The water encircling the tree withdraws through the bark, the tree groaning slightly at the intake of water. Where the water had been is a ring of tiny salt particles. The specks of white fall from the air, released by Maia's will as she lowers her arms, the strange wall touching her will withdrawing. A smattering of salt grains patters the floor. Maia associates it with an audience's applause.

Feeling somewhat relieved as well as having an odd sense of pleasure as if she herself drank some of the water, Maia turns to Greg. When she sees his face, her stomach does a flip.

Greg's mouth is open, stretching his long face longer, and his eyes are as wide as two full moons. "How did you do that?" he asks, finally managing to close his mouth.

"How did I feed the tree?" Maia asks, thinking at first it's a trick question since it seems like an easy enough thing to do for any practiced Elementalist like Greg, until he speaks again.

"You didn't just feed the tree, Maia," he says, incredulousness building in his voice. "You energized it. You caused a massive scale osmosis in a second! And dialyzed the water so that the tree had the proper chemical components. How did you know to do that?"

Maia doesn't understand several of the words he uses, though figures out the gist of it. "The tree wasn't accepting the salt, so I flushed it out of the water," Maia says. "Don't you know how to separate individual particles like that?"

Greg shakes his head to clear it. "Yes, but that's something you learn only when you have a grasp of controlling all the basic elements. What doesn't make sense to me is how you got the tree to... energize."

"All I did was feed it," Maia says lamely, rubbing an arm with a hand, something she did when she was embarrassed or nervous.

"No, feeding a plant, or anything for that matter, is simple. All you do is put the nutrients in proximity for the organism to feed. What you did was bypass the feeding process entirely and cause photosynthesis. My lord, you even managed to draw from the air around the tree to do it."

"Hold on," Maia says, holding up a hand. "What did I do?"

Greg walks over to her, talking fast. "Essentially, the tree had some amount of energy. You just caused the tree to gain a considerable amount more energy."

Maia is still confused. "So..."

Greg drops his head, then lifts it again to look her directly in the eyes, finding the right words. His hands rise as he speaks, his gestures growing wilder as he goes on. "Energy is the basis of life, Maia. Only the individual organism decides when to create, intake, and/or use it, and you just caused that tree to create a whole lot of it. You made energy via—sorry, through another living thing. Other Elementalists, like me, can only move other living things that have weak wills, like moving a branch, but not to the extent of forcing a tree to give up its branch. To cause something living to do what you want, like manipulate its own form or function completely... No Elementalist has ever done that."

The potency of what he is saying, along with how he says it, hits Maia like a runaway cart. "Are—you sure no one's done it?" she asks.

Before Greg can answer, the other two occupants of the room round the tree, walking toward them briskly. "Oh, lord," Greg says under his breath, brushing a hand through his short brown hair. The two magicians are as Maia assumed, a guide with her apprentice neither of whom Maia has seen before, though both walk with an air of purpose that causes her stomach to turn again.

The tingling sensation from metaphysically touching the wall surrounding the tree lingers. Flexing her fingers, Maia realizes she isn't mentally drained in the least. In fact, she feels like her body is larger than it actually is. Her thoughts skip around, trying to make sense of it as the two magicians near her and Greg. Greg's words repeat in her mind: Energy is the basis of life... Had she borrowed some energy from the tree?

"What in the world was that?" the magician guide asks Greg without looking at Maia, stopping just short of him and crossing her arms over her chest. Her apprentice, a girl that looks no older than Maia, mimics her guide's stance. Thinking about it now, the guide looks slightly younger than Greg. Good, that should give Greg an edge the other guide would have to respect.

The quiet that ensues, save for the faint crashes of waves outside the tower, makes Maia uneasy. She looks at Greg, who appears to be thinking hard.

"I was just expounding the extent to which our magic can influence biotic entities," Greg says decidedly.

Maia rolls her eyes at his choice words, though is grateful for his... shoot, she had heard a big word herself to describe indirect language from her mother but it slips her mind. Well, she's grateful.

"Don't lie, Greg, I can feel the tree practically buzzing," the guide snaps, gesturing to the root at their feet.

Maia hadn't noticed, what with being too preoccupied by her own newfound energy, but sure enough she can sense the root's imperceptible movements.

Greg now crosses his arms, favoring his left leg with his other bent slightly forward, a casual pose. "You undoubtedly witnessed the tree consume water. You know trees need water, Jenna."

Somehow when he talks plainly, it sounds even more condescending, though Maia can see its effectiveness on Jenna. The girl uncrosses her arms. "Well, I've never seen a tree consume so much water so fast."

"Do you know what kind of tree this is?" Greg asks.

The question causes Jenna to pause long enough for Maia to realize that, while she herself doesn't know (weird that she had never asked Greg about it before), neither does Jenna. "All right, Greg," Jenna says, giving Maia a cursory glance before walking off. "Though don't cause so much of a disturbance next time!" she calls over her shoulder.

Greg nods at the apprentice who is somewhat flustered by Jenna's sudden retreat. She begins following her guide back to their spot on the other side of the tree.

"Well, that went well," Greg says more to himself than to Maia, then looks at her. "By the way, I actually don't know what kind of tree this is either." He winks at her, causing Maia to both laugh and blush. "However," he continues, "that also makes your feat all the more mysterious."

Maia's face, which was starting to feel flushed, suddenly feels very cold. Greg notices and lets out a single laugh, surprisingly light and clear compared to his normally deep voice.

"Don't worry, Maia, I'm certain you didn't violate any fundamental Elementalist laws like Bel's 'Living things should not be trifled with' shtick. I don't know how you did it, but I know for certain you did do it. Which then means…" His voice trails off at a subtle tremor in the tower. A low rumble, and quick, small throbs cause the tower to quiver.

All at once the tremors cease. "What was that?" Maia asks.

"Master Kellen opened his office," Greg says with a frown.

"Wait, there really is an office at the top of the tower?"

Greg laughs again. "I've never lied to you, Maia. Anyway, something as mundane as a hermetically sealed office shouldn't be surprising to you right now."

Tilting her head, she gazes up past the branches of the tree clinging to the ceiling. As ever, the light radiates across all surfaces of the tower normally, though she senses some large portion of the tower far above has moved. "Circumlocution!" Maia cries triumphantly, causing Greg to jump.

"What?"

"That's what you use! Circumlocution… hehe!" She can't help but laugh at herself for saying it, it being such a weird word.

Greg smiles at her, nodding. "It seems I've been found out. Now I'll need to find a new tactic." The smile fades again when the clear sound of shoes clapping against the floor reverberate down the steps. He looks up to where the stair joins the floor above.

Maia, following his gaze, watches as a pair of feet, each fitted with a silvery boot, takes the steps down quickly. The form of a middle-aged man appears to whisk his way along the tower wall round and round. "Master Kellen?" Maia whispers so that only Greg can hear. Greg nods.

Master Kellen reaches their floor in what has to be a record time, and hurries straight for Maia and Greg. He wears a smart deep blue jacket over a pure white buttoned shirt tucked into black pants that widen at the end, each leg's cuffs hovering above the tops of his silver ankle boots. He stops short, appraising each of them individually, then his gaze follows the root of the tree to the trunk and then all the way up. He turns back to them, gathering himself up in a formal posture, looking to Maia like he is about to say something important. His shoulders fall, and he lets out a deep sigh.

"Ah, Greg. And Maia," Master Kellen breathes more than says. "It's good to meet you, Maia. And, of course, see you again, Greg. You probably noticed me open my office…" He stops to laugh breathily as if he made a joke. "Well, I'm here, so that should be doubly obvious. I'd like to speak with both of you, individually, if it would be all right."

The way he talks sounds oddly relieved, though coming from the man dressed like he's at some festive party it is welcoming.

Maia doesn't answer, waiting for Greg to acquiesce for the both of them as any guide is required to do for his apprentice. Greg gives a faint "Of course," which Maia knows well enough as not due to timidity but respect.

"Come!" Master Kellen says warmly, turning and racing away and up the stairs at the same impossible speed he came down them.

Too afraid to match his speed for fear of falling on her face, Maia pumps her legs quickly enough in an effort to at least not lose sight of him.

"You don't have to rush," Greg says behind her. "He's patient, and doesn't expect others to be nearly as fast as him."

"Why does he do it, then?" Maia asks, panting slightly as she slows down.

"When I asked him, he told me he liked the rush. He also muttered something about magicians never exercising physically, though personally I don't know where anyone would find the time and energy outside practicing magic, an already exhausting hobby."

Maia's breath evens out, now taking her time marching up the steps. At least someone else thinks it's exhausting. "Does he know what I did?" The question comes out calm, though the sudden appearance of the tower's master and all its implications has her awash in nerves.

"He's not banning you from the tower, if that's what you're getting at," she hears Greg say. There's a pause as they circle up the stairs, both of them attentive to Jenna and her apprentice looking up at them from below. "If anything, he's extracting us from eavesdroppers so that he can explain something important to us."

Maia nods, though "something important" only paints what she did as all the more sinister.

The two emerge on the next floor up, though Maia doesn't risk a glance at Renauld or any of the others. She doesn't have to look to know what they're thinking, because the floor is deathly still, not even one soft kiss from a magical breeze to ruffle her hair.

The rest of the walk up is silent, though Maia is curious about the two upper levels she rarely gets to visit. Both contain furnishings, also made of sand, unlike any of the other floors which are primarily for practicing purposes. In each floor, several magicians occupy the sandstone couches, none of them doing any magic, all deep in conversation when Maia and Greg appear, though they hush when they see the pair.

When Maia's legs begin aching from all the steps, they reach the top floor, vacant save for more elaborate furnishings. In addition to the molded sand couches, tables, stools, and even a bookcase, there are various glass objects, most of them vials, resting atop the tables, full with different colored liquids. One dark blue liquid has a steady flow of steam rising from it, though the steam doesn't evaporate and instead lingers several inches above the floor in a thin layer of vapor. Maia's feet break the vapor's surface as she steps down, though she then realizes the stairs continue up straight into the ceiling and stop there.

When she turns to Greg with eyebrows raised, he makes a shooing motion. She continues up, apprehensive at first. Unbeknownst to her, as she climbs, a hole opens up where the stairs meet the ceiling, and at reaching the floor's height and glancing up she sees it. Without pausing to show surprise, she steps up into a room vastly different than the rest of the tower.

The walls curve inward overhead, though are largely masked by wood. The wood, also curving with the wall, starting from the floor up, consists of shelves packed with books towering over Maia, and end with individual columns of planks reaching and meeting at the center of the domed ceiling. The floor itself is covered with overlapping rugs of varied sizes and shapes. Where Maia stands is a blue-and-white ocean-patterned ovular rug, whose edges cover another ovular rug sporting the sword-and-tree crest of Lanmar, whose edges cover another rectangular rug dominating the room and featuring a blazing fire pattern surrounding a circular object at its center, whose edges are covered by many more rugs Maia doesn't bother to admire. Atop the rugs before the far wall is a table with four unremarkable chairs, three facing the outer wall and one facing toward the majority of the room. This chair is occupied by Master Kellen, who is fixated on a book opened before him on the table.

Maia moves to stand on the fiery rug slightly before the chairs, too uneasy to sit down, while Greg takes one of the chairs. Master Kellen looks up at Greg, an apologetic frown forming on his face.

"I'm sorry, Greg. I wish to speak with Maia first. Alone." He speaks with the same smoothness as a released breath of air, something Maia would otherwise consider peeving, though coming from the wizened man it is relaxing.

Maia watches Greg lower his head once, a nod, and he exits. As he passes Maia, he whispers, "I'll be waiting right below." Once he's gone, Maia is left to stand uncomfortably in front of Master Kellen's soft yet penetrating gaze.

"Don't be alarmed," he says, "I didn't summon you here so that I can analyze you. Though I would ask you to be willing to analyze yourself." He says this last sentence with a tonal change that is still breathy, though sharper, as he enunciates the words.

"What do you mean?"

He beckons her over, turning the book on the table to face her. "What you performed to that tree, or for that tree, is not something any Elementalist magic can do," he says as Maia moves to see what's written in the book. She looks at him in surprise. "Please, don't be surprised. I am called 'Master' of this tower for a reason." He pauses. Maia wonders whether what he says is self-praise or explanation. "By the way, please don't call me by my title. I prefer Kellen."

Explanation, she thinks decidedly. Looking down at the pages before her, she finds a table of contents that lists the different chapters in the book. Each chapter is titled with what appear to be different fields of magic, starting with Elemental, and continuing through a variety of others Maia had no idea existed. There are so many she can't believe no one she knows has discussed them with her, much less believe she herself hasn't found written about in a book from her town library.

"Mast—" she cuts herself off, excitement and nervousness confusing her thoughts, "I mean, Kellen, are these... are there really more types of magic than Elemental?"

"Why, of course. Haven't you heard of the magician Dunlon?" It's not meant to be cutting, especially in the slow airy way he speaks, though Maia can't help but feel embarrassed she had never considered or questioned it.

"Well, I have, though I don't know much. I just thought he was a really powerful Elementalist. Wait a minute, how come no one told me about other types of magic when I first came here?"

Kellen frowns, only for a moment, before the calmly vacant face returns. "Telnas has… use for magicians with potential. Elementalists are lowest on their radar, and I make it a point not to teach beyond the specialty of this magic."

Why? Maia wants to ask why for everything he says, though Kellen is still talking.

"Although, I suppose I should have a word with Greg and the other guides to make sure there is some sort of baseline of knowledge students are being taught. Let me bring you up to speed, starting from what you may already know. This tower was named the Tower of Bel after one of the lesser first-known magic-users, during a time when names were commonly four letters or less, save for the more prestigious individuals. Like the magician Bel, the residents of the Tower of Bel have always been, and are, Elementalists, which is to say they specialize and perform in nature, one of the many realms of magic. Elementalists are considered basic since they cannot spontaneously create nor destroy that which they manipulate, and the nature they do manipulate is always tangible and simple matter.

"Dunlon, one of the greatest magicians, if not the greatest magician, was known to have dabbled in the Elemental to see if he could transform the genetic makeup of a porpoise's fin into a bat's wing, but ended up only influencing the porpoise's behavior to flap like a bat. Many chalked his trials up to him not being well-read and practiced in Elemental magic, though even the best Elementalists after him have tried to transform matter to give it new properties, with no luck. Bel, who lived before Dunlon, argued things were not to be changed drastically from what they were, especially living things, lest the natural order be disbalanced. Most Elementalists agreed with her logic, mostly because they feared the thought of a magician transforming one of them into a stone or some other object. That didn't stop many of them from trying."

He pauses momentarily, then nods. "Ah, well, now you know more. Now, as to why I brought you up here other than to take a look at all the fields of magic, I want you to consider several options."

Maia's face twitches. She barely kept up with the history lesson, her thoughts still stuck on the sinister way Kellen mentioned some in Telnas looking for magicians. Now, the topic of conversation is becoming eerily similar to every other one she has had with her parents regarding her future and finding a job.

"It is up to you to decide, though I'm here if you want advice," he continues. "Take your time reading each field—there are synopses on the first page of every chapter—and when you're ready, tell me which field you find the most intriguing."

Slightly overwhelmed, Maia plops into the middle of the three chairs and pulls the book closer to rest on her forearms. The thought of abandoning all that she has practiced in Elemental magic—moving and solidifying water, creating tiny daredevils out of still air, and even molding a small section of solid rock—seems like a waste. She hasn't even gotten to really manipulate fire yet (the feeling of combusting a pile of wood is a real rush). Though, if there are other fields of magic, perhaps she could find something as exciting, if not more exciting, than whipping up a gust of wind to fly over the country on.

She turns to the first chapter, deciding to reread what she already knows of Elemental magic. The book describes it as a lesser magic (for what reason Maia does not know) and it, as she already knows, involves manipulation of the elements. The next chapter details several subfields of Elemental, as well as overlapping ones, and one of them Maia finds particularly fascinating: Shapeshifting, or as the synopsis says, "changing the material of oneself." It lists various uses, such as shrinking, expanding, and even turning invisible.

The following chapters go over the subfields of Elemental magic in more depth (air, water, fire, earth, and synthetic), though Maia skims these since she knows the gist of each. Coming across another chapter reveals a new field for her: Spatial. There are two primary subfields listed: Teleportation magic, in which the user can displace objects or herself without moving, and Void magic, in which the user can simply open and close space. Maia wonders what the uses of Void magic are, though shudders at the thought of moving space to form simply nothing, and reads on.

Again, the following chapters describe the interplay and overlap between the previously discussed fields, though a small section catches her attention. It explains different techniques and approaches to conducting magic, noting somatic (the text doesn't define this for Maia, though she deduces its meaning from the next word to be related to the body) and cognitive practice, as well as verbal. The mention of spoken word magic catches Maia's attention. She was unaware she could manipulate elements using her voice. She stows this news away in her mind before continuing.

She's nearing the end of the book, and though she is taking her time, she is too drawn in to apologize to Kellen. Another chapter details theoretical approaches to Mind

Control, which Maia breezes by. She's uninterested in manipulating other people (the thought is too scary for her to entertain). She finally reaches a new field of magic. Conjuring, the title says, then continues with the magic of creating from nothing. That's literally the extent of the synopsis before it goes into applications and approaches, which only go on for the next two pages. Such a tiny chapter for a magic that has seemingly endless possibilities confuses Maia, though she is already reading the title of the next chapter.

Enchantment. This intrigues Maia deeply, and she scans the synopsis. She is delighted at what she reads. Being able to impart effects to an object for the object to then impart effects onto its environment is very appealing, and Maia can think of multiple practical uses. She could create a necklace that allows its wearer to breathe underwater, clothing that protects its wearer from heat, boots that make its wearer light-footed to walk on water, perhaps even on air, and travel great distances, a ring that makes its wearer very strong... Maia realizes she's caught up in a daydream and looks up at Kellen, who is watching her thoughtfully.

"Have you found a new field of magic you're wanting to practice?" he asks.

Looking back down, she flips over the last couple of pages until she reaches the bindings. Written on the inside cover next to an asterisk are the words Fields of magic are listed in order of power and difficulty. She closes the book and slides it back onto the table, thinking hard. "What if I want to continue learning Elemental magic?"

Kellen spreads his arms, palms open. "By all means, continue doing so."

Biting her lip, the answer not quite helping her decide, she thinks some more. "What do you think?" she asks finally.

His mouth twinges upward, seemingly pleased at the desire for his opinion. "You are young, Maia. Even the most aged magician can start learning magic if she hadn't known she could do it before, but she is forced to choose a single field which she must then attune to."

Maia tilts her head, confused.

Kellen says, "I know you don't know what I'm talking about, because I don't tell anyone who doesn't have the potential to change fields of magic. Most of the other Elementalists here don't know, and those who do I ask not to discuss it openly so that other Elementalists don't feel left out. It is somewhat insulting as a magician to learn that you are restricted to a certain field of magic. I imagine it is something like what non-magic folk feel about magicians.

"I don't like to think in levels of magic, though the different fields undeniably have varying difficulty, as you no doubt noticed from reading the inner binding. That said, it is unfair to say Elemental magic is the weakest since it is the 'easiest' to learn." He makes quotation marks with his fingers. "And it is unfair to say it is the easiest to learn since it is the 'weakest.' Neither is wholly true. Magic comes to us subjectively, and such general terms like strong and weak, easy and hard, are only measured from averages. Remember, Maia, it is never wise to determine one's potential from an average."

With a nod, Maia arcs her back, feeling the stiff muscles pop and loosen. Then she asks, "But what field do you think I would be the best in?"

Rubbing his fingers, Kellen sits forward, elbows resting on the table and hands clasped for his head to rest on. "That is a more complicated question to answer. Given your already extensive ability to do Elemental magic, you would seem well off staying put. However—today's event revealed you also have a certain propensity for something different. The nature of it is unknown to me, unfortunately," he says with a sorrowful sigh. "If I had to guess, what you performed is a mix between Conjuring and perhaps some form of Mind Control."

Maia's face blanches. "Mind Control?"

"Not in the sense you forced dominion over the tree," Kellen says hastily, "though to some extent, you did influence the tree to do what it did. And before you ask, yes, a tree technically has a 'mind,' though not a brain. I suppose the colloquial term we use for it is will."

Maia relaxes, easing back into her chair. "Okay. Conjuring and Mind Control. But wait, hold on a minute, you said older magicians are forced to attune to some sort of magic. What does that mean?"

"At a certain point in every magician's life, usually around full maturity when they reach 20 years old, they choose a field of magic that they will forever favor above all others. They may still be able to perform others, though only at the most basic level and never to the extent of magicians specializing in that field."

This makes Maia worried. What if she chose a field of magic she would later hate? Would she grow up longing to be practiced in another field than the one she chose?

"It does have an ominous note of finality to it, doesn't it?" Kellen continues. "Of course, you're still only thirteen. You have a rather large head-start compared to other magicians in making such a decision. So, what would I suggest?"

Maia perks up, eager for some solid advice.

"Read some books about other fields. Study."

Instantly, Maia deflates. She doesn't want to study. She wants to do stuff. Suddenly Kellen bursts into laughter causing Maia to start, his svelte frame rocking back in his own chair.

"I'm only joking, although you're free to do so if you wish. What I'd really suggest is to visit the other Occult Towers and practice under each to get a feel for different magics."

"Other... Occult Towers?" Maia has only heard the Tower of Bel described as a singular Occult Tower.

"Yes. There are two others, one on the eastern border of Lanmar and another in a low valley a little north of Telnas. I suggest the far east tower, known as the Tower of Vern, who was a very fine Conjuror, for you to start."

"You're saying I should travel all the way to the other edge of Lanmar," Maia states more than asks.

"It's quicker travel than you think. Plus, I can call upon someone to get you there."

Still a little stunned, she asks, "Who?"

"Just a second." Kellen turns his head to watch a section of the tower's wall that peels away under his gaze. Maia stares in awe, aware that she is witnessing a master in Elemental magic perform in front of her. She feels a light breeze waft over her, though senses the tingling of magic and focuses her mind to understand what Kellen is doing. She only notices an unnatural wind current, like a tunnel of air, reaching through the opening and ending at Kellen. Kellen's mouth then moves as if he's talking, though Maia hears nothing. He stops, turning back to Maia, and the hole in the tower closes. The air becomes still again.

"What was that? What just happened?"

"I was calling Darren. He's a Teleporter, and hopefully will get here within the next few minutes. My message may get somewhat distorted since air isn't a great conduit and can't hold sound reverberations too well and the distance is far, but he'll know it's me."

She is about to ask the same questions a different way, though decides to drop it. Whatever it was, it was too controlled for her to make sense of even by directly observing it, much less try to practice it herself. "So…" she starts slowly, "You called someone who can teleport."

Kellen raps a knuckle on the desk. "Right. Darren is one of those who I mentioned before: a magician in Telnas who—let's just say he works closely with the guard. I trust him, but just because I do doesn't mean you should."

That's ominous Maia thinks. "Wait, hold on!" She notices she's developed a bad habit of telling people to wait for more mundane things, though at this moment the phrase seems acceptable. "You expect me to leave now!? I haven't decided if I want to go yet! I mean, what if I want to stay?"

Kellen chuckles softly at her building hysteria. "The youthful sure are complex. It seems you are not always prone to rush into things."

Maia feels like this is one of those condescending adult things she gets with her father, though Kellen doesn't wait to bask in her annoyance.

"Don't mind my banter. I have a bad habit of observing things aloud—sometimes I catch myself narrating my own life. As for your questions," he pauses, his eyes sincere when he looks at her, "what do you want?"

Most of her warring thoughts are blown away by the question, though a single one remains.

"I saw the way your eyes lit up a few times while reading about certain fields," he continues, apparently going to give her the answer she already knows. "I have a feeling you want to explore. And, what better time than now?"

He stops, waiting for Maia. She takes a breath.

"All right. I want to learn different magics."

Beaming at her, Kellen closes the book on the table, the satisfying thump like a gavel affirming a final verdict. "That's wonderful! You won't have to worry about your parents, for I have associates in Fairbreeze that can notify them. You can, of course, take your time telling them yourself—"

"That's all right," Maia says quickly, already thankful she won't have to listen to another spiel about life choices from her parents. "Though I was wondering, what magic does the other Occult Tower practice? The one north of Telnas?"

"Vale Tower. It got its name for being in a valley, and the taxonomists were known for their ingenious names for things," he says dryly. "They practice Spatial magic."

Her face falls. "What about the other magics? Like, where do Enchanters learn?"

"Enchantment... hmm, those who practice it are few and far between. Most magicians tend to specialize in the more active magics. I don't think I can name you an Enchanter off the top of my head, though my knowledge only spans as far as Lanmar. To be honest, the only thing I know regarding Enchantment is the Solar Flare, illustrated in the rug behind you."

Maia turns to look over her shoulder at the rug with a crimson stone at its center surrounded by flames. "An enchanted rock?"

Laughing, Kellen says, "Well, yes, though it is said to house the fire of a nearby star that vanished long ago. No one knows how, who, or why this story came about and whether it is simply a myth, though I suppose it is best such an item doesn't exist, or at least never resurfaces given the potential for chaos it would bring in the hands of an Enchanter."

"How come?" Maia asks, more curious than frightened of the rock now.

"Hmmm... how to put it. Well. In the hands of an Enchanter, an enchanted object's power is infinite. Say, for example, you enchant a mask to allow underwater breathing. An Enchanter can use it literally forever, though the Enchanter's natural life ends quite a bit before then. Someone specializing in another field of magic or someone non-magical can use the mask for a limited time before its magic is expended. Imagine the power of a star in the hands of an Enchanter."

If Maia could whistle, she would have. There's a small pause in which she lets everything she's learned sink in.

"Tell you what," Kellen says suddenly. "I'll research Enchanters for you so when you come back, er, that is, if you decide to come back, even just to visit, I'll know where to tell you to go if you want to learn Enchantment."

Maia brightens, nodding thankfully.

"I'm glad that that's settled. One last thing. Ah." He says this last part as if pleased with something. "Darren's here. Come, let's go downstairs and meet him. You can catch Greg up on the way down."

At first she doesn't understand why he emphasizes "you," but she remembers what Greg told her about Kellen's exercising just as he springs up and rushes from the room, almost galloping down the stairway. She supposes, slowly standing up from her chair and making her way out of the room, when you grow older you naturally develop such eccentricities.

Chapter 8: **Not**

Any town worth staying in has to have a tavern, and any tavern worth having has to have a distillation of the finest beer in Lanmar: Midnight Delight.

"Seriously, what is it with you and that wimpy alcohol?" Idrid asks across the roughly sanded table, nursing her own beer. "Summer's Fire is the most popular, and for good reason."

I ignore her jab. I grab my mug and carefully place my elbows down, avoiding the coarse spots of the table so as not to get splinters. "It's not about which tastes the best," I say, reverently moving my mug around in my hands to cause the pale yellow liquid to swirl. I glance around the room. We've chosen a table far enough back and in a corner to have a good vantage so that we can't be snuck up on. Satisfied by the mellow tavern-goers, most sitting individually at meticulously placed seating, creating the lovely sense of controlled chaos that only a tavern could perfect, I look up at Idrid. Her figure is, as ever, imposing, though the dim atmosphere of the tavern softens her largeness.

"What's it about then?"

Giving her a knowing smile, I reach into one of the three pouches I keep attached to my belt on my side, and I pull out a vial the size of a thumb containing a golden liquid. "Remember that whole bar fight back in Ferry when that guy took my sword? Well, before any of that happened because someone had to aggravate an already rowdy patron, I was enjoying the miraculous work of my beverage." I flourish the vial at her before pulling out the stopper and pouring it into my drink.

"You really like Midnight Delight, huh?" It's only when she's inebriated that Idrid ever says anything redundant, though I encourage it since it gives me more openings to hear myself talk.

"The drink by itself isn't enough," I say, again placing my elbows down to carefully swirl the drink in my hands. "It's the supplements that really put it in a league of its own."

"Where do you get that from, anyway?"

"Gold hops. Plucked from the fields we pass by all the time, being travelers and all." True to their name, they give my drink an ironic warm yellow color as fine as a midmorning haze. What I don't tell her, not because I don't trust her but because it's too complicated to explain, is I've added chemical components that give the beer a strong drowsiness effect. The reason I fell unconscious during the bar fight after mistakenly intaking some of it. Well, I don't really consider it a mistake, since the drink had been thrown in my face.

Idrid takes another large sip from her own mug and slams it down, the sound joining the charivari of tavern noise. "I never see you drink it," she says. I eye her fourth Summer's Fire, its golden color comparable to my tweaked Midnight Delight. "Why don't you ever drink it?" she continues, rubbing her face groggily.

"I've told you before, I have to wait for maximum effect." That is, full potency. "Come on, I'll bring you up to our room so you can sleep. We'll be continuing on our way early tomorrow." This last part is obviously not true, though we both know it since we define "early" to be after noon.

Standing, I leave my beer on the table and take Idrid's arm. Getting her up is the most important part since I could hardly carry her, much less up stairs, and I always take care to get her to our room before she falls into a daze. It works out well since it would be suspicious if I did my work accompanied by a half-Giantess.

She obeys my pull, and I guide her across the room, weaving between the strewn tables and tall chairs, then up the stairs, and finally across the threshold of our room. We were fortunate enough to be one of the few travelers to have snagged the room; most everyone downstairs appears to be a resident of the town.

"Get some sleep," I tell her softly, waiting by the open door and watching as she muddles to the beds I pushed together to fit her frame. Once she's lying down and I hear her breathing begin to relax, I quietly close the door and go back downstairs.

Looking across the tavern I see my drink hasn't moved. Leaving it alone in the first place was a tactic that worked half the time. Greedy tavern-goers can't resist the sight of a full mug of any beer. From here I can't tell the difference between it and Summer's Fire, signifying my mixture has mostly mixed in.

Crossing the room again, I sit down facing away from the wall and nurse the mug as the other patrons do with their own drinks. Across the walls are windows, though the blinds are closed to retain the soft amber light sifting through the air from individual lightbulbs hanging across the ceiling. I aim to find a target that looks remotely wealthy, or at least not wearing commoner clothes.

Mostly everyone keeps to themselves—only two groups of three gathered around their own respective tables and a woman chatting up the bartender. When running this scheme, groups are never any good to attempt a pickpocket, so I turn my attention to the others scattered throughout the room. Many wear drab tunics, only some with a wool jacket thrown over their shoulders. To give them credit, they all have a potential swagger that seems to be the norm for common folk, which makes sense, given they do the dirty work. I only note this because it makes me feel better about taking from anyone in the upper class, which constitutes anyone marginally richer than a commoner.

My eyes return again to the woman at the counter. The wall behind the bartender has alcoholic beverages lining the shelves. He is leaning over to talk quietly to the woman. I observe him more closely; his cheeks are rosy, though his eyes are too sharp for him to be tipsy (I've known tavern keepers to drink on the job); sweat beads dot his forehead under his thinning brown hair; he maintains a slight smile as his mouth moves; and his lean is all too forward to be casual. All signs point to him being attracted to the woman.

Hold on a minute—this woman is seducing him! I've seen the same techniques used by many a prostitute—not ones I paid for, since I'm above that, though not above following the prostitute and their buyer to their room to steal a little something—and the way she carries herself I know she's refined her skills over much practice. When she isn't talking she holds her rosy lips apart, as if part-surprised and part-delighted with what the bartender says. Most of her back is facing me, though I can see the subtle animations of her face from the side as well as the not-so-subtle nods of her head, her long dark hair bobbing slightly from its neatly tucked hairpin, like a swishing pony's tail. Come to think of it, that's probably how the ponytail hairstyle got its name. I can be such a dunderhead sometimes.

The woman is not dressed the part of a prostitute, but I've had enough experience to know the tricks of the trade, so much so that I once doubled as a prostitute myself in order to get a man alone and knock him out. She wears a tight black blouse with a matching shawl, a look both mysterious and alluring. From the look of her long, slender arms she hasn't undergone the tasking work of commoners that would build at least some muscle. Could she be royalty?

She turns her head and I duck my head down close to my mug as if to sip while fixing my gaze to her. She scans the room back and forth, as casually as any tavern-goer, then continues jovially attending to the bartender. Something about it was off and it took me a second to register it; her head and face remained still and composed, though her eyes had flicked between each individual; some she double-checked, as if evaluating them. Royalty would have reason to be distrustful... I stand up. It looks like I've found my target, though I'd better hurry before the bartender gets too attached.

Grasping my mug, a visual facsimile of Summer's Fire, I saunter slowly toward her, making sure to get the bartender's attention. I stop two stools over from the one she sits on, giving meaningful glances her way. The bartender, thankfully not a confrontational fellow, steps away, clearly more intrigued by how I play this than worrying about his "claimed" territory. Perhaps he's counting on me messing up or the woman turning me down.

"Hello there," I say, striking a balance between shy and forward, tilting my head and turning it slightly to peer at her sideways.

"Hello," she says. Her voice is slightly deeper than expected, though not as deep as Idrid's, and drawling.

"You wouldn't by chance like a drink?" I ask. I shift the mug across the counter a couple of inches in a nonassertive offering. "I can't bring myself to drink another."

She doesn't even look at the glass, staring at me. She slides a hand onto the top of the stool between us and scooches into it. Gingerly, she moves an arm to take the beer. I release my grip, slowly enough to allow our fingers to brush for a moment. The middle finger of her right hand has an appealing ruby ring encircling it that I mentally note as something worth taking.

"Such a kind offer. Thank you," she says, sliding it the rest of the way to sit in front of her, but doesn't drink it just yet. "You don't look like you're from around here. A traveler?"

Thankful for the opportunity to talk more openly, I begin my act. "Oh, I've traveled quite a ways. Just yesterday I was in a little town called Ferry—ever heard of it?"

She shakes her head, her ponytail oscillating behind her.

"Well, trust me, you aren't missing much. It's far to the southeast with nowhere to go for miles. Except the Talwood, though not many would dare to enter such a place."

"Such a ways," she says with a smile. "What brings you to The Bludgeoned Boar of all places?"

"What else?" I say, gesturing vaguely to the mug she holds in both her hands.

"Beer?"

"I meant the one holding it."

"HA!"

Together we look at the bartender, who barked out the laugh. He shakes his head, a massive grin on his face. "That's one I haven't heard. Good on you!" Without another word he walks off to a corner behind the bar counter, still smiling.

The entire time I had been talking to the woman he hadn't been making much of an effort to appear like he wasn't listening, and I was afraid he would persist in wooing her. I put on a bashful face, turning back and smiling somewhat stupidly at the woman. "Hah… I'm not usually so forward…"

For her part, her face does not redden in embarrassment, though she pretends to blush behind a raised hand. Her other lifts the mug, and I watch as her performance freezes so she can enjoy the drink. My smile deepens.

She turns back to me, daintily licking her lips, her coy smile returning. "What is it?"

"Like I said, I'm never this forward. To tell the truth, I've never flirted at all..." Not the truth at all, though the change from confident to shy is another quality people generally find attractive. Something about appearing honest and vulnerable pulls them in and weakens their defenses.

She lets out a soft, charming laugh, again covering her face with a hand. "You're cute," she says, taking another sip from the mug.

I feign embarrassment, tilting my chin down and rubbing the back of my neck with a hand. "Would you... like to go out for a stroll? Maybe show me around Chalman?" I ask this knowing that it is unlikely she lives in this town.

"Why, of course!" She steps down from her stool and moves for the door, her pace surprising me. I follow. We step outside, and she asks, "What would you like to see first?"

"How about... someplace quiet? Uncrowded?"

"I know just the place," she says, and walks briskly down a well-trodden dirt path leading away from the main thoroughfare of cobblestone, around the back of the tavern. It stretches a ways to a lone cottage with an orange grove just beside it. I can picture an idyllic orange luminescence warmly emanating from the square windows reflecting off the wavy green and brown wildgrass and vibrant leaves of the orange trees, though the lights are off and the setting is of muted colors. As it is, the silhouette of the cottage is more unwelcoming than anything.

As we approach, I notice littler details that are off; an outside shutter discolored from aged paint hangs off one of its hinges; the grass is more untamed than the simple charm of a slightly unkempt lawn; and the door to the cottage is open. I don't recall it being open.

"What is this place?" I ask to her retreating back.

"It's my home," she says pleasantly without stopping. "Come on inside."

Her voice is sickly warm like the taste of too much butter. Weird, my tongue picks up the same unpleasant taste. She passes through the doorway first, turning with an outstretched hand. I follow, taking her hand and letting her pull me inside.

The second I step through the threshold, the place lights up. I freeze as the door closes behind me of its own accord, only my eyes moving to follow the woman, who lets go of my hand and walks into a living room, plopping herself down on a sofa.

"Now… what to do with you?" she muses to herself, and the look on my face causes her to chuckle not at all like she laughed before. "You're a fine specimen of man, much better than that bartender."

I consider my instinct to go still. The dull, sickening taste of too much butter lingers on my tongue. I finally understand she's using magic. "You're a magician," I say, taking a step toward her. If she's part of the Guild or Guard, I need to act quickly.

"Stop." A wave of wind rushes up in front of me like a wall, and the air becomes still. Not the sort of stillness of regular air, but the air in front of me is literally not moving.

"Elemental magic?"

"I'm impressed," she coos, her voice fainter as if coming from several rooms away, then I realize it is, since sound waves can't really travel through whatever magic she is doing. "You know more than the average man about magic." She goes silent, watching me.

I look at her through the weird air wall. Every sort of magician I've come across has had a strange effect on me, all to do with taste and smell. I always questioned the reaction since it evoked a bit of nausea, and over my encounters I developed a sort of tolerance. I never got rid of the ruddy tastes, though.

"You lured me here?" I prompt, taking a step away from the air wall. Behind me and at the door I feel another rush of air and know that I am trapped in the entryway. Well, to her I'm trapped.

"Yes." She stands up, moving in front of me on the other side of the air wall. "You're going to give me what I want."

I raise my eyebrows, noting her taunting. "And what is that?"

"All of your gold."

My eyebrows go higher. There's little sense for royalty to need money. Then again, they do go out of their way to get as much as they can. I shake my head. The walls around me are withered and cracked all over the place, so she certainly isn't royalty.

"You're in no place to refuse," she says, mistaking my movement as me saying no.

"Uh-huh." I cross my arms and lean back on one leg. Any minute now and the drowsiness should kick in.

For the first time she frowns, looking mildly upset. "You don't seem to care that I have you trapped in my house. Would you prefer suffocating until you pass out, or will you comply?"

She is getting pushy. I take a moment to think. A prostitute who uses her charm and magic to rob people is better than a royal, but still seems unfair. I'm not saying I'm much better, though technically I come by my money through honest scamming and not the kind that no one can help falling for. If I were to play the hero, if only for a moment, how would I prevent her from terrorizing this town?

"Just give me your damn money," she says peevishly, getting impatient. "I don't want to use force, but I will."

"Is there a guard outpost in this town?"

Her smile returns. "It doesn't matter—no matter how fast you can get them I'll simply leave."

I nod. "All right. What's your name, if you don't mind me asking? It won't matter since you'll most likely change it, but I want something to remind myself of whom to direct my anger toward for losing all my money."

She considers this, eyeing me. She yawns, shaking her head. "Jasmine. Now, would you—" She yawns again.

I step through the air wall. It parts around me, and she takes a sluggish step back, her eyes conflicted between drowsiness and shock. In a swift motion I take her arm, pull her close, and gather her up in my arms. She is heavier than I anticipated, though I manage to carry her to the sofa.

"What is this?" she breathes, her eyes slits, though I see her dark pupils looking up at me.

"You'll wake up soon enough," I say quietly, laying her down. I watch for several more seconds until her clenching hands relax and fall to her side. My eyes fall to the ruby ring she is wearing. Despite its appeal, it has an engraving indicating it's likely a personal item. Stemming my greed, I peel my eyes away and wander around the room, searching for anything that would both sell for a high price and not be so suspicious that it would turn away buyers. I very much doubt Jasmine really lives here. Its interior is rundown, explaining the decrepit outside lawn and furnishings. The electricity works, though, which I figure was one of the few things she managed to salvage of this place.

I take a quick tour of the house, doing a sweep to look for any hidden nooks or crannies that a magical seductress who picked up strangers in the night for money might hide something in. Every room looks as unappealingly drab and untenanted as the rest, save for the bedroom, which has several layers of silk sheets, each a different monochromatic warm color, covering the bed. I recognize the cloth to be as sybaritic as Jasmine's dress, and stop beside the bed, turning in place. The room is set in a corner of the house with two doors leading out, one to the kitchen and the other to a T-hall conjoining the bedroom to both the living room and entryway. Still, the floors, walls, and furniture are well aged. A curved vanity rests beside the wall opposing the bed, and I walk over to it, admiring myself in the mirror.

I brush a hand across my bangs, which are growing shaggy. They hang just above my glinting eyes. Looking away from my dashing looks, I slide open all of the drawers. Nothing but variously sized hairbrushes.

As I take several steps back from the vanity, I notice something about the room is different from the rest. My eyes follow the wall behind the vanity up to the ceiling. This room is the only one where the roof is slanted. In the corner, above a knee-high trunk, is where the ceiling is the lowest. Stepping over to the trunk, I unlatch the lid and pull it open. It is entirely empty. I close it again, looking up at the ceiling several feet above me. A slightly discolored patch of wood stands out from the rest, though it is otherwise as much a part of the ceiling as any of the rest of the decaying wood.

I step onto the trunk and finger the dark spot. It's as coarse as the rest. As I touch it, I begin to take my hand away for fear of splinters, though I feel the wood budge. Slowly, I push up. The wood recedes into the ceiling, and falls away to the side. It's a hidden compartment, half the size of the trunk I stand on. Excellent.

Reaching further, I feel around. My hand brushes something thick and soft. I pull out a long article of clothing I don't recognize that barely fits through the gap in the ceiling. A bag—no, a purse that was resting on top of it falls to the floor with a loud chink that perks me right up. Before I drop down from the trunk to scoop up the purse, I remember the cloth I'm still holding. Holding it in front of me for a better look, I gasp.

It's a hoodless cloak, its rayon a striking royal red with a meticulous embroidery that offsets the red with a deeper red pattern like that of a checkerboard. Though, a checkerboard has too defined a pattern, for this fabric is so interwoven it could easily be mistaken to be one shade of red or the other, depending on which caught your eye first. Its collar is stitched together around the chest, then splits elegantly around the area of the solar plexus. The hem ends along my lower calves, pretty much a perfect fit for me.

I appraise it warily, considering the costs and benefits of wearing such clothing. I know it to be the same clothing worn by high-level magicians, specifically those in contact with the Royal Court of Lanmar, though how a simple Elementalist came by it is a mystery. It is undoubtedly a beacon for trouble if recognized—however, only royalty and the most powerful of magicians would truly know what the cloak signifies. Not even the majority of the Guard would know much, other than it being a mark that deserves reverence. In that regard, it is invaluable.

I feel along the inside of the collar, and my hand snags on an unusual protrusion of fabric like a sleeve. I pull on it lightly and reveal a black face mask smoothly knitted along the front neckline. Grinning wickedly, I mentally commend Jasmine for the ingenious feature. Of course she would want to hide her face in her line of work.

Finally, I step off the trunk and pull the cloak over my head. It wraps loosely around my shoulders, and falls gracefully around me. I tuck the face mask back behind the collar and scoop up the purse from the floor. I peer in to see a small fortune inside.

The cloak lacks pockets, though I notice simply by touch that there are dagger sleeves concealed within as well. Jasmine must like to play dirty. Thinking about her pulls my mind back to what I should do about her. I'm not one to go out and report a criminal, though that seems like my best option, since I don't want her following me.

I hold the purse in my left hand and walk out of the house, my new cloak's heavy fabric only minutely shifting in motion. I resign myself to the duty of reporting that an Elementalist on the outskirts of town commandeered a house and tried to rob me. Then again, that can wait until morning. The effects of my tweaked Midnight Delight will continue for another six hours, and I could use some rest myself.

Idrid wakes up with a shudder. She throws the covers off both the beds and rises stiffly. I watch her swivel her head around in the reflection of the mirror I am admiring myself in set against the wall next to the door. Her eyes meet mine, then drop to the cloak. "What are you wearing?"

"A cloak," I reply, running a hand along its smooth exterior. It ripples with a sheen much like velvet under my touch.

"I can't tell if it looks ridiculous or majestic," Idrid muses in a monotone, then rises from the beds slowly. She begins her daily routine of dredging for clothes.

Disappointed by her lack of awe, I leave to allow her to dress. Taking the tall stairs one at a time, I find a table close to the exit and sit down, adjusting my sword and sheath so that it isn't digging into my back. It's the early afternoon, just past a commoner's luncheon, so no one but the bartender from last night is lounging around. I draw back the curtain of the window set above the table and peer outside.

The carriage we rode in and its horses are still outside, and the nasally driver rests on his perch, which is surprising. I expected him to lose patience and leave, though perhaps he is used to royals taking their time. I hear Idrid's heavy footfalls on the stairs and get to my feet, scraping the chair back with the back of my legs.

"Let's at least eat first," Idrid says gruffly, and I fall back into my seat. She walks over to the counter and says something to the bartender, the bartender doing his part not to look too wary of how she is a head shorter than the tall alcohol racks behind him. After he disappears into a door set in the back corner, Idrid comes to sit opposite me.

She observes the carriage outside, then her eyes return to my new clothing. "Where'd you get the cloak?"

"An Elementalist tried to rob me last night, so I robbed her," I say with a smile.

Idrid's eyes narrow, her mouth stiffening. "You got the attention of a magician?"

"Hey, I just offered her a drink." I pat my pouches resting along my waist knowing she can't see beyond the edge of the table.

She gives me a short, withering look. "We should get going, then."

"I'll have to tell the town guards about her before we leave."

"You do that, I'm staying here."

I note her change in attitude, though I don't push it. I've been down that road before, and it's never good to make Idrid angry. However, eventually I would like to ask her about her disdain for magicians that rivals my own.

"Mind the carriage," I say, rising once again from the seat. Outside, the streets are relatively quiet. The quaintly thatched and curving rooves of the double-story buildings contrast with the fired brick walls. Several children taking turns jumping on the cobblestone, careful not to step on cracks, notice me and begin staring in the unabashed way children do. The man resting atop the carriage's front seat also sees me and waves me over. Not wanting to be rude, I walk briskly across the street.

"James, good afternoon! My, what a lovely cloak you're wearing! Are you ready to proceed to Telnas?" It may just be that I have finally become accustomed to his voice because it actually sounds pleasant.

"Not just yet," I say, then add, "and I'm Not James. I'm going to go notify the town guard about an Elementalist gone rogue."

"Oh dear, oh dear. Well, very well, sir," he says with genuine concern.

I leave him and continue up the street. I can spot the cottage a ways behind the tavern and other buildings as I pass them by. Other side streets between buildings seem to continue to other roads in the main part of town. More people are walking on the next parallel street, so I take one of the small roads to join them. I hesitate before stepping out, my eyes searching for the green-and-white of Guard chainmail. Or robes, I think, chewing the inside of my cheek at the thought of more magicians. Though standard issue, the Lanmar gear and colors tend to be worn only by those loyal to the king, or the Royal Guard. From what I can fathom it is a silent show of disapproval toward the ruling class. Or, at least, King James. Some may choose not to show their alignment to simply be on better terms with common people. I've overheard more than a thing or two about their view of King James. It would be rare (which isn't impossible, I tell myself) for the district guard to uphold all of the king's rules. Steeling myself, I press into the thick of the crowd.

On this street there are stalls set up along the backside of the buildings I pass in between. A stall I go by coming out onto the street holds a variety of springs, coils, wires, cogs, and many other miscellaneous mechanical gadgets I lack a name for. A grimy man within holds out a hand filled with gears and barks "D'ya wanta biyagya?"

I shake my head, processing the words through accent. Do you want to buy a gear? I raise my hand and shake my head again with a small smile, turning away in my best quasi-sorrowful manner to join the stream of people. The unabashed staring of a child gripping his mother's hand points at my hair as they pass by. "It's like snow!" he exclaimed. "Mmhmm," the mother says, pulling the kid along quickly without looking. I allow a small smile before clamping it down when more begin to take notice. They peer at me warily. I don't blame them; compared to their tanned skin from who knows how many hours spent in fields I must look like a cloud. I catch a few murmurs of "Northerner," and I relax my shoulders. For now, I'm unrecognized.

Most of the other stalls boast various tillable foods, one even selling the raw basics of wheat and seeds, and like every good (or as Idrid calls it, "good for nothing") marketplace, this one has a curiosity shop. None of these hold my attention for long, and my darting eyes spot the one stall I need to steer clear of: the pawnbroker's.

Unfortunately for me, several guards stand in semi-formal attention around the stall, each head moving back and forth so that their gazes sweep over the street in patterned intervals. Biting my bottom lip, I continue to follow the current of people. I would stand out like a boulder in a corn field if I changed direction. To be fair, I already did stand out with the people moving around me allowing me a lot of leeway.

Sighing and bracing myself for the worst, I decide to march straight over to the guards. They spot me and place their hands over their swords' hilts. Well, that is telling enough that they do not recognize the cloak I wear as a grand magician's. No guard would dare attempt attacking one, so the gesture is likely hostile. Appearing royal can very easily get commoners and the guard who aren't loyal to James set against you on sight, a sentiment Idrid and I share. Even though I'm contradicting myself by wearing this cloak, a signifier I'm basically the enemy of the people, there is always another worse enemy. I'll win the guards over by reminding them of that.

"What is your business?" one guard says. He's taller than the others with a nasty boomerang-shaped scar on his upper left arm, though like the others he wears plain light chainmail with leather arm guards.

"I'd like to report a crime." I pause to allow the guards to wonder about what exactly the crime could be and so that I can get a view of the pawnbroker. It's a man I don't recognize wearing tan cotton trousers, a spring green waistcoat over a long-sleeved yellow shirt, and a shrewd half-smile. Whether he recognizes me or not is uncertain. Continuing, I say, "A woman tried to rob me."

The guards' hands fall from their sword hilts. The tall one remains serious for his part, while the other three attempt to stifle smiles. "Excuse me if this comes off as uncaring, but that sounds a little ridiculous. We also couldn't arrest a woman for attempted robbery since they technically did nothing wrong."

"Your hair is peculiar," one of the guards comments.

I glance up, noting the grey tips of my bangs. "Yeah, well, it's rather common where I'm from," I say truthfully.

Another guard says, "I don't think I've seen anyone with hair color quite like that. What is it, silver? Did you dye it?"

Patting my hair self-consciously, I say, "It's natural. Um, about that being robbed thing…"

"The king has grey hair." The tall guard eyes me closely. "Or so I'm told. I've never been to the palace to see the king. But I'm sorry to tell you, there isn't much we can do about a crime that didn't happen."

So either these guards haven't heard about James's twin or don't care. Good luck for me.

"King James has a bounty out for someone who looks like him," the first guard says.

Crap. My shoulders have gone back to being rigid and it's all I can do to keep my hands unclenched and arms hanging casually at my sides. "So he does." I shift my feet. The light weight of my sword pressing on my back gives me some assurance. "I suppose it's a problem if none of you have seen what he looks like."

The tall guard's eyes narrow before the lot of them throw their heads back in laughter. "Like we'd care who the bastard has it out for!" He grips the scar on his left arm with his other hand causing me to wonder if it's relevant somehow. His head lowers when he's finally composed. "It's enough putting up with the abysmal rises in crop output. Like we could force the people to make plants grow faster, right? Anyway, sorry to say we can't do anything about some would-be thief, especially a woman. Not until there's a crime, anyway."

I let out a breath. Having also counted on the leniency women get with the law, I reveal my trump card: "She's an Elementalist."

The guards freeze, their smiles dropping immediately. The tall guard shifts his legs uneasily. "An Elementalist, you say?"

"She trapped me in a cottage on the outskirts of town and tried to suffocate me by manipulating the air."

"How did you manage to escape?" Despite the question I can see the guards' eyes are all serious with hints of fear.

"She was talking about how she would knock me out and take whatever I had on me. She turned her back to me and I managed to throw a pan at the back of her head." It isn't a perfect lie by any means, though the guards are now suddenly on my side.

"When did this happen?" the tall guard asks.

"A few minutes ago," I lie, then take the chance to capitalize on their fear. "Are any of you acquainted with magicians?"

One guard shakes his head, but the others all nod stiffly. The tall guard says, "Most of us have been terrorized by them, yes. It is why we joined the guard."

I nod sympathetically. "She will probably wake up soon, and it would be easier to bring her in while she's unconscious."

"You said on the outskirts of town. You mean the cottage behind the tavern?"

"Yes."

The tall guard nods to the other guards and they all cross the street. "Thank you for notifying us," the tall guard says.

I stand still for a moment, looking over my shoulder to watch them march between the buildings and out of sight, then turn back to face the pawnbroker. He's eyeing me, though it's with the look of any shopkeeper trying to interest a customer.

"Overheard you were nearly robbed," the man says casually. "Need some quick money?"

"Luckily I still have my money. But thanks for the offer." I wave to the man and turn to make my way back to the carriage, Idrid, and, soon enough, Telnas castle.

Chapter 9: **Maia**

In the Tower of Bel's large sandy entrance chamber, Master Kellen introduces Maia and Greg to Darren, who apparently is a Teleporter. He looks to be about in his mid-twenties, has short dark curly hair, a tan complexion typical of the native people of Lanmar, and wears a peculiar velvety red cloak around his shoulders.

"Pleased to meet you," Darren says, eyeing Maia skeptically as he says this. "Kellen told me you're looking to dabble in other magics, huh?"

Maia shakes his offered hand, then crosses her arms over her chest, unsure how to take the sudden attention Greg, the tower's master, and now a Teleporter are giving her. "Nice to meet you too." Kellen's earlier message springs up again. I trust him, but just because I do doesn't mean you should.

"So," Darren says, "you want to travel across Lanmar to the Tower of Vern? Will this be a quick journey, or perhaps do you want to learn some about Teleportation on the way?"

Maia feels it would be nice to learn about it before being teleported, though doesn't speak. Instead Greg speaks for her, still playing the part of guide even after she and Kellen told him she'd be leaving.

131

"There's no rush, though there's no need to bother inundating her with Teleportation jargon either," Greg says, winking at Maia. Maia figured Greg would ease up on his wordy use of language around those with greater authority, though she takes it as his way of giving her something familiar to latch on to.

"But of course," Darren says with a smile. The way his lips freeze in their upward arc makes his face appear tight. Then it's gone, his eyes moving slowly back on Maia.

Kellen taps his booted foot rhythmically on the floor, his fingers also tapping on his forearms, seemingly absent from the conversation.

"You're sure you want to go?" Greg asks Maia for what could be the hundredth time.

"Yes," Maia says. Just then, she remembers that Kellen mentioned only those with the potential to learn other types of magic were told about them and how they would have to specialize in one of them. "Wait, did you practice other magics?"

"No," Greg says. "I never wanted to."

"Why not?" she asks.

"Elementalism is the most versatile magic."

Darren gives a wry smile, saying, "Which is really the only thing it has going for it."

Greg makes an unimpressed noise that sounds like a duck's quack being cut off.

Kellen's tapping stops and he suddenly looks at Maia. "Well, are you ready to go?" His breathy voice seems to dissipate in the air quicker than voices normally take to dissipate.

Stifling an excited, worried, and slightly regretful sigh, she says, "I guess."

"All right, then," Darren says. "If you would, please," he adds, speaking to Kellen and turning around to face the wall of the tower. A moment later the wall splits, stretching outward in two places like a double door. The water around the tower is already solid ice, which must also be Kellen's doing, and Darren takes a confident step onto it. He turns again, beckoning Maia to follow.

More tentatively, she moves to stand beside Darren. "Take us as high as you can, Kellen," Darren says.

Kellen's face turns into a wicked smile that sends a shiver down Maia's spine. "You don't want me to take you that high," he responds, and the last thing she sees are his silvery boots disappearing as the ice beneath her feet shoots upward, causing her to buckle from the momentum.

Maia flings her arm out to grip Darren's, who preemptively held it out for her to hold, and the ice stops climbing when they reach the top of the tower. She shivers at the sudden temperature drop, the sharper winds nipping her bare skin. She feels cool frost cling to the soles of her shoes numbing her feet and shivers again. Sure that her balance is back, she peeks her head over the edge of the ice platform they're on. A square pillar of ice suspends them, plunging all the way down into the sea.

"Keep hold of me," Darren says, placing his other hand over hers.

Maia looks up at him, though his gaze is fixated on the distance somewhere north of the cliffs and path she walks along from Fairbreeze. She straightens, then the next second she's not standing on the pillar of ice.

Like a lightning flash, except without the effect of being momentarily blinded, Maia takes in her new surroundings. Somehow she thought it would be more disorienting, though she doesn't feel disoriented, nauseous, or like she'd get a headache. She stands in a field of low-growing paspalum that is common along the subtropical inlet of the Sterling Sea. Darren allows her to now let go, and she turns in place, wide-eyed. Behind them is the tower in the distance, a thumbtack against the horizon. For a moment she swears she can see the shimmering cyan pillar of ice recede into the sea. "Whoa."

"Cool, right?" Darren turns around to look back as well. "We're about an hour's travel from the harbor. For a Teleporter, the trip is instantaneous."

Maia's eyes search the mostly flat fields for a sign of her home in the distance though can't find it. It's probably obscured by the few low hills surrounding them.

"Is there anything you'd like to know about Teleporting before we go again?" Darren asks.

Maia, not missing a beat, asks, "How does it work?"

Laughing slightly, Darren looks across the landscape. "As liberating as being able to disappear only to reappear somewhere else at will is, it still has its limits. To be able to teleport somewhere, you need to have the place in sight."

"So that's why you wanted to get high," Maia states.

"Expert Teleporters can travel quickly, using their teleporting in succession. From an outsider's perspective it would be quick enough to be considered a hallucination. It isn't as simple as looking at a spot and poof, you're there, though."

"How draining is it?"

"It depends on how far and how much you're teleporting. Teleporting actually has a formula, if you want to indulge me."

Maia nods enthusiastically, her hair tickling her face in the light breeze.

"The formula is $T>=(S+M)/D$, which means teleportation can only occur if S, span, plus M, mass, quantity divided by D, displacement, is less than or equal to T. Everything has mass except for what exists in the vacuum of space, and since there is nothing to displace, or no technical space to move to in space, the formula doesn't work and you can't teleport to it. Void-users specialize in empty space, and unfortunately even I don't know exactly how that works. Span typically has yards as its unit of measurement, since most Teleporters have a capacity of travelling only so much distance, and the mass most definitely makes it more challenging the more you have to move."

"What's T, then?" Maia asks, managing to keep up with most of it.

Darren continues, his smile increasing as he speaks. "That's just short for teleportation potential, and it varies with the Teleporter and consists of its own precise calculations. The formula I gave you is only a simplified version that doesn't account for more complex factors like gravitational pull, initial velocity of the mass of the objects you want to teleport, practical calculations for why displacement actually makes teleportation easier, and planetary circulation. Let's just say the complete formula has its own subset formula to calculate what T is."

"Hold on a moment," Maia says, scolding herself yet again for telling someone to wait when they obviously would. "Planetary circulation?"

"Oh, that's primarily factored in when teleporting into thin air. You know. Like, for example, it's easy to simply look at a spot on the ground like I did and mentally evaluate the distance to it, since you and the spot on the ground are both moving at the same velocity due to you both being on the planet that is rotating. But focusing on a space in the air, that's trickier. You can't really use anything as a means to gauge exactly where you're trying to go, and you may end up teleporting much too far into the sky that you could end up too high in a layer of the atmosphere. Then gravitational pull will play more of a part, which in turn affects the velocity you're going and before too long it would be extremely difficult to correctly account for where you may end up teleporting, if you can still. It's happened that a Teleporter accidentally went up and fell to his death."

"Yikes," Maia says, pulling a wisp of hair behind her ear.

"That's enough rambling from me for now. You ready to really get going?"

With a nod, she takes hold of his arm once again, and they teleport to the furthest of the low hills in their field of view. Five seconds pass in which she realizes he's going slow for her sake, and before she can tell him to go ahead again they're at the top of another low hill. The tropical grass is beginning to thin out where they now stand, and further on she can see the hills fall away to a totally flat spanse of short prairie grass.

The next moment they stand in that prairie grass, and she can't believe how wide and empty it all is. Maia had never traveled anywhere other than the magician's tower, though her father mentioned a far green field to the northeast called the Passerine Flatlands. This has to be the Flatlands, she thinks.

"There's a house I pass by in these fields whenever I travel between Telnas and the western Occult Tower," Darren says. "It's a nice farm, and you'll get to see some chickens."

Maia can't help but laugh at the quaintness of how it sounded. "I don't think I've ever seen a live chicken."

"You're about to." The farmhouse appears in her view. It's fairly large, at least two stories high and lengthwise would take up a quarter of a block on a street in her town. With the next teleport, they stand directly beside it. Its wood is a faded brown, constructed of planks travelling up, the second floor and roof supported by beams along the building's exterior. To Maia, it fits the stereotypical image of what a barn would look like, even the angled triangular roof.

Maia can hear the pleasant sounds of clucking coming from around the building.

"Go ahead and take a look around if you want. On the way to pick you up I didn't get a chance to say hello to Lauren, who runs this place."

She decides to do just that. Darren walks along the wall to go around the right side, knocking on a window as he passes, while Maia goes around the left. A low barbed wire fence coming up to her ankles travels perpendicular to the building and forms a wide coop for the chickens which strut about in large groups. Their feathers are a variety of whites, browns, and mixed colors of white and brown. Each seems to have a little red spiky hairdo on their head, and their beaks are cutely angled downward toward their claws.

The claws are the only thing that appear treacherous about them. They all move as a mass like the ocean's waves. Each chicken's beady eye seems to be looking at her, even though their heads are angled in all sorts of directions. Their soft clucks are even cuter, as if urging her to try and pet them, though she stays a couple feet away from the wire fence. A flash of grey in the mass of chickens catches her eye, though it disappears the next second.

Searching a few seconds more for which chicken could be grey, she gives up and turns to look back over the distance she came. Her eyes drop from the fuzzy horizon to the nearby grass. She had not noticed various dark spots scattered randomly across the field. Inside the dark spots new grass is just beginning to grow past a quarter of an inch. In a weird way, it is like some sort of Giant jumped around on one leg and trampled the ground. It's the best she can come up with to explain them, anyway.

"Hey, Maia, this is Lauren."

Maia turns to her right to see Darren and Lauren, a tall woman in her early-to-mid-thirties wearing a patchy, grimy shirt, peer out of an open window set in the building. "It's nice to meet you," Maia says awkwardly, giving them a wave.

"So you're a magician looking to study different types of magic?" Lauren says, her light voice contrasting with her rugged appearance. "Out here I don't get much news of the goings on of the popular world, but from what Darren tells me, it's uncommon."

"What's uncommon?"

"Magicians looking into other fields of magic. Then again, I'm just a common farmgirl," she says with a wry smile.

"She's also a mechanic," Darren says, causing Lauren to turn on him.

"I don't do much mechanical work anymore," she says in a grumpy but restrained manner, and Maia senses there's something more to their relationship. "I worked on making mechanical creatures a while back, though the only stuff I could make come to life were small animalesque machines like chickens."

More confused, Maia looks back into the chicken coup. "Why would you want to make machines that look like chickens?"

"All sorts of reasons," Lauren says, embarrassedly scratching the back of her neck. Her head jerks toward the chicken coop. "Oh no. Darren," she says, pointing.

Maia follows where she points to the spot of grey she saw earlier, which is now approaching where she stands by the fence. The chickens surrounding the grey mass cluck, aggravated by its purposeful, jerking strut toward Maia as it pushes them out of the way. It's obviously a chicken, Maia thinks, though its movements are not fluid. Finally the chicken's head rises above the others, a tall cylindrical neck of... wires?

The metal sheen forming the dome of the chicken's head faces Maia as it moves toward her, its eyes unblinking in the sense that the chicken is literally mechanical and does not have eyelids, but also blinking in the sense that lights behind the tightly fitted red lenses of what substitutes for eyes are flashing progressively faster.

She feels her gut constrict in fear and stumbles away from the fence, falling onto her back. The mechanical chicken is making menacing coos at her, still jerking toward the fence. Out of the corner of her eye, she sees Darren extending his arms in two directions, one arm aimed at the chicken and the other aimed upward.

The chicken's eyes are flashing like fireworks now, but just before it reaches the wire fence, it disappears. Coincidentally Maia being sprawled on the ground already put her in a position where she could see it reappear in midair a couple dozen meters above her, where it promptly explodes. Small charred bits of fractured metal rain down from the fading black cloud of smoke. Maia's Elementalist training kicks in, and she forms a weak dome-like barrier over herself out of the air. The bits and pieces bounce off the air and slide to rest on the ground; other pieces fall inside the chicken coop, causing several clucks of surprise.

That explains what Lauren meant by "all sorts of reasons," Maia thinks.

"Sorry about that," Lauren says, patting Darren. "Quick work on your part, Darren. I don't normally go out much anymore, save to feed the chickens, and must've missed that one. I've forgotten how many of them I made, though with luck that should be the last one."

Maia looks over the various dark spots with the newly growing grass. "So exploding chickens are what made those marks?"

"More or less, yeah," Lauren replies.

"Why would you keep an explosive chicken in the coop with the rest of them?"

Lauren huffs out a breath, blowing her bangs out of her face. "It's not like I put it there; it must have gotten in itself. I left the exploding chickens to roam the fields just to keep the wrong sorts of people away, but as you just witnessed I couldn't make it so the chickens could register normal people and bad people, so they go off on seeing anyone. Except for me, of course."

"Still a pretty ingenious invention," Darren says admiringly. Lauren mutters something derisive under her breath, though Maia can see her blushing. "Well, that was fun," Darren says, "Would you like to stay a bit more, or continue on to the Tower of Vern? We could always stop by more places along the way, if you're interested."

Lauren scoffs, "Oh stop, Darren, are you trying to recruit her into your guild? I tell you, Maia, Teleporters are mischievous people. Too hard to keep track of."

The guild. Apprehension at all of Darren's previous talk floods her, and she is back on her feet. Fairly certain she also doesn't want to stay to witness what else could transpire between them, Maia shakes her head. "We can go now."

Chapter 10: **Jasmine**

Groggy, dazed, disoriented, and all other sorts of out of sorts, Jasmine awakes to the sound of clomping and metal, as if some of the town's guard are in her house.

"Great Dunlon, she's awake. Quick," a voice says, and the resounding footsteps surge toward where she lies.

They are in my house! Jasmine's eyelids fly open just as two of the guards grab her wrists, yanking her up. A wave of nausea passes over her, though her thoughts are lucid. She just needs time to assess what's happening.

"Don't try anything," the same guard says, who she now sees is standing in front of her with a sword drawn and pointed at her chest. Without looking away from the guard, she focuses her attention on where the others have her arms locked in theirs.

She speaks one word: "Sever." The air rips the men's hold on her and they stumble away. "Thicken."

The guard in front begins a lunge, but his sword bounces off the air. He curses, taking a step back. Jasmine, for the moment free, collects her thoughts. The night before she brought a man here, and she had him trapped. But then… she can't remember what happened after. He somehow escaped and got these guards to capture her. She needs to make an escape and find somewhere else to work.

"Constrict." As the three guards gasp from the sudden tightening of the air around them preventing them from moving, she shakily makes her way to the bedroom. Hitting the doorframe with a hand to steady herself, she half walks, half stumbles to the chest and climbs on top of it. Focusing on her feet, she reaches a hand up to the false board, and touches nothing. For a moment she stops, unsure if her senses aren't fully back, and wriggles her fingers around. Her hand brushes the edges of other boards, then she looks up. The false board is gone, and upon stretching her arm out to feel within the hidden compartment she realizes everything inside is gone too.

Anger fills her, and she almost falls off the chest. There was something peculiar about that man, apart from the fact he managed to rob her. How did he do it? How did he even find her stolen items? Why did he steal from her and then call the guards on her, other than the obvious?

No honor among thieves. With the anger rising to numb away her stupor, she stomps onto the floor and walks to the entryway. The guards surge toward her, taking her off guard. She stumbles back as a sword arcs an inch from her chest. She loses her balance and falls back through the doorframe into the kitchen. Her head knocks against the side of a counter drawer. The dull pain helps diminish her muddled mind. Unscrewing her eyes, she sees a wrought iron pan handle sticking out from the countertop. She grasps it in both hands and hurls it at the first guard almost on top of her. It connects with his ribs and he collapses to the floor, impeding the other guards. "Constrict!" she shouts, and once more they still, wrapped in pockets of air while struggling desperately to move. Without saying anything, she stands and cups the back of her head where an ache blossoms.

She exits the building, mapping out her next move: find that man, then kill him. The fading grass surrounding the pathway that stretches towards The Bludgeoned Boar quivers as she storms away from the abandoned hovel. On the bright side, she'll no longer have to stay there.

Jasmine comes upon the face of the tavern and looks back and forth. She cuts across the street and moves between buildings on the opposite side to a busier street. Here the townspeople bustle back and forth between market stalls. She moves to join the streams of people. Looking both ways, she quickly finds the person she is looking for and moves toward him.

"Hey. You."

The pawnbroker drops a wooden doodad onto the countertop of his stall and sits back in his chair. "What can I help you with?"

She meets his brown eyes and sees a glimmer of recognition, as if he knows what she's looking for. "I'm looking for a man."

"You've found one," the pawnbroker says.

"Yeah, well, this man stole from me and I want a name."

"Hm." His eyes screw up while he rubs his chin. "That's not a lot to go on. But, you're in luck for ten."

"Ten what?"

"Ten gold pieces."

Jasmine laughs. "You heard I was robbed, right?"

"All right," the pawnbroker says, his eyes flitting to her hand. "How about your ring?"

"How about my fist?"

"Easy, Elementalist," the pawnbroker says, raising his hands.

Jasmine freezes, unclenching her hand. "How do you know that?"

"Like I said, you're in luck. Since this info was given to me freely, I suppose I can give it freely as well. A man wearing a dazzling red cloak came by not too long ago saying a woman Elementalist had tried to rob him."

Passing townspeople flinch back at hearing the word "Elementalist" and hurry away.

"Absurd," Jasmine says. "That was my cloak."

"Well, he drove off in a carriage, so I assumed it was his, given his stature."

"Which way did he go?"

"I saw the carriage going south on the street over, but…" He trails off when a child runs around the stall and jumps in his lap. The child whispers something in his ear then jumps back off his lap and races off. "Ah," the pawnbroker says. "Another stroke of luck. Apparently this man you're looking for left the carriage just outside of town and walked off toward the hills."

"Great, thanks." Jasmine pushes away from the stall.

"What do you plan to do if you find him?"

She turns to look back at him, eyes alight. "Since it's technically your business, I plan on killing him."

The pawnbroker nods with a sympathetic smile. "He did rob your precious cloak."

"It's a Guild magician's—" Her eyes narrow. Curses. He'd got her talking so easily. Pawnbrokers are too shrewd.

His eyebrows rise in satisfaction. "Even thieves can't trust thieves, it seems."

Jasmine reapproaches the stall slowly and lays her palms flat atop it. "Do me a favor," she drawls while her fingers curls in, nails leaving light scratches in the fine grain.

"You can threaten me, though there's no point. Once the network knows it, it's known."

Her face blanches before swiftly setting in a light smile. "Do me a favor and hold this info for a week—"

"Pah!" he scoffs. "Information has a timetable of usefulness. I can't withhold it."

Hands now fists, she presses her knuckles against the wood, ring digging into her middle finger. "You are part of the network, so you wouldn't be breaching any protocols." She leans in closer and flutters her eyes.

"What's in it for me? Have you more info to share?"

"You've gotten quite enough. Do this," she rushes over his humorless laugh, "and I'm willing to not... harm you."

"I already told you threatening me—"

"Not you, dear," Jasmine says. "Your superiors. Those in Flwihhndg. I hear they're not pleased with the kingdom's deforestation?" She lifts her hand and lets it fall to her side.

Directed by Jasmine's eyes, the pawnbroker looks down to where her left hand had been. An abjectly charred mark in the wood resembling the shape of her ring has a faint stream of smoke rising from it. Slowly, he nods. "Info for info. A good transaction. I'll hold it for the time being." He picks up the wooden doodad from his stall and begins to fiddle with it nervously as Jasmine turns away. He glances once at her retreating back. "Perhaps I should tell her about the Giant that man travels with. Or who he is. Eh." He shrugs and in a single motion collapses the object into itself to form a solid sphere.

Jasmine remerges into the flow of people, heading toward the south exit of town. She smiles to herself. The less people the better. She can confront him alone and take back what's hers, as well as what's not.

Chapter 11: **Maia**

Upon reaching the edge of the long fields and the first sign of consistent civilization Maia has seen outside her home, Darren strikes up conversation again.

"You know, Teleporting is a good way to earn money."

Maia raises her eyebrows at this.

"People pay for someone to move objects around easily. Like I moved that mechanical chicken. All it requires is your will. With training, of course."

"Are you trying to recruit me?" Maia asks.

"Of course." Maia is surprised by his honesty. "The way Kellen put it, you have oodles of potential. There aren't many good Teleporters, let me tell you."

Maia's eyes return to the double-shaded red cloak he wears. She decides it's time to test Kellen's warning about trusting him. "Lauren said you are a part of a guild. Is it a guild specific to Teleporters?"

Darren follows her eyes, then shakes his head. "No, the guild she was thinking of consists of officials. You know, part of the Royal Court, that sort of thing."

The sudden jolt of discovering his status hits her like a cast-iron pan. The fact that she of all people is traveling the country with someone who isn't just some magician with the ability to teleport but is also a part of the Royal Court causes her to become more self-conscious. "Wow. Um. Is that an official's cloth?" she asks, gesturing to the cloak.

"Only for the highest magicians, yes."

"Is—does Kellen have one of those cloaks?"

Darren sighs. "I'm afraid not." He paces several steps away, the sound of his brown suede shoes brushing the blades of grass similar to the sound of a brush straightening hair. He stops, facing the town just ahead of them that Maia doesn't know the name of. "The Guild... I apologize, I can't give away the name for political reasons—even though it's absurdly obvious it hardly matters," he mutters.

"What?" Maia guesses, "Is it called the Magician Guild?"

Darren gives her a withering smile. "The Guild does not view Elementalists as worth having in their ranks. It's a decision upheld by the line of kings up to James, and the earliest magicians, knowing full well Elementalist magic was technically the easiest to learn, were all too happy to create a magical hierarchy. The people I work with, they're not all good people."

"Oh." Maia doesn't know what to say. She is mostly unaware of the political system in Lanmar, and all she does know is from listening to what her father mumbles about at mealtimes. He'd always said King James was a selfish dictator who constantly held lavish dinners, and the only good thing about them was that they kept Lanmar in the good graces of foreign countries. But understanding now that such a system would exclude a group of people—magicians—simply because they practiced a different magic is... frustrating.

"Elementalist magic isn't easy," Maia says, her voice tight. "Sure, it's accepted as the most common type of magic, but that doesn't make it easy."

"I agree with you," Darren says. "I became friends with Kellen for that very reason. Elementalists are invaluable in ways other magicians take for granted. Even before I became a member of the Guild I've been clandestinely looking for magicians with the drive, the ambition to push for a change to the system."

Maia mentally thanks Greg for his endless vocabulary that taught her what clandestine meant. "So you're not only looking for Teleporters," she muses, rubbing the sole of her shoe against an itchy spot on her ankle.

"Do you really want to know why I want you to become a Teleporter?"

Slowly, expecting him to turn to her with a serious face, though he simply keeps looking over the town, she asks, "Why do you?"

He breathes in deep, chest expanding, exhales, then turns to look her in the eye, a playful inquisitiveness quirking his mouth up. "Do you know all the magics?"

The question confuses her. "Kellen had me read a book briefly that had fields of magic, sure."

"That's good. Could you list them all to me?"

Unsure where this is going, Maia decides to oblige him. "Elemental magic, or controlling the elements. I remember reading something about subfields, like Shapeshifting, though I forget the other subfields."

"Those are simply the basic elements, like air, water, fire," Darren fills in for her.

"Then there is Spatial... which is what you do."

"Teleporting, yes. There is also Void, but that has limited use and is largely forbidden."

Kellen didn't mention there were forbidden magics to her, and now she wonders why he didn't tell her before prompting her to decide what magic she wanted to learn. "All right. Then there's Conjuring, simply making stuff from nothing, right?" Darren nods at this, and Maia continues saying, "Mind Control—"

"It's more manipulation, since you can never really force someone to do something they genuinely don't want to do, which is also largely forbidden, but go on."

"—And finally Enchantment. Enhancing things to do... other things, essentially."

"Very good," Darren says. "Now, tell me, if you were to fight another magician, which is typically what Elementalist magicians are used for in the Royal Guard, how would you fight, say, another Elementalist?"

Truth be told, Maia had daydreams, and even just dreams, of getting into tight situations with her peers in which she would command the tide to roll in and sweep her enemies away, and even a tornado to scare off the other Elementalists she knew only by name. None of the dreams were realistic, of course, since she could only create small gusts of wind to blow for several seconds. "I suppose... I would use the earth to trap the Elementalist so they couldn't move."

"That's a good way," Darren says. "They could still talk, though as long as you're vigilant they would have to speak very quickly. What about in a fight against a Conjuror?"

This is tough for Maia to consider, since a Conjuror could unpredictably produce anything, like a sword or a crossbow. "Would creating a barrier between me and them with the air work?"

"It would indeed," Darren says approvingly. "Conjurors can only create things that are in close proximity to themselves, and shielding yourself from them would virtually render them useless. Now, how would you go about fighting someone like me?"

She should have seen the question coming, but it surprises her. She blinks, her mind going blank, and the next second Darren is gone.

"You see?" he says calmly into her ear from behind, causing her to leap forward. "Fighting a Teleporter is another game entirely. Sorry for scaring you, by the way."

Maia, her breathing getting rapid, nods.

"They always have the element of surprise. They are always the fastest. You cannot trap them. The only way you could fight one is knowing in advance if they are coming, and if they are predictable." He folds his arms underneath his cloak, his face becoming somber. "No matter how special the other magicians in the Guild think they might be compared to others, like Elementalists, a single Teleporter could take them all out within a minute. They're actually lucky the Elementalists that are part of the Guard don't care one way or another about holding a higher position, otherwise I'm sure we'd be looking at a different political system."

"What if I blinded you?"

Darren stops, now his turn to be confused. "What?"

"You said earlier that a Teleporter has to be able to see where he, or whatever object he is teleporting, is going," Maia says.

He considers her for a moment, then his face breaks into a smile. "You're very right. That would be a great way to stop a Teleporter."

She savors the feeling of being right before considering all he's said. He seems earnest in trying to recruit her, and there's nothing ominous standing out about him. Except maybe that he didn't give the name of the Guild he's in. Why did Kellen say not to trust him?

"All right, I think we've had enough of a talk," Darren says, interrupting her thoughts. "Let's go the rest of the way so you can get to learning." He strides over to her in three steps, gingerly taking her arm again. "Ready?"

"Yeah." A street of the town they were just overlooking flashes into view around them, enlarged and occupied by several civilians. A dusty brown dog lying beside a building picks up its head and barks at her, then the dog and street are gone and they're on a new street. The streets flash by, soon replaced by images of fields once again, though more towns emerge on the horizon, and soon again they are past. "Have we—passed—Telnas?" Maia asks between teleports.

"Yes," Darren says, face forward as usual, his eyes darting back and forth looking for the next best place to go. Taking a moment to stop at the bottom of a valley he says, "We just left it, actually. The last scattering of towns we went through are all connected to it." When he finishes, he teleports to the top of the valley hill and freezes. Maia feels his hand stiffen around her wrist. She follows his gaze and realizes they aren't alone.

Chapter 12: **Not**

"I'm telling you, it's way faster walking this way," I argue, hooking a thumb over my shoulder. "That carriage would have taken us all the way around to the southern entrance of Telnas, a route much too convoluted when we can go straight there on foot."

"What about those fancy red curtains I was supposed to wear?" Idrid asks, her face set in a deep frown that she only had when she disagreed with me. "Should I throw them away, too? Wasn't it your idea I wear something fancy to blend in?"

"Pah. You still have them, but we can find something else for you to wear. I always come up with something, and if it gets hairy I have a sword."

"I know," she breathes out angrily. "Still, it's not like we don't have time. Why are you so eager to get to Telnas all of a sudden?"

"The faster this is over, the faster I can..." I stop, smelling a strange scent like rotten eggs on the breeze. I gaze over the low fields stretching toward the town we'd just left, then turn around to see a man wearing the distinguished magician's royal red, and a girl in trousers and water-colored shirt with elastic cuffs stitched in at the end of her sleeves that snugly wrap her forearms. I curse to myself, though put on a genteel smile. "Hello there!"

The man, who is holding the girl's arm, whispers something to her, then they both pace a few steps forward. "Hello," he says, studying my face.

I feel the impending recognition coming, so I drop the façade and say, "Not," just as he says "James?"

"What?" the man asks.

"It's Not. My name is Not." I glance to Idrid, who has her arms crossed and is looking at the two menacingly.

"You're not kidnapping that girl, are you?" Idrid asks.

"What?" It's the girl who speaks, her voice high and emphatic. She gathers her flowing, shoulder-length brunette hair in a bunch and lets it go, the futile gesture something like a nervous habit. "No, not at all! Why would you say something like that?"

Idrid tilts her head. "I can't think of many other reasons a man would be found alone this far out of town clutching an underage girl. He's wearing the same cloak as you," Idrid adds softly to me. "Do you know him?"

"Of course not," I whisper harshly, then say louder, "Well, if this isn't a kidnapping and you two are just passing through, we'll be on our way."

"Hold on," the man says, "what do you mean your name is Not? You look exactly identical to the king."

"Exactly identical, huh?" Idrid muses. "I really want to see what this king looks like now to see if it's true."

Sighing, I say, "Let's cut to the chase already. What's your name?"

"Darren," Darren says.

"Nice to meet you Darren. Do you not know that the king recently set a bounty for someone looking exactly like him?"

"Why would you tell him that?" Idrid whispers, turning to look at me. I ignore her, watching Darren.

"I did not." Whatever pretenses there were are gone now, and Darren has the feral eyes of one observing his prey. "Maia, I'm afraid I'm going to have to get you somewhere safe for a moment."

Curious, I watch as his eyes wander from mine to a space behind me, and then he vanishes, along with the girl.

"Where'd they go?" Idrid gasps, suddenly in a panic.

"He teleported," I say, feeling nervous excitement urge my face to break out into another smile. This will be interesting.

Idrid looks at me in horror. "No. I'm not sticking around to face another magician. Find me where you first found me."

Confused by what she means by "another," I watch her bound down the side of the valley and away, arms pumping. I don't have time to worry why she has always been flighty around magicians, but abandoning me to deal with something alone is unlike her. I'll have to force an answer out of her next time I see her.

Standing still and letting the steady breeze blow over me, I relax while focusing on my surroundings. Up here there is about a twenty-yard space of flat ground before the top of the valley curves back down on either side. I am vulnerable from virtually all sides, though I hear my instructor's voice from years ago echoing in my head. Quick opponents will take advantage of the limits of sight. You must listen and feel more than you see, then react. Instructor and I had not known it then that I could sense magic with smell and taste; it had been an invaluable sense getting me out of several tight spots with magicians.

The wind around me shifts, blustering my hair back and forth. I feel it rush through the back of my hair and blow my bangs around. A tiny infraction of the wind causing it to unnaturally wane and the smell of sulfur simultaneously set my senses on high alert. Within that second, I debate whether or not I should move away; a Teleporter would take advantage of my momentum and catch me out if I overextended, and, for a Teleporter, most movements are overextensions that can be taken advantage of. I remain in place and turn my head to look over my shoulder at Darren. He is surprised by being noticed, but for his part doesn't teleport away again.

"Where's your friend?" he asks, taking a moment to look around.

"She ran off. Said she didn't want any business with magicians."

"Fair enough. James wants you caught, does he?" He begins walking parallel to me, stopping in a place roughly in the center of the ridge the same as I am. When I nod he asks, "Why?"

"You'd have to ask him," I say, keeping my body facing him.

"I didn't know the king had a brother. Is it a family thing?"

"Most definitely." I know he is trying to goad me, get my emotions stirring, though at the moment I'm enjoying myself. No one thus far, except for Idrid, had reasoned I was James's brother, and I am curious to see what conclusions Darren draws.

"You aren't denying being his brother," Darren muses. "Yet I find it hard to believe. You may be a lookalike, but you're also a thief."

"Think what you like. I'll continue as I am."

"Are you the rightful heir to the throne?" he asks.

"Like Dunlon's Holt I am," I snap, annoyed at such a banal assumption.

He tilts his head. "You don't deny being the king's brother, but deny being the heir. If you won't say who you are, then tell me, why are you headed for Telnas?"

Unsurprised that he had overheard Idrid and me talking, I shrug. "To clear my name? To put an end to James's tyrannical rule? Something heroic, though I haven't decided exactly what my real reason is."

"What happened to the former king and queen?"

I still, caught off guard by the question. Luckily Darren waits for my response rather than attacking. "You don't know?"

Darren's gaze is fixed on me. He truly expects an answer. I look off to a puff of cloud drifting on the horizon. My parents. Everyone related to me by blood is rotten to the core, especially them, so I'd assumed their sins caught up with them and caused their demise. If not, then... "I suppose that's my reason," I murmur.

"What was that?"

"Nothing. I don't know."

Darren sighs. "Have it your way." His eyes fall to my cloak ruffling in the breeze like his. "I'm guessing you stole that from one of the other Guild members."

"Actually, I stole it from someone who stole it from someone else who was probably a Guild member. Or is, assuming they're still alive."

He shakes his head. "Look, I don't really care how you got it. You must be something special to have gotten it, but why did you steal it?"

"I liked the color," I say.

Darren stares at me blankly. "That's it? That's your serious answer?"

"Mmmhmmm."

He looks at me for a moment longer, then sighs. "Well, I'm disappointed and regretful that I have to take you in. A thief is trouble enough with everything that's going on, if what you say about James wanting you captured is true."

"It is."

"Damn. Well, again, I'm sorry I have to take you in."

"Me too." I take my sword out of the sheath across my back.

"What are you doing?" he asks.

I look at him, then at the empty space beside him, as if there are other people standing here making up an invisible audience, then back at him. "Fighting you?"

Darren looks at me incredulously. "But you're not even a magician!"

"Nope."

Darren curses, then disappears and reappears in the spot behind me. I know this due to the sudden overwhelming odor of sulfur filling my nose. Whirling, I bring my sword around to slice the air where he was standing.

The smell almost vanishes, though is fainter, and I turn again to see he's back where he was standing before. He is breathing quickly, though not from tiredness.

"How are you predicting where I teleport?" he asks.

"I wasn't predicting," I say. "This," I continue, stopping for a second to swing my sword quickly to my right where Darren reappears, keeping my swing short before I cut him, "is predicting." Darren eyes the sword pointing at his chest and teleports to the side, keeping enough distance between him and it.

"You're something, I'll give you that."

I smile politely. "Well, thank you."

He brings his arms around in a hooking motion, and then suddenly he has them tucking around my own arms tightly. "Twenty feet up should only break your legs," he says, tightening his arms in a bear hug.

We stand there for a moment awkwardly pressed together before he realizes nothing is happening. I thrust my head back, hitting him square in the face and causing a bit of pain to throb around my skull. He keeps his grip around my arms, though I jump up and back. We both fall backward.

I land on him and he finally lets go. Rolling off, I stand up and face him. He is clutching his nose, a trickle of red spreading over his fingers. "You know, you're good," I tell him, leveling my sword at his chest again. "I probably should have told you before since you seem a decent fellow, but I'm immune to magic."

He looks up at me, not with the anger of someone who had his face smashed but with newfound interest. "You're... immune to magic?" he repeats, taking his hand away to observe the blood there.

"It's a gift," I say.

"HEEEEEY!"

The scream cuts through the wind, and I look down toward the town to see a woman with long dark curls rushing up the incline toward us. Her speed is impossible from simply running and I see her feet hover above the ground. Boar crap, it's Jasmine. "I don't know if you're a friend of Jasmine's, but I don't have time for this. I'm out." I turn, put away my sword, and sprint down the hill, leaving Darren.

"Who are you!?" the woman asks when she reaches Darren. "Why do you have my cloak?"

Darren takes a moment to stand up, pulling out a white handkerchief and dabbing his nose. "This is mine," he says, putting the newly dotted with blood handkerchief away.

Looking behind him to watch the man who called himself Not tearing across the valley floor to the other side without looking back he adds, "I assume you're the one Not stole the cloak from."

"What? Who?" The woman is panting, frustration obviously overtaking her.

"Honestly, I don't know myself," Darren says with a sigh. "But unfortunately, that must mean you are the one who stole it in the first place, because I don't recognize you as a Guild member."

"I don't know who you are, but I don't care. How about you give me your cloak and I won't hurt you?"

Darren teleports in front of her and punches her jaw hard. Her head rocks away, and her eyes cloud up. Pinning her arms behind her back in a swift motion that takes him behind her, he focuses on the other side of the valley and teleports with her.

"Ah, piss!" Not cries somewhere to Darren's left.

Darren, unaware he had teleported right beside Not, who is now angling away and sprinting southwest, simply ignores him and continues to teleport rapidly toward the palace. Nothing to be done with that anomaly. Not yet. In another seven teleports, he is standing atop the easternmost wall where two Elementalists are lounging around. They both jump when they notice Darren holding the dazed woman.

"Put her in one of the prison cells that can hold Elementalists," Darren instructs them. "Keep her there until I come back." He doesn't have to wait, knowing that the cloak he wears will be enough for them to obey him without question, and teleports his way back to the town where he had left Maia.

He pushes in the tavern door and finds Maia sitting nonchalantly at a bare table. She looks up at him and stands up quickly.

"What happened to your face?" she asks. "Are you all right?"

Darren sees no reason not to tell her everything, since none of it made much sense in the first place. "The guy, Not, headbutted me," he says, beckoning for her to leave the place so that the bartender couldn't continue eavesdropping from behind the counter.

"What? How?"

"I couldn't teleport him."

"What do you mean you couldn't teleport him?"

"I mean exactly that." He sees Maia recede a bit at his snappy retort, and adds, "Sorry. It's been a strange day. When I tried to teleport him, it was like trying to teleport a building. No, it was like trying to teleport the world itself, not that I've tried. He was just immovable."

They continue to walk silently to the edge of town, behind the tavern, where there's a cottage and an orange grove. Something clinking in Maia's pants pocket every step she takes catches Darren's ear. "What is that noise?"

Maia, wide-eyed, sticks both her hands in her pockets, muffling the sound. "Nothing. Just a necklace."

Forgetting about it, Darren looks eastward. "Well, we're almost there. I'm going to take you the rest of the way then leave you outside the tower. I have business to take care of back in Telnas."

"The guy... Not?"

"No, someone else."

"Is he actually the king? I mean, the rightful king?"

For the first time in a while, Darren laughs. "If he's the king, that would have been a heck of a convoluted ruse. I highly doubt he's the king. Probably just somebody going around causing mischief. Plus, he denied it. Although that doesn't explain the current king's interest in him." He mumbles the last sentence.

"Someone who looks like the king and is immune to your magic doesn't seem like just somebody," Maia states more to herself than to Darren.

"True. We most likely will never see him again, or whoever he was with. We should get going now." He takes her hand. Immune to magic, huh? A smile creeps on his face. He could work with that.

I find a farmhouse in the fields and debate whether to hide there, in case that Teleporter decides to pop up again. No, I want to make it to Telnas as fast as possible and find that good-for-nothing half-Giantess. The past few days she's been ditching me at almost every sign of danger and it is starting to complicate things.

I continue my run at a light jog, getting a rhythm with my arms and legs as I calculate the direction I'm heading by the angle of the sun. It's almost too bad that I'm immune to magic, because I might have liked it better having Darren unwittingly take me to the palace within an hour so that I could get this whole ordeal over with.

Rows of apple trees aesthetically aligned in the soft, tilled soil catch my eye, and I forget myself for some moments while I get lost watching the trees line up in perfect rows, only to spread out and realign again. The orchard abruptly stops, and I focus back to where I'm going. I should still be going west, given the sun is beginning to shine somewhat in my face, though it is partly shaded by puffy clouds. Knowing Idrid, she could very well have already run into and through the next town over. Her large legs can carry her for miles, and she rarely tires. Another farm, this one growing wheat, spreads out to my right. I spot a road travelling parallel to me on my left. The hard-packed dirt road would be easier to jog on, so I angle myself over and continue jogging.

For some reason I thought the road would travel more south, though I guess my memory isn't so good. Minutes pass while I try to focus on other things apart from how far I'm going to have to go, and my mind returns to what I'm going to do when I get to the palace in Telnas. I can picture James, a smug king sitting on the throne or at the head of the dining table. I reactively snarl when I see him in my mind's eye—a man that looks just like me. In my earliest memories I didn't know my brother too well, though I was told we were identical twins. It was all due to Mother living separate from Father, and she never told me why, even though I implicitly knew. All I can remember of the time before the separation are the large windows that let sunlight ignite the carpeted floors at the front of the palace. But Mother took me away before I could make any real memories. We didn't leave Telnas, and instead stayed in a well-to-do complex for higher-ranking officials.

I don't follow the train of thought, not wanting to dig up that part of my life again. Something white, probably a cart, becomes a speck in my vision on the road ahead. Idrid was right that staying in the carriage was more of a smart move. I pick up my pace, not wanting to continue running for much longer. Slowly I gain on the cart, though as I get closer and it gets bigger, I notice familiar gilded ornamentations along it that glitter in the waning sunlight. No, it can't be.

Minutes later reveal that it is indeed the same carriage we left in Chalman. I run to catch up to the driver, who is also, just as I remember, sitting haughtily at the front. His head turns toward me, surprise raising his eyebrows. I give him a wave, and he stops the carriage.

"Your majesty!" he says in a way much like a paean, rising from his seat in a swish of his colored fabrics, "I thought you had abandoned me! What are you doing running along the road like a commoner?"

"What is going on this time!?" a voice within the carriage bellows, and the door flies open. I peer inside at the same two angry-faced foreigners I had originally taken the carriage from. Their eyes light on me, and they are suddenly all too affable. "Oh, King James! Come inside! We were wondering where you ran off to when we found our carriage abandoned in the last town!"

It is probably better that I don't force them to leave a second time, lest I lose their trust. However misguided their belief I am truly James, it is for the moment providential. I prepare myself for the journey of playing the part of James, and warmly smile at them, taking the short step up and into the carriage.

The man who spoke closes the door and taps on the roof. "So, James, how is Telnas?"

This is going to be a long trip. "Uh. It's fine."

Chapter 13: **Maia**

The Tower of Vern is more like a traditional tower than the Tower of Bel—at least it's closer to what one looks like in Maia's mind. Darren left her just outside in a rush, repeating that he needed to take care of something back in Telnas, though he refused to say what it was exactly. She appreciated the information he gave her about Teleportation, though despite the appeal of traveling across the entire country in a day, she does not think she will try learning the field. Maybe it is the head-achy equation Darren discussed. It just seems too dangerous to get wrong, she thinks, holding a hand to her head. Or maybe he's one of the corrupt politicians of the king's Royal Court her father always mentioned, and maybe that's why Kellen warned her about trusting him.

She stands silently outside the tower, gazing up at its twisting masonry. In addition to being taller than the Tower of Bel, at least visibly, it is wider, and even has a door. The door itself, singular and arched, has a metal ring set into its left side and doesn't seem to have a lock. The tower itself is nestled in an alcove of land that rises up to the edge of a forest, which, when she looks in both directions, seems to stretch on limitlessly either way. Maia paces up the four stone steps that jut out from the tower's door and pulls on the metal ring.

The door swings outward easily, in fact much faster than Maia anticipated, as if it is shocked at her touch. It bangs loudly against the outer stone of the tower. Embarrassed, she waits a moment before stepping inside.

"Who are you?"

It takes her eyes a few seconds to adjust to the dimmer light. She is now aware there is a crowd of at least seven people gathered around the entryway. Many others in smaller groups busily chat with each other along the tower's perimeter, unintrigued with Maia's entrance. The flickering lights of tall candles in candlestick holders jutting out of the stone walls in a spiral match the spiral of a wooden staircase. That reminds her of her own tower, only the steps don't rise to meet the next and are instead individual boards. The banister on the outside of the stairs appears treacherously unsupportive, consisting of only a long, encircling wooden handrail with scarce posts holding it up.

"Who are you?" Maia lets her gaze fall to look again at the one who asked. It's a boy around her age, arms folded, with dark eyes glittering in the candlelight.

"I'm... Is the tower master around?" Maia says, glancing at the other kids, also roughly her age. She realizes she must have come in when they were all training.

"The master?" the boy scoffs. "Who are you that would be important enough to meet with Master Aveve?"

Maia turns to look at the others who stand motionless, their arms hanging limply at their sides like a bunch of lifeless puppets. "Look, can you tell her Master Kellen sent me here with Darren?"

The boy unfolds his arms and puts his hands on his hips, trading one arrogant pose for another. "If you so badly need to see her, she's up there," he says, pointing up. He turns away to whisper something to two other kids, who follow him to the farthest wall.

Looking around at the others, who look at her dumbly for a few more moments before turning away, she sighs and makes her way to the base of the stairs. She braces herself for the long climb, then starts taking the steps up. She stays to the inside, wary of walking too close to the banister in case it decides to give out and plummet her to an inconvenient end. Each step creaks under her foot. She is tired from all the day's events and the flickering orange lights on the stone walls seem to call out, trying to mesmerize her eyelids to close.

Yawning, she presses on. The stairs even out at a landing for a bit, and Maia is caught off guard that there is another floor. She looks around at even more faces that glance at her but then turn away without a second look. Stepping gingerly toward the banister for a moment, she looks over it.

She can see all the way down to the bottom, where the shadows of the kids mill about. Apparently the floor only travels around the edge of the tower, leaving a humongous hole in the center. Looking up, she can see the ceiling climbing to a single point at the center. Not much further now, Maia tells herself.

She continues up the steps and passes two other donut-like floors with people talking to each other, interrupting themselves to look at her for a moment. At long last, the stairs cease beneath the point where the ceiling angles inward; she's made it to the final floor. She doesn't have to ask anyone here where the master is since the only person older than twenty years is a woman pacing around the tower's stone walls while reading a book. She wears equally ridiculous attire to Kellen's: a white, gold, and blue-patterned dress with similar high ankle boots, though the boots aren't silver and are simple plain leather. Also like Kellen, she wears the outfit rather than the outfit wearing her, as Maia's father would say. Come to think of it, Kellen didn't make one mention of Master Aveve aside from her name.

For a moment Maia admires the woman's long, straight dark brown hair forming a perfect halo around her face, then timidly pads over to the woman, all too aware that the students watch her. She doesn't know why none of them are practicing. "Um, excuse me," Maia says.

The woman tears her eyes away from the page she marks with a finger and looks up at Maia. "Oh. Hello. Who are you?"

"Maia. Master Kellen sent me here so that I could learn about Conjuring."

"Oooh!" the woman coos with admiration, closing her book with a solid thump, causing the other students who weren't already staring to swivel their heads in interest. "So you're an Elementalist looking to change fields? This is exciting!" She sweeps past Maia, stuffing the book in a perfect space in a bookshelf and returns to her. "Did Kellen say anything about little old me? I haven't heard from him in weeks."

"Uh," Maia says, awash with relief that the woman is immediately accepting of her arrival.

"You don't have to answer that," the woman blunders on. "In fact, he probably told you not to say anything about him to me, he's such a mystery. Oh! I forgot to introduce myself! My name's Aveve, and around here I go by Master Aveve, though," Aveve adds conspiratorially, stepping up rather close to Maia, causing her to feel unsettled, "you may call me Aveve since you were previously a student of Kellen."

"Oh. Well, actually, I'm not entirely sure I want to stay a Conjuror forever," Maia says while Aveve winks at her and steps back. "I'm more here to see how I like it, then maybe go learn some other magics."

"Hmmmmm." Aveve considers her with a smirk. "Talented too, huh? I should expect nothing less from Kellen."

Maia is at first disgruntled that the woman attributes her "talent" to Kellen, whom she hadn't known until today. This woman seems to have an odd focus on him.

"Have you already visited the other tower? What other magic do you know?"

Still acutely aware the other students are listening, Maia stammers out, "I only know Elementalism."

"Oooooh!" Aveve almost swoons, rocking back on her heels in extreme pleasure. "How thoughtful of Kellen to have sent you here first! I assume Darren was the one who took you? He's such a helpful guy, always there in a pinch. Here, come with me," she says suddenly, moving toward the stairs and shuffling down them rapidly before Maia can so much as reply.

Maia notes the way Aveve moves down the stairs is also similar to the way Kellen shoots up and down them. It is possible all the tower masters are equally eccentric, she decides.

"I'm sure you're very tired," Aveve tells her. She stops at the next landing and moves around the handrail that extends in a circle, separating the floor from the empty space at the center of the tower. The students make way for her, Maia quick to fall in step behind her. "There are a few beds here you can stay in while you're with us. Maia, is it?"

Blushing slightly, Maia tells her it is.

"Such a nice name. Well, here's a bed. Practice has been over for about an hour, though most everyone is still here." Aveve frowns, sweeping her gaze around at the students, who seem to recede under it. "The tower is technically open at all times, though I would think kids your age would have things to do. Not you, of course," Aveve adds to Maia. "You just got here. I'm sure you'll make friends soon enough. Oh, and if anyone here gives you trouble, make sure to tell me. I don't like having drama under my nose."

Maia decides to say nothing about the rude boy and simply nods. The bed is a simple single bed with cotton sheets and an attractively fluffy pillow.

"Go on, you should rest. I'll make arrangements with some of the other students to get you started on Conjuring tomorrow. This is exciting," Aveve repeats, moving away and swiftly climbing the stairs again.

Taking advantage of the students watching Aveve leave, Maia sits on the bed and considers everything that has happened. She started off the day making ocean water crawl up a tree, then everything spiraled out of her hands. She doesn't regret doing it; in fact, energizing that tree had been the most exciting thing she'd done in ages. And, as uncomfortable and dizzying as the past few hours have been—what with learning that other types of magic existed, being teleported across Lanmar with one of the highest ranking magicians, meeting the mechanic Lauren and almost being a victim of an exploding chicken, stumbling upon a man who called himself Not and who, according to Darren, looked exactly like the king and was immune to magic, and finally reaching this tower and meeting Aveve—each event was fun in its own way.

Maia becomes aware that two students are approaching her, both girls wearing matching deep blue dresses. "Are you a new student?" one of the girls asks. She has wild medium-length hair that is a lighter shade of blonde than the other girl, who also has medium-length hair. Both their bangs are cut in a straight line just above their eyebrows.

"Yeah," Maia says. "I'm Maia."

"I'm Tricia," the lighter blonde girl says.

"And I'm Lin," the other girl says. "We started just last week. Don't know many others here since people tend to keep to themselves, though Paul's a friend." She points a long finger with a near-equally long nail at a boy standing across the gap on the opposite side of the floor. "He came in around the same time we did."

"That's cool," Maia says, eyeing Lin's suspiciously long fingernails. "Do you all live nearby?"

"Yeah, we live in Chalman, which is just west of here," Tricia replies. "Where do you live?"

"Well, here now, I guess," Maia says, attempting a joke. When the other girls smile, she continues, "Actually, I live across the country. A harbor called Fairbreeze."

The two girls gasp. "Why so far?" Tricia asks.

"I, uh… well, I'm originally an Elementalist."

Tricia and Lin's eyes widen, glancing wildly around at the other students, who have more or less gone back to milling in small groups.

"What?" Maia asks. "What's the matter?"

"Nothing," Tricia says. "It's probably best you don't tell anyone else that, though. Most here think poorly of… You know, Ellies."

Maia bursts out in laughter, slamming her hands on her thighs. "Ellies?" she splutters, "Is that a real nickname? That's amazing!"

"Shh!" Tricia hisses. "It's meant to be derogatory."

"So you were practicing magic all the way over at the Tower of Bel?" Lin asks, sitting down next to Maia in an aggressively friendly manner. "What's it like? Who's the master there?"

"How did you get here?" Tricia joins in the questioning, sitting on Maia's other side.

Maia makes a mental note that maybe the general magic community, and not just the elites, disfavors Elementalists. "Well, a Teleporter took me here as a request from my tower's master. Master Kellen."

"Master Kellen?" Lin squeals. "I've overheard Master Aveve mention him. I'm pretty sure she likes him. What's he like?"

"I only met him once, but he wears weird clothes like he's going to a party."

Lin nods wisely. "Just Master Aveve's type, I imagine."

"Wait, you got to travel with a Teleporter?" Tricia asks with a hint of jealousy. "Man, I wish I got to do that."

Maia settles for a shrug. "The tower is unlike this one. It's constructed entirely out of sand and sits offshore in the ocean."

"Sand?" Tricia shares a teasing look with Lin, their cheeks dimpling. "Ellies are better than we thought." Tricia looks at Maia. "Sorry. We don't know much about what they can do."

"Speaking of," Lin begins, and Maia knows where she's going, "could you... perform something so we can see?"

When Maia finally nods, both girls go silent and watch her, clasping their hands in their laps. Slightly flustered by the attention, Maia wonders what she should do. She doesn't want to disappoint them with something lame like a gust of wind, which is really all she has managed to do with air outside of making the air solid for a few seconds, but there aren't many other options. They're three floors up from ground level, and she doesn't want to walk all the way down and leave the tower just to manipulate a piece of earth.

Rubbing her legs through her pants with her fingers, she feels the lump of silverware in her pockets. Oh, that's right, Maia remembers. She had stolen a knife and a fork from the tavern while Darren was dealing with the man called Not. It'd become a habit of hers to take whatever; the thing didn't matter, so long as she could fit it in a pocket. She remembers when she was a lot younger a stranger in the port market tried to make off with a bucket of salmon roe after directing the seller's attention away. He'd rounded the corner where she was watching and almost bowled her over. Though she forgot his face, the thrill of the seller shouting at them caused her to act on her own. She pulled his hand and somehow found herself in an alley hiding alongside him. She forgets his face, though remembers him smiling and saying, "Thievery's a crime only if what's taken is irreplaceable." He offered her some of the roe, and that's when her life changed forever. She learned she hated fish, but more than that a different kind of excitement that rivaled performing magic.

Reaching a hand into her pocket, she pulls out the fork.

"Why did you have a fork in your pocket?" Tricia asks, wrinkling her nose.

"So I can eat pork on the go," Maia jokes, and to her surprise both the girls laugh. More confident, she focuses on the metal. Despite popular belief, earth and man-crafted components of earth are the easiest to manipulate, alongside water, at least in Maia's point of view. Fire, for whatever reason Maia had never thought to ask Greg, she also has a knack for controlling. She has the most trouble with air. Picturing the fork in her mind, she urges the individual prongs to meld together and elongate. The metal obeys, stretching out, then turns to curve in on itself, wrapping up into a silver band.

"Great Dunlon..." Tricia breathes in awe.

"Cool," Lin mimics Tricia's awe. "That is so cool."

Embarrassed, Maia says, "That's not much. Kellen— er, Master Kellen can have the wind carry his voice great distances, I think all the way to Telnas."

Neither of the girls say anything at that, their hanging mouths enough for Maia to tell they are clearly impressed.

Tricia is the first to recover. "You said the tower is in the ocean. How do you get to it?"

"I turn the water to ice and walk across."

"Unreal," Lin says.

"You're going to have to show us that one sometime," Tricia says.

Maia shrugs again, fingering the metal band. "You know, I don't really need this. Would you like to wear it?"

"You'd give it to me?" Tricia asks in a hushed voice that almost causes Maia to burst into laughter again.

"Sure. Just a sec." Maia holds the band out and widens it so Tricia can stick her hand through it. Once it's around Tricia's left arm, Maia eases the metal to nestle snugly against Tricia's skin.

"Cool," Tricia says, reverently stroking the metal.

"Oh, I probably should make a way for you to be able to take it off," Maia adds, snapping a finger at the metal, causing a perfect, thin crack to emerge. A little portion of the metal protrudes across the crack to work as a clasp.

"Thank you!" Tricia says, giving Maia a warm smile.

For a moment Maia is lost in an oddly happy feeling, though is drawn back at the realization she hasn't given Lin anything. "Oh, I also have a knife! I can make you one, too."

Lin, who was longingly watching Tricia stroke the metal band around her wrist, lights up. "Oh, you don't have to," she says politely, though her eyes are eager.

"It's nothing," Maia says, pulling the knife out of her pocket and working the same magic on it. Maia takes extra care to avoid having the metal scrape Lin's long fingernails as she slides the identical metal band around her arm. "There," Maia says.

"Thank you!" Lin says, bubbling with excitement. "This is all so incredible. I can't believe everyone here thinks Ell—Elementalists," she corrects herself, "are lame."

"Hold on," Maia says with a smirk. "Can you show me your magic?"

"Oh, let me!" Tricia exclaims, scooting to the edge of the bed, leaning forward and cupping both her hands out in front of her. Her hair falls in a swath over her face. Maia wonders if the girl can see anything, though Maia is more interested in what is going to appear in her hands.

Several moments pass, and then the sound of a small pop is accompanied by the appearance of a long wooden staff around ten feet balanced in Tricia's hands. The girl grips it at the center.

Maia flinches back, surprised by the largeness of the object. She'd expected something like an apple. "Yikes! Holy cow, that's huge!"

Tricia beams at her. "You like it?"

"Yeah! Just curious, why'd you choose to conjure a staff?"

"Oh, the basement of the tower is a massive storage room for all the items conjured here. Last time I went down I remember seeing a long row of staves lining a wall."

"Whoa," Maia says. "What are they used for?"

"Staves? I think Master Aveve said they help hone magicians' magic, though she found the inconvenience of using them to be more bother than training students without them, so she stopped having students use them. I bet students used to whack each other with them."

Admiring the smooth length of wood, Maia dares to ask Tricia for it.

"What?" Tricia looks confused. "You really want a staff? They're not that great."

Maia is sure she wants it. With all she's learned already, she is still eager, if not more eager, to learn more. "I think practicing with a staff could be helpful."

"If you really want it," Tricia says with a shrug and hands Maia the staff.

Gripping it in both her hands, it is only slightly heavier than Maia first thought. She is sure, though, that she could get used to the weight. "Thank you!"

Tricia stands up, and Lin stands as well. "Well," Tricia says, "I guess we should start heading back to Chalman. Almost everyone else has gone home already."

Now that she mentions it, Maia notices that there is only one group of three standing by the stairs, preparing to leave as well. "Okay. It's nice to meet you both."

"Nice to meet you, too," Tricia and Lin say together, sticking up a hand to wave. "See you tomorrow!"

Maia waves as they move to the stairs and start climbing down with the other three students. A wave of tiredness rushes over her. She realizes how drained she's become from the magic she's used, in addition to the day's events. She rests the staff in the space underneath the bed and pulls the sheet back. A tiny bubble of excitement rises in her stomach, reminding her that tomorrow she will be learning a whole new type of magic. With a yawn, she moves under the sheets, pulling them up to her neck and rolling on her side. So far, things aren't going so bad.

Chapter 14: **Not**

"Actually, things are going bad." My smile is sarcastic to match my words, though both the foreigners aren't picking up on it. A part of me wishes them to so that I could cut them both down and be done with this abysmal carriage ride. "The people hate their king, the Guard is barely staying in line only thanks to the Magic Guild, a civil war is most likely on the horizon, and I'm pretty sure Ferry is the most poverty-stricken town in the spanses, let alone the kingdom."

"Oh dear," says Jean (I'd gleaned their names earlier in the conversation). "Though I'm sure you can handle it. After all, you throw all these extravagant parties."

"I shouldn't, though!" I say, looking at them both. For a moment they're confused, then I give a sharp laugh that causes them to laugh in turn.

"Oh, James, you are a jokester!"

My smile turns feral. Just until the next town, I tell myself, then I can throw away the stupid façade. "I try," I say, letting out another laugh that reignites the two men. My eyes wander to the left window of the carriage that would've been covered if not for the missing curtains. I shiftily glance between the two before opting for staring at a dark spot in the fabric of the floor.

"You noticed the curtains, then?" the man to my right speaks. His name is Halette. His voice is gravelly, unbefitting his leaner body shape. "You mustn't blame yourself. Thieves run rampant in the north as well, one must've snuck in at some point."

I roll my head in a half-understanding, half-regretful manner while my thoughts turn to Idrid who now has them. "At some point."

"But hey," Halette continues as if trying to cheer me up, "the annual beard shaving contest is taking place soon!" My eyes fall to his brown beard that reaches his chest, and I refrain from making a remark as to why he'd be the one to bring it up.

"I suppose it is," I say, unaware such a contest existed. I'm about to ask how far until the next town, though catch myself at the last moment. I'm getting too restless. I know I'm using the ride to distract from how close I'm getting to the capital and the king. I cross my legs to keep from bouncing them. Asking where we are wouldn't matter with the destination being all the same, and it'd only result in more backhanded talk. "Are you looking to enter?" This is not backhanded, but genuine curiosity.

"I am indeed!" Halette says.

"Remind me, what is the prize for winning?"

"A hundred gold pieces."

"Are you going to be shaving it yourself, or does someone do it for you?"

"Me, of course!" Jean speaks up. "You speak as if you've never attended!"

I haven't. That's what I would say, though I see no reason to have them question my identity any further, even if they couldn't already piece together who I'm not. "It's been a while. I assume you'll split the prize money. But what does the competition itself look like? How does one judge the best... uh, beard shaving?"

"That's easy," Jean says smugly, whipping out a foot-long pair of scissors. "The bigger the beard, the longer or harder it takes to cut, which means extra points. The minimum length cut needed to place is two inches, and after that every extra inch gives additional points. Then it's all up to the barber to add a unique style and flair to the mix. Something complementing, exciting, flavorful."

I lean back against the carriage's cushioned seat, still eyeing the abnormally large scissors. "Fascinating." In all honesty, the prospect that someone came up with this is fascinating in and of itself.

"There's more to it," Halette says, leaning forward conspiratorially.

"Do tell."

"The judges favor uniqueness. That gives us the edge." He turns to chuckle with Jean, a chuckle that could be considered evil in any other context. Jean stashes his scissors back within his coat, flashing me a grin.

I get the feeling I'm supposed to be invested here. But I'm anything but. "Oh no!" I shout suddenly. "I forgot my dignity!"

Halette and Jean reel back in shock. "What?" they ask in unison.

"I mean, my diadem! Forgive me, my friends, I must away! We will meet again, at my palace!" Throwing the carriage door open, I hurl myself out and tuck into a roll that brings me around into a crouch on a wet turf of grass. I glance back at their worried faces peering through the early shadows of a young night. "Worry not about me! Go onward!" I stand up and pace away from the road, looking to put enough space between us so I meld into the shadows.

"I must away," I mutter to myself. "That's a good one." My breath comes out in puffy clouds, an early sign it will be a cold night. Still, better than inside that carriage. The grass is uneven, almost as if each new space I step on is on different layers of ground.

The vapor from my breath joins a thicker layer of mist that wavers around me. It takes me a few moments to realize walking across uneven ground through mist at night is a disorienting experience. There are no stars out, and the previously clear sky is now covered by clouds. The Mol Star in the east would've been a helpful guide, but I guess I'll have to travel in the general direction the road travelled. Speaking of the road, it seems I'm no longer in sight of it.

I glance around at the minimal space visible in dark and mist. In addition to only being able to see ten feet in all directions, the sound of my breath is muffled. I can hear no other sounds.

Turning back to what I think is a southeasterly direction that should return me to the road, I step forward. Not so much as the crinkling of grass reaches my ears. I look down to make sure I am in fact walking, then look back up. The mist moves, drawing toward me in wisps, dispersing in gentle waves when it brushes my skin.

Shivering, I pull my cloak tighter. An arm claws through the blanket of mist ahead of me, its pale flesh consistent with the lifeless air, then disappears just as fast. I gasp, though elicit no sound. I snap my fingers. Nothing.

Another grey hand pushes forward at me, slender yet sharp knuckles pointing down with its palm up. I have to stop before walking into it, and three more hands join the first. The arms stretch out of sight.

Hesitantly, I reach my own hand out and poke one of them. As soon as my finger touches the hard skin, the hand drops to the ground. I quickly step forward, parting the mist to see who the arm belongs to. Kneeling, I find, to my horror, the arm isn't attached to anyone. Looking wildly at the other arms hanging in the air, I see three forms still attached to each arm, which are still reaching toward me palms up. They're androgynous, inhuman, solidified shadows against a backdrop of shifting silver. They lack features of any kind save for the general four limbs, torso, and head, though the mist forms over their faces' makeshift mouths and eyes. The effect is like someone tried to make puppets out of charcoal.

Eerily like puppets pulled along by invisible string, they glide motionless in a semicircle, closing the gap left by the fourth creature whose arm I step back and away from. Pulling my sword from my sheath, I slice it through the air once and then stab it into the patchy grass that is being coated over with mildew before my eyes, a challenge for them to come closer.

Simultaneously, the creatures ball their hands into fists and point at me. I wrench my sword out of the ground and wait for an attack. They don't move. Slowly, I step to the side. They remain motionless. Moving my head, I follow where they point.

Sticking straight up out of the dirt is the long handle of a shovel, its head buried in the ground. Seeing as they haven't attacked me yet, I conclude it best I be directed by these creatures and see what happens. Heck, I'd just accidentally detached one of their arms, it's the least I can do.

I put away my sword and step over to the shovel, sliding it out of the ground. The wood of the handle is coarse, and the dull metal of its head is caked with faded red stains. Turning back to look at the creatures, I find that they are all pointing at the ground in front of their feet. Warily, I walk forward, stopping three feet in front of them. Raising the shovel, I swing it down into the ground.

Each figure, still pointing at the spot where my shovel is now buried, glides motionlessly away, the tips of their extended fingers the last to be enveloped in the swirling mist. I pry away the piece of earth, flinging it to the side, and continue digging. At the very least my shivers have turned to cold sweats, though I'm unsure if it's from the exertion or the scuttling fear that has crept inside me since the mist appeared.

The ground around me starts to cave in and I quickly leap away. The fallen ground forms a four-by-eight foot hole, six feet deep, the dimensions particular to a royal's grave. The first thing I see at its center are pointed feet in boots half beneath the ground. I look over the body's legs, arms, chest, and head, all half-buried. I can't make out the face, so I step closer, very aware that I am stepping into someone's grave.

The moment I make out the face I stop short. It's my face. Looking closer at the clothes the man is buried in, I see the same crimson fabric I wear, but it is so faded with age and obscured by dirt it matches the grey atmosphere. This doesn't make any sense.

Death is your future.

The thought stumbles into my mind. I force myself to think only about the man lying on the ground. I wonder if it's a hallucination. Or James.

Wishful thinking.

In a flash my sword is drawn and I'm about to drive it into the corpse, but in that same time the man has burst from the ground and has an identical sword leveled with mine. I stare into the man's grey eyes that are as lifeless as the mist around us. His mouth quirks up. "See you soon."

All at once the air is released, and the usual darkness of night surrounds me. The mist disperses, the man dispersing with it, and I'm alone in a field holding my sword up at nothing. It's only then I detect the receding smell of copper. I appraise myself to make certain I'm not bleeding from some unknown wound. Glancing to my right, I see the road only fifteen feet away.

Whether a dream, hallucination, or real, I know that it's best I find the nearest town quickly before it can happen again.

Chapter 15: **Idrid**

She walks alone through the night along Telnas's red-light district, the northwestern-most area of the capital. It was constructed that way long before, to serve as a barrier between the well-to-do residents and the nearby thieves and pickpockets in Picaroon. Even so, the past kings heralded the area as a "gift" to the people, generously phrased as "recreational." Back then there was also the nearby menace of the Giants in the Dagger Hills. Her people.

Her strides carry her down a memorized path, weaving in and out of streets and side streets in such a way that she wanders in circles. Every corner she turns she imagines seeing them all again like she used to as a kid. It was a good thing Not came around when he did, otherwise she may've become lost to that fantasy. Making a game out of stepping between the arch-patterned cobblestone, she looks up. The main attraction, a large square building whose face rises high and swings forward to provide an overhang where electric lights on a string hang like icicles, houses all sorts of oddities (and not just people), and she finds herself coming back around to gaze upon it again and again. It is the only building in the area whose business profited enough to allow electricity.

She pauses in front of one of its seven doorways, a flimsy, red-tinged opaque curtain in each substituting for doors, and gazes up at the large letters inscribed in pitch across the wall.

"Ferry Fancy," she mutters. A play on words, she knows, to elicit thoughts of mystery. She half wonders if Not got his idea of wordplay from this brothel.

A figure wearing no shirt and a pair of ballooning pants at the hems shifts behind the curtain, glinting eyes looming over a cloth facemask. "Whatever your fancy, the fancy is the journey," comes a husky voice. "And we serve to make the journey to your fancy."

She can't help but smile. She waves an apologetic hand, and the figure tilts his head in a nod before moving away. Stepping out of the way of an eager young couple who unabashedly charge on through the doorway, she begins walking again.

Subsequent buildings are lit invitingly by fires in stone sconces between archways. Beyond the arches are large open interiors that serve as social hubs for either food, gambling, or the more lascivious activities. She averts her eyes as a scantily clad woman lies down on a couch beside a man and looks to the opposite side of the street. Similar open areas are segregated from the street by arched pillars, though there are also elevated platforms, several of which are attracting crowds.

Crossing the street, she stops and leans against a pillar to watch what has one of the crowds excitedly buzzing. A pair of men stand facing each other in a standoff on the stone platform, each holding a one-handed sword. The man on the left is taller, though Idrid isn't sure if it is due to the prideful way he carries himself or an actual two-to-three inches' difference. He wears a fine tan tunic closely fitted and a matching pair of tan pants. His blond-brown hair is cut neat and short, and his eyelids droop lazily, his common soldier sword held out in such a way that the tip vaguely points in the direction of the other man. Clearly he's overconfident and isn't taking his opponent seriously.

The other man is starkly different, almost the opposite. He stands sideways, body angled slightly, wearing a well-worn grey cloak that falls around his shoulders. It's tattered in most places along with the simple pale shirt he wears. His dark grey pants are the only thing he's wearing that isn't tattered. His long raven-colored hair falls in curls and barely touches his shoulders. Between the curls of his long bangs she can see his eyes, sharp and intent, focused on the confident man. Idrid thinks about leaving, having seen her share of swordfights between Not and someone else, but she halts, noting the scraggly man's sword. It's shorter than the soldier's sword, though it's curved wickedly, with a looped hilt. She has read about the swords in the South crafted like it—the book referred to them as scimitars. Preferred by the desert people of Lynnor, it is good for quick movements, particularly slashes while on horseback due to its light weight. She supposes it has a unique edge, no pun intended, in duels, but it is at a disadvantage against the balanced weight of his opponent's broadsword.

The way the man holds the scimitar is also peculiar. He grips it in his left hand, something Idrid has only seen Not do, though the blade-side is pointing forward from the underside of his hand. The grip is something she would expect for a dagger. The scraggly man has his elbow bent, resting the hilt against the center of his chest with the sharp end pointing straight out at his opponent.

A deep voice resounds across the crowd and bounces against the large pillars; it's an announcer's voice. "A'right, this bout will last until a fighter leaves the boundary, a fighter becomes incapable of continuing, or a fighter surrenders! Death is a possibility that the owners and landlord take no responsibility for. Nor are bets gone awry! Are the fighters ready?"

The confident man waves his sword lazily in the air and nods, smiling slightly. The scraggly man shallowly lowers his head.

"Begin!" the announcer's voice shouts.

The confident man moves first with a leap forward, closing half the distance. His sword pokes forward, testing the reaction of the scraggly man. Idrid took him for foolhardy, though he apparently is giving the fight some thought. Perhaps his confidence is earned. That is what she would have thought were it not for the scraggly man's next move.

His scimitar spins forward and slams against the confident man's sword, surprising him with the force that causes his sword-arm to bounce back. The movement was fast, too fast to be certain of how it was done.

Idrid's eyes narrow and focus on the scraggly man's left hand gripping the scimitar. The confident man, no longer smiling and his eyes wider in concentration, recovers quickly and brings his sword back in front of him.

The confident man lunges.

Again, somehow, the scimitar arcs sideways and outward, knocking the confident man's sword away with unthinkable force. If Idrid hadn't been watching the man's hand, she would have missed it again. His hand flicked around, spinning on the axis of his forefinger, to grip the scimitar traditionally for only the moment in which he swung, and then flicked back to grip the hilt in his underhand. What added to the strength behind his swing was the relaxing of his elbow, like a coiled snake snapping in an instant.

The confident man, now desperate, attempts to get the scraggly man off balance with a forceful horizontal slice aimed at his protruding left elbow. The confident man steps further forward to add momentum and get closer.

This time the scraggly man keeps his scimitar in his underhand and twists his left arm while extending it out, so that his elbow faces outward. The scimitar's blade is angled toward the ceiling, perpendicular to the way his elbow is pointing. In the same moment, he kneels down.

The men's swords collide, their metal shrieking violently. Idrid recoils at the sound, putting her hands over her ears. The confident man loses his footing as his swing follows through, his blade sliding along the curve of the scimitar.

The scraggly man, still in a crouch, steps forward, his scimitar angled at the other man's chest. The confident man catches himself before he falls on the blade.

The two men stay there, frozen. The audience realizes the scraggly man could have killed the other. The audience reacts a moment later, erupting into applause and cheers. Idrid steps back as the two men separate and walk away from each other. The confident man shakes his head angrily at the result before she turns away.

She walks along the outside of the pillars, letting her feet carry her to the end of the main thoroughfare and down one of the larger side streets. She can't help thinking about the scraggly man's swordplay. With how quick his movements were, he would prove a match for Not. She does not know how Not or anyone would counter the scraggly man's interchanging grip of his scimitar.

The street she's now on leads north to the sketchier part of the district, although it is already sketchy enough as it is, with prostitute houses lining every street. Several pairs of people, civilians whose arms are linked with those of prostitutes (she can tell by their mascara and showy dresswear), shuffle down the street toward her, merrily talking and laughing. They show no wariness of Idrid, something she found typical of the commoners in the red-light district and why she tended to wander around there specifically rather than elsewhere in Telnas.

A man steps out a side door to the larger building where the duel took place and begins walking toward her. She recognizes the long curls of hair swaying with his steps, his scimitar in a curved scabbard at his side. The confident man steps out the door two seconds later and points at the scraggly man's back.

"Hey!"

The scraggly man stops walking but doesn't turn. Idrid continues her progress toward them, unperturbed by the potential fight between them.

"You're just going to walk off? What about a rematch?"

The scraggly man notices Idrid approaching and nods at her wearily. Idrid pauses, looking over his shoulder at the confident man.

"Are you mute?" he shouts, taking a step forward. Idrid balls her fists and takes a step forward as well. The confident man retreats a step back. He eyes Idrid a second longer before turning and returning through the side door without another word.

"Hah," the scraggly man breathes, his stony face turned vaguely at her. "Thanks." His voice is deep and clear. Without another word, he walks past her and continues down the street slowly.

"Who are you?" Idrid asks, curious.

He stops again, though this time he turns to look at her. "Tang," he says.

"I mean who are you?"

"I'm a guard," he responds.

Idrid silently watches him. He appears to be in the early stages of adulthood, the same as Not.

"You're a half-Giant," he says as if introducing her to himself. "Giants lived in the hills north of here but were eradicated. I'm sorry."

Idrid blinks at the bluntness of his words. "What do you know about that?"

"I am a guard at the southern border of Lanmar where the plains meet the desert," he says. "What I know I've told you."

"You had no part in it." He would've been too young.

"I've had dealings with Giants. They're large, but people all the same, with virtues and vices." Tang scratches the side of his head with a finger.

"You say you're from the South," Idrid says. "Your swordplay is like that of the desert people of Lynnor. Are you from there?"

"You saw my fight earlier." Tang's eyes flash as he tilts his head left and right, his long hair swaying like willow branches around his face. "I'm from Lanmar. The riverside town Brelen." He taps the hilt of his sword. "Have you ever been there?"

"I've passed the river that runs to it, but never been to the town."

"Not Brelen. Lynnor."

Idrid hesitates. Another couple passes by under an overhang of a hole-in-the-wall restaurant whose windows warmly illuminate their rosy faces. Perhaps she's asked too much.

Tang's eyes stay on the couple's backs as they walk by Idrid. "Where's Not?"

It takes her a second to process the question. "What?"

"You should've expected talk of the king's double to be popular here of all places," Tang replies. "It's not like he's the only one in the stories, either. Many have heard of the one who accompanies him."

Her mind races to find a way to distract. None of the stories would include Not's name. "You believe these stories?" she asks.

For the first time Tang smiles, but it's only his mouth. "No one descended from Giants would come here alone after the way the former king treated them, unless they had the force of an army with them."

"I don't have an army," Idrid mutters, shifting, expecting the worst.

"I said the force of an army. It isn't my best analogy, though the devastation Not could bring is comparable." Tang steps to the side and begins to walk slowly back toward her.

"How do you know Not?"

"We grew up together."

She barely hears him as he passes. Whirling around and putting her fists up in preparation for an attack, she opens her mouth in surprise at his continued pace.

"I've no interest in spoiling whatever plot he's cooked up," Tang says with a sigh, stopping several feet away with his back facing her. "Or you, if you somehow managed to convince him of something."

"You're not the king," Idrid states, thinking aloud. "I wasn't aware the nobility here had the privilege of friendships outside of family."

He glances at her over his shoulder. "I'm not noble in any meaning of the word." Turning around fully, he narrows his eyes. "I hope you succeed. If you do, would you do me a favor?"

Realizing she still has her hands up, she lets them fall to her sides. This man is sharper than his sword, and clearly knows Not somehow. She curses herself for being so obvious. "What do you want?" she asks finally.

"Visit my home. It's a gatehouse along the southern border. Just follow the road travelling south of Brelen and you'll find it. The road divides a lovely patch of grass from a barren canyon floor where nothing grows."

Idrid shakes her head. "Why?"

"You'll bring Not too, won't you? If he doesn't come, don't bother."

"Why?" she asks again.

"So I can kill him."

Idrid steps forward and raises her arms again, ready to pound the man's head in. He jumps back several feet, widening the gap.

Tang laughs, sweeping his hair to the side. "You're pretty loyal. I think you'll be able to convince him to come." Several moments of silence pass as Idrid glares at him. "Don't get me wrong," he continues, "I don't want to kill you also. That would only make him mad, which none of us want. If you could, though, do me that favor and bring him to where I live."

Idrid freezes, noting the way he's now talking. It's casual, confident, almost charming, while underneath lies dangerous intent. It's the same way Not speaks.

"I'll be on my way unless you want to talk more." Tang turns back and walks off, his hair bouncing against the top of his shoulders. He disappears around the corner.

She takes another step in the direction he went before getting ahold of her thoughts. She realizes she is very angry; her heart is racing. She didn't like the idea of someone who knows Not wanting to kill him. Wherever he is now, she prays they don't meet. She shouldn't be worried, but there was too much similarity between them for her comfort.

Thinking better of going after him, she continues in the direction of the hills to the north, following the same paths until Not would arrive.

Chapter 16: **James**

"…and then he looked me in the eye with a sudden clarity you wouldn't believe, it was like looking into two lakes, and he said, 'Clocks tick, but ticks don't clock.'" Up and down the dining table came uproarious laughter, the sound quirking James's mouth up marginally. He had been thinking about the upcoming deadline for the science project the magicians in Vale Tower had been hard at work on. "Then he took a bite of his fork and had to be immediately sent to the dentist. Suffice it to say he had had one too many drinks."

James lets his smile widen a bit as the laughter of others reignites, despite only hearing the latter part of Seph's story. He allows himself to chuckle, which gets the attention of Seph.

"King James, I'd like to hear you tell a story," Seph prompts, covering his mouth in an effort to stifle his laughter.

"Yes!" several of the other royals murmur their agreement.

James waves his hand lazily over the tabletop and shakes his head. "I don't have many funny stories to tell."

Finally in control of his face, Seph lays his hand on the table next to his plate. "I'm sure you have some interesting ones, funny or not."

James tilts his head, the tips of his silver-grey bangs falling just above his eyeline. He places an elbow on the table to prop up his chin. "Not many of you here knew my parents."

The guests hush, all eyes focusing on the king.

"I hardly knew them," James continues, rubbing his chin thoughtfully. "I knew my father better than my mother. When I was young, they separated. It wasn't an official divorce. She simply started living outside the palace. And he continued to live within, taking care of me. It was too early in my memory to recall everything accurately, though I remember enough to know what the reason for the separation was.

"I had a brother who was younger than me. He went with my mother to live outside the palace. I occasionally got to see him and my mother, and we got along well. We would build sand castles on the shores where the channel met the Sterling Sea. My most vivid memory is of him trudging determinedly into the waves at high tide. They were so tall and strong, I couldn't hear anything else other than their crashes when I called to him to stop. I had a fear of the water back then. He did it only to lessen my fear of the water… he must've been four at the time."

James smiles slightly, shaking his head. "I couldn't believe someone so young could do something so reckless just for the comfort of someone else."

A steady silence settles over the guests. Seph speaks up. "That's how he died?"

No, James thinks, but only says, "An unfortunate event."

"So this person who is currently going around and who looks like you—?"

"An imposter."

"That's horrible." Seph's wife, Mira, pauses to sip her wine. "For someone to use the identity of someone dead…"

"Some magicians can take on the form of others," Filento says. "Though, it's impossible to do it perfectly."

"You said you knew the reason for your parents' separation," Seph recalls.

"My brother wasn't the reason as most people think," James says. "The reason my parents separated was because of the eradication of the Giants."

"The Giants in the Dagger Hills," Seph mutters. "Not many agreed with the king's decision."

"It was both my parents' decision."

Guests collectively drew in breath. "What?"

"They knew such an act would cause contention. In order to make it seem like the Royal Court was split in the decision, my mother moved. It was a sort of fail-safe, so that if people lost trust in their king, the queen could return to take over the throne. They didn't live long enough to regret their decision to kill the Giants, though, if they ever regretted it in the first place."

The guests murmur among themselves, and James puts on a presentable smile. "I wanted to go live with my mother, rather than have my reputation tainted by my father's action. But, some things are unavoidable."

"You disagreed with his decision?" Seph asks.

"He killed a race of people. What about that would I agree with?"

Seph pulls his hand off the table slowly, placing it in his lap. "Apologies."

James taps his chin several times before removing his elbow from the table. He feels a hand on his shoulder and looks over to Filento. Filento jerks his head toward the door. Standing just on the inside of the door at their side of the dining hall is one of the Magic Guild's magicians. Darren, James recalls. His hands are weakly bunched into fists that hang by his side as he nervously makes eye contact with the king.

Nodding at the guests and murmuring, "I'll be back," he leaves the table and strides over to Darren. "Is there something important?"

"Somewhat," Darren says vaguely. "I've taken an Elementalist down to wait in one of the special cells. I found her chasing after your double outside Chalman."

"My br—"

"Take us to see her," Filento instructs, somehow at James's side without him noticing.

James flinches in surprise before composing himself. He nods to his advisor, grateful he caught him before a slipup. "Filento. Yes, I'd like to see what she has to say. Filento, please stay here and entertain—"

"I could be of some assistance," Filento interrupts again.

Darren's eyes become slits as he appraises the advisor. James pauses for a half second, then waves his hand. "Fine. Take us to see her," he tells Darren, who appears unperturbed by Filento's rudeness in interrupting the king twice.

Darren turns and pushes open the door for the two to follow through. He leads them down a corridor, then another, and finally to a stairway descending down, the furnishings diminishing as they go. At the base of the stairs, he turns right toward the underground prison. Just inside the guardroom is a desk occupied by a guard repeatedly flicking a quill around his thumb before grasping it again. The guard stands up fast at the sight of James.

"Remain where you are," James tells him. James continues after Darren, who turns into one of the prison complex's hallways. Their footsteps echo off the stone floor and walls.

Darren stops at a third cell near the center of the hallway and looks down. James and Filento take up positions on opposing sides of the metal grate built into the floor that leads into the cell. Through the grate they can make out the dark figure of a woman lying in a cot thirty feet below. "I knocked her out, so you'll have to wait a bit before she wakes," Darren says.

Filento lets out an impatient breath, and James tells Darren to fetch the key. Darren squats down and glides his hand over the lock on the thick bar intertwining with the grate to hold it fast with the prison floor. Lifting his hand and moving his other, both palms up, the bar disappears from the grate and reappears instantly in his hands. Placing the bar next to the grate, he lifts the cell open as he stands.

"Only Teleporters can open it," Darren explains. "A lock would be too simple to undo for an Elementalist."

James nods. "Ingenious. Take us down."

Darren lightly grips the sleeves of the men on either side of him and teleports them all to the floor of the cell.

"She's awake," Filento announces with his hands behind his back, sharing a clandestine look with James. Darren readies himself as the woman rolls over, her eyelids just opening.

"What's your name?" James asks the woman.

"Jasmine," Darren answers for her as she slowly looks between the three men, sitting up.

"How do you know my brother?"

Filento inhales sharply at James's question, casting a quick glance at Darren. Darren, for his part, shows no reaction, only crossing his arms over his chest.

"I don't know him," Jasmine, unmoving, says in a monotone. Her dark hair hangs around her face, obscuring it from view.

"Why were you chasing him, then?" James asks.

"He stole from me," Jasmine says.

"He's a thief?"

"Yes."

"And that's all you know?"

"Yes."

James sighs, then turns to Darren. "You saw him, too. Did you get a chance to talk with him?"

Darren looks between Filento and James, then down at Jasmine. "Why isn't she moving?"

Filento takes a near-imperceptible step toward Darren, and James asks again, "Did you talk with him?"

Darren stares at Filento, his face set in concentration. After a long moment he says, "No. He did not tell me anything." He leans to look around Filento. "What are you doing behind your back?"

Filento brings both his hands from behind, revealing he's holding nothing. Darren relaxes. Then Filento snaps his fingers. "You can continue sleeping, Jasmine."

Jasmine finally moves, shifting her legs onto the cot to lay on her back. Her eyes close and her chest rises and falls in the manner of someone deep in sleep.

"What—?" Darren's eyes freeze as Filento's thumb presses against his temple.

"We interrogated Jasmine but did not learn anything," Filento says. There is a flash of warmth that discharges from the skin of his thumb into Darren's head. Filento draws his hand back and moves to whisper in James's ear. "He won't remember my magic, or that the man is your brother."

Darren's eyes stare blankly at the spot where Filento had been standing. A few seconds pass before Darren blinks several times, then looks at the two other men. "Should we get out of here, then?" he asks.

"Please," James says.

Darren takes both men's sleeves once more and teleports them up out of the cell. He kneels, shutting the grate at the top of the cell, then replaces the metal bar in the center of the grate.

James nods. "Please return to the dining hall, Filento. I'll be there shortly."

Filento bows, Darren saying, "I'll go, too." The two men exit the hall, leaving James standing alone still beside the cell.

James drops his head to look back down at Jasmine sleeping peacefully on her cot in the corner on the floor far below. He watches her for several minutes, deep in thought. He shudders once, then makes his way back to the dining hall.

Chapter 17: **Jasmine**

It has been hours since she awoke to find herself in the bottom of a cell, and Jasmine is just about prepared to carry out her plan. The cell allows her a space twelve feet long and wide to pace, which she has taken advantage of fully while coming up with a way out. She ignores the cot in the corner, for she can't bear the thought of sleeping anymore.

The area is likely somewhere underground. Two Elementalists had put a bag over her head before dropping her into the cell. The fall must've knocked her unconscious yet again, or the guards did something to make her unconscious, since it's the last thing she remembers. She is surrounded by four stone walls, a stone floor, and a grate far above made out of some metal she couldn't move when she tried to use magic. The stone she can move, though the grate continues into the stone and forms a cocoon around her cell.

That, she assumes, is the "trick" they use to keep in Elementalists. Really, though, it isn't much of a trick. It's as clear as day that she's actually in a cage rather than a walled cell, and she lets out a quiet, short laugh at the idea that any other Elementalist wouldn't notice it immediately. She has to give the magicians who came up with the idea some credit, though.

The material does make it difficult to do anything, since it is so perfectly ingrained with the stone that any Elementalist who tried to manipulate the stone would only get a centimeter's length of rock before meeting the immovable metal. Not much can be done with a centimeter-long rock.

The obvious oversight the designers made is that the cage, while very carefully interwoven, isn't a whole surface. Jasmine assumes none of the magicians here have met an Elementalist capable of compressing stone to a space less than that of a thimble, though it could also be none of them managed to do it without exhausting themselves. She doesn't complain since it's lucky for her.

She is ready now; the only thing keeping her here is her doubt about what she'll do once she gets out. Crouching to the floor, she taps a finger on it and mentally pulls the stone. Beneath the floor she can feel the cylindrical mass she wants shift upward, passing between the cocoon of metal. She pulls it carefully, and it rises smoothly.

Soon enough there is a miniscule cylindrical stone pillar touching the metal grate above her. She draws in a considerable amount of stone to thicken the pillar somewhat, then breaks off its base. Now, she manipulates the pillar of rock to shift its base so that it rests on the most supportive spot of the metal cocoon beneath her cell. Another oversight: the base of the metal is much stronger than the overhead grate, due to its interconnectivity.

She positions her pillar of rock so that it wedges against the weakest spot on the grate above right beneath the handle which only opens on the other side. In theory, for every action there is an equal and opposite reaction, and she hopes to make the action of forcing the stone pillar up against the metal grate to also push against the metal cocoon beneath the floor, which will cause a lot of tension. Then, it will be up to her to keep the stone pillar from snapping, so that with enough tension the metal grate above will snap open.

Focusing herself, she begins the process. With adamant will, she applies pressure onto the stone, which in turn puts pressure on the metal. The pillar visibly begins to thin, the stone pulling into itself in an effort to lengthen and push up and down as the pressure builds.

Jasmine begins to sweat, but keeps the pillar steady. She realizes the pillar is getting too thin and she's running out of stone. With minimal additional effort, she draws from the stone making up the cell walls and floor itself, building the pillar some more. Soon enough there are no more stone walls, and the floor she stands on recedes into the pillar. She now stands on the metal cocoon itself, and the pillar is staying strong.

Above, the grate is groaning but holding. This is a good sign. All she has to do is wait.

Seconds tick by. Jasmine's upper lip is slick with perspiration, but she holds on to the pillar. Almost when she feels like she has to take a break, the grate above snaps open, the pillar pushing upward and slamming through the ceiling above. Fantastic.

She takes several breaths before swirling her hands around to create an air current. With the ease of an acrobat, she flies from the floor and up through the opening, landing on the solid surface past the metal grate. Appraising her work, her pillar of stone now a fixture in the ceiling, she looks around for an exit.

The metal grate serving as the entrance to her cell is set in the middle of a hallway with five other metal grates just like it travelling both ways. Only one end of the musty hall has a door, and she goes to it.

Prying it open just a smidge, she peeks out. It's another hallway travelling left to right, though this one is furnished. Green banners hang over the stone walls at all too carefully spaced intervals for an underground prison system, each sporting Lanmar's crest. The floor has floorboards, unlike the concrete hall she stands in, with a long red carpet stretching the length of the hall. Not a single guard in sight.

Jasmine steps into the hall, shutting the door while dusting off and straightening her clothes. Toward one end of the hall there is a desk with a writing quill and a large, closed manuscript with thick pages. It must be a guard's station, though why there is no guard stationed there Jasmine can't fathom.

Walking briskly over, her two-day-worn dress brushing the floor, she stops at the desk and flips open the manuscript to the first page. Numbers with corresponding names are scrawled in order by date, going down to the bottom of the page before continuing in another column on the same page. She flips somewhere halfway into the book, coming upon blank pages, then quickly flips back to the latest entry. Her name is at the end in relatively fresh ink.

How did they discover her name? No matter, she needs to get out of here. Or, she thinks the next moment, she can stick around for just a bit. After all, that Teleporter unwittingly got her inside the royal palace itself. She couldn't very well leave without taking something.

Flipping the manuscript closed once more, she pads over to the door and exits. Here there are wooden steps ascending straight for at least two stories, which she takes. The stairs level out and the room ends at double doors. Pushing them open, she is yet again in another hall travelling left to right, this one considerably better furnished. Sconces line the walls, their flames flickering warmly, and the floorboards are padded with a thin fabric. Jasmine chooses to go right, admiring an occasional iron suit of armor positioned along the hall.

The first person she sees steps into the hall from a room. It's a man, undoubtedly a servant, given the refined manner he holds a tray of various fruits and cheeses, wearing a simple white buttoned shirt and untarnished black pants. He eyes her lazily, then turns and walks off down the hall.

Fair enough. Jasmine enters the same room, shutting the door behind her. It's a storeroom filled with food. One glass cabinet stands by the door with several bottles of wine, several giant sacks of flour and potatoes rest on the floor along the walls, and rows of barrels labeled with fruit names occupy the majority of the room. Dried fruits don't interest Jasmine, so she leaves.

Following the direction the servant went, she finds another door leading off to the side. The door swings outward, pushed by a man wearing foreign clothes of bear fur thrown over a formal shirt that barely contains his muscles. Jasmine takes several steps back before she freezes when the man sees her.

"Jasmine." His voice is surly to match his intimidating frame. His eyes are pale green, offset by a brown bushy mustache. He steps out into the hall, followed by the same servant she had seen earlier. "Impressive you managed to escape a cell designed to keep Elementalists in."

Jasmine curses to herself. She should have knocked the servant out. "How do you know me?"

"Darren," the burly man says, and the one she had briefly met before he promptly punched her jaw exits the room to stand before her.

"Darren doesn't know me," Jasmine snarls, focusing on the corners of her vision for anything that would help her escape.

"Not does," Darren says.

Cocking her head, she asks, "Who?" As soon as the question is out, yet another man exits the room. This one Jasmine recognizes. But it can't be. He stands between Darren and the burly man, the spitting image of the man who somehow knocked her out the previous night and took her things. "You…"

"Me?" the man says, a mocking smile plastering his face.

"…aren't him."

His smile drops, anger flashing in his eyes. "What?"

Jasmine ignores the doppelganger and looks at Darren. "Are they brothers or something?"

"Aren't you perceptive," the burly man states rather than asks.

"And who are you?" Jasmine spits.

"Filento," he says. "So he goes by Not."

"How did you know he's not the same man?" Darren asks. "Does Not look more handsome?"

Jasmine looks back at the doppelganger, whose face is blanching with anger. Aside from the obvious undignified expression, he is more or less the same as the man who stole from her; same short grey hair (albeit better combed), same grey eyes, same body type. "The other guy was more sincere," Jasmine decides.

"What!?" the doppelganger repeats, his fists balling up. The servant behind the three men looks just as offended.

"Didn't you say he stole the cloak that you stole?" Darren says.

"He did, which is why I'm going to get it back after I kill him." Jasmine rubs the ring on her right hand with her thumb, thankful they hadn't taken away anything from her. That would've made her mad. Now that she thinks about it, the man who is apparently Not could have taken the ring for himself at the tavern as well. Why didn't he?

"That's interesting," the doppelganger says, finally reining in his anger. "Because that means our interests, in this case, are aligned."

Jasmine frowns. "What do you mean?"

His arrogant smile returns. "His existence threatens the kingdom."

For a moment Jasmine is silent. She looks at the way the other two men stand by his side like bodyguards, and suddenly she understands why the servant looks so offended. "You're the king?"

"The only reason I let you talk to me so is because you may prove useful in luring Not here," King James continues, basking in her shock.

"Your brother actually goes by the name Not?" It's somewhat ridiculous, though she has to admit the name is clever in its own way. Learning his name will be helpful finding him.

"I attribute his antics to an individuality complex," James says.

That doesn't seem quite right to Jasmine, since Not didn't have a care posing as some random guy to infatuate her, a tactic she herself was trying to pull off that night on him. The thought riles her up, though she forces her expression to remain neutral. She wouldn't let these men know more about her than they have to.

"So, would you like to help capture him?"

Jasmine thinks it over. It is appealing, and would place her on their side. "If I help capture him, what do I get?"

"Your freedom," James says.

Jasmine wrinkles her nose. The threat is clear, probably the only thing he's been straightforward with. "What do you plan to do with him once you have him?" Jasmine asks, changing tactics.

"Like I said, his existence is a threat to the kingdom."

Filento curls his fingers in the way Jasmine knows is the gesture of a magician, though she is unsure what kind of magician he is. Darren, on the other hand, blinks, glancing at James uncertainly. His eyes fall to Filento's fingers, and they widen.

Looking up thoughtfully at a sconce just above her head on the wall to her right, she sighs. "That's a shame. A bribe would have been a better offer than a threat."

"You're refusing?" James says, smirking at her. "You're not exactly in a position to refuse." As he says this five guards outfitted in Lanmar's colors exit the room into the hall behind him. They draw their swords with their right hands, holding them pointed diagonally at the ground.

She eyes them warily. They don't seem to be magicians, though they don't appear all too concerned. Her gaze returns to Filento. Either they underestimate her or place a lot of trust in this magician. "Aren't I?" she asks rhetorically, then sidesteps a knife the servant behind the men throws. Filento's fingers curl and uncurl faster, the servant behind him reacting and moving toward her. "Concilium!" Jasmine spits disdainfully. "This kingdom really is corrupt if the king rubs shoulders with brainwashers."

Before anyone else can make a move, Jasmine thrusts her right hand into the flickering fire in the sconce above her. The servant freezes, eyes glazed over. Filento, James, and Darren, whose face is sickly pale, share a confused look.

The flames lick around her skin; dull cracking and spitting noises erupt, though her hand remains uncharred. The ruby ring on her index finger begins to vibrate, and the flames flickering around her hand curl into the ring as they're drawn in.

"What are you doing?" Filento asks, his hands stilled by apparent curiosity.

Jasmine doesn't answer as the ring's vibrations grow in intensity. As soon as the ring feels like it's going to tear her finger off, she wrenches her hand back, holding it up with her palm toward her, gem facing outward.

Filento stays still alongside James, who looks equally confused. Understanding dawns on Darren's face, and he looks at Jasmine for a moment. Jasmine is worried he is going to teleport the ring off her hand, though he nods at her. The next moment he's gone.

Grinning wildly, she sets her other hand's index and middle finger over the gem on her ring. It glows brilliantly beneath, a raging fire quivering in anticipation of being let loose. Jasmine obliges, drawing the fire out in a rush.

"GET DOWN!" she barely hears Filento yell a second too late, as the flames rush forward in a wave. The servant is engulfed in flames, and that is all Jasmine sees before the fire creates a wall reaching from floor to ceiling in blazing glory.

Still, the stream of fire exits her ring. She aims the ring at the floor, making sure to ignite everything she can. The last bits of fire sputter out of the ring, lighting in patches on the matted floor. Turning, she flees away from the fire and the awful magician and king.

Chapter 18: **Not**

"Again!"

I pant, sweat dripping down my face in waves despite the cold mountain air. Raising my practice sword, I lunge forward. Instructor dodges easily, hitting my back with the edge of his own practice sword, making me buckle down in pain.

"Again!"

Gritting my teeth as the pain in my back swells up and travels up and down my body, I force myself to stand. I turn, trying my best to look at Instructor through the sweat in my eyes. He stands several feet away. I note that he has the advantage of being in his prime; twenty-five years old, healthy, and a solid three feet taller than me. I drop my sword, allowing it to clatter on the ground and rest on my right foot as I wipe a hand over my eyes, swiping the sweat away.

"Are you giving up?"

The question comes out in a dangerously low voice. I swipe another hand over my eyes then hair so that the strands cling to the side of my face. Instructor advances, his stony face a telltale sign of his anger, pulling back his sword, about to strike.

Before he does, I kick my right foot up, sending my sword flying into him. He reacts quickly, though not quick enough. He turns so that the sword ricochets off his side, and then I grab it out of the air and take advantage of his turn by getting behind him.

From there, I swing my sword in a downward arc and kick the back of his knees with my foot. Instructor defends his head, blocking my sword with his own, though is caught off guard by my kick, and stumbles.

I curse, my size once again not giving me the strength to cause him to fall. Instructor whirls around, sword pointed at me, though I have mine already leveled with his. His eyes are alight, face set in concentration. Suddenly, he breaks his form and stands upright.

"Good. That was good." Instructor nods at me, then walks along the rocky surface to a ledge, and sits atop an outcropping of rock to gaze out across a valley hidden behind a multitude of hills.

Panting, I follow him and sit on the hard ground beside his rock, crossing my legs. We sit side by side for some time, me considerably more winded than Instructor.

"Not," Instructor says after a minute without looking at me, his clear blue eyes distant. I follow his gaze over the countryside, spotting a sparkling river in the distance nestled in the spring fuzz of the barrens. It's familiar. The highlands overlook Lanmar, so maybe I passed it when I ran away. "I've found it."

I turn to look at him, my panting cut off with a gasp.

He meets my eyes, his own tearing up as he repeats the words. "I've found it."

My breathing hitches, and I startle awake, crashing to the floor. I put a hand over my chest, feeling my heart pumping fast. Slowly, I remember where I am. A kind farmer found me groggily treading through his wheat field the previous night. He'd told me I'd stumbled onto the outskirts of Telnas and offered me his place to stay in exchange for me not culling the field for him. Whether politeness or a skepticism of my mental state, I let him lead me to the residential district. Finally, I had made it back.

I stand up, appraising the bed I fell out of. The sheets are darkened with moisture. My sweat. It's been a while since I've dreamed. I see images of Instructor's eyes lingering against the back of my eyelids every time I blink. My eyes fall to my sword resting across the arms of the chair beside the bed. I'm the same age he was at the time.

Shaking my head, I throw the cloak I left hanging on the back of the same chair over my shoulders. I take the sheets off the bed and roll them up. At the very least I can help wash these before I leave. The homeowner—Andy, I recall—sits at a dining table, taking small bites out of an apple while reading a flier.

"Good morning!" he says through chomps. "I hope you slept well. Don't mean to be rude, but last night you looked ghastly."

"I bet," I say, standing at the other end of the table. "What's that you're reading?"

Andy turns the flier to face me so that I can read it while he answers. "The beard shaving contest is tomorrow. Not my kind of event, though I enjoy seeing the crowds." He notices I'm carrying the bedsheets. "Oh, you don't have to do that," he says, standing up.

"I insist," I say, stepping toward the house's exit. "The river's out here?" I don't wait for his answer, knowing perfectly well a stream runs close by. Outside there is also a wire tied on a hook implanted in the house travelling to another hook implanted in a tree. Andy comes out behind me as I walk toward the water's edge.

As I dip the sheets in the trickling water, he asks, "So you're a travelling swordsman?"

"Yes."

"Sounds like an adventurous life."

"More or less." I finish soaking the sheets and move to hang them up to dry.

"I've heard rumors of someone travelling around Lanmar impersonating the king." I freeze for a millisecond before pulling the sheet over the wire. "I haven't ever seen the king," Andy continues, "though descriptions of the traveler say they're identical. Grey hair, grey eyes."

I straighten the sheet out then cock my head to look over at Andy, who is standing just outside the doorway. His pose isn't threatening; in fact, he looks slightly nervous. "What would you do if your entire life you looked like someone else and you were never recognized for anything other than who that other person was?"

Andy folds his arms, unfazed by the question. "I would change myself to be different."

I move away from the hanging sheets and walk over to him. "I'm not who the rumors say I am. I'm not an impersonator, nor am I the real king."

Andy lets out a breath and visibly relaxes as if a problem plaguing him for some time had been solved. Then he takes a cautious step back behind the doorway. "Who are you, then?"

Smiling slightly, I tell him. "I'm Not. Not is my name."

He blinks. "Not? Do you have a last name?"

I suddenly laugh, making Andy flinch. "Not James."

"Not James?" Understanding washes over his face. "So you are the king's brother? Did your parents name you that to tell you apart?"

Laughing again and reaching inside a pocket to produce the bag of coins I took from Jasmine, I say, "No, I gave myself that name when I ran away."

"Why did you run away, if you don't mind me asking?" he asks, watching me pull out several gold coins that I offer him. Slowly, he takes them. "What are these for?"

"One is for letting me stay the night. The other three are because you didn't try to murder me while I slept." At the look of horror that crosses his face I burst into a fit of laughter. Composing myself, I add, "I ran away for many reasons. I haven't told anyone this, mainly because I thought it unimportant. Basically my presence caused tension in my family and I had no interest in the throne. Pretty standard elite-type stuff."

Andy is awash in revelations, though he allows me to step past him and head for the bedroom to collect my bags and sword. When I come back to the door fully outfitted, he gives me a strange look. "I never knew any of this about the royal family. It makes sense they'd keep the personal—well, personal. But why is it you've returned to Telnas?"

"Well, if you've heard the rumors then you've probably heard something about James sending most of the Royal

Guard out to get me. If it happens that they find me, I can only assume he'll kill me. He always was possessive of what was his. I'm looking to stop him from bothering me any longer."

Andy nods, somewhat more agreeable than I would imagine someone to be after being told their king's life is being threatened. "I don't know if you've been living here quietly until now the past couple of years," Andy says, "but the people here don't think fondly of the king. If he's looking to kill you simply because you exist…" He pats my shoulder. "Then I'm on your side."

"Well. Thank you." I nod once at him, then make my way out the door and away from the house without looking back.

Chapter 19: **Maia**

Maia wakes up slowly, as one does when they've had a satisfying night's sleep, and lets her eyelids rise to stare up at the ceiling. The flickering of candles across the wall reminds her where she is, and a sudden burst of excitement forces her to sit up. Her bed sheets tumble off, her hair spilling over her face, though not before she catches Master Aveve watching her from the stairwell.

"Good morning," Aveve says warmly. "And yes, it is morning. It can be difficult to know the time of day when you're in here since there aren't any windows on this floor, but your circadian rhythm seems to be on point."

Swooping her hair back behind her ears with both hands, Maia blinks the rest of her sleepiness away. "Circa-what?"

"I see you've got a staff," Aveve says. "Do you plan on using it?"

Remembering that she left the staff Tricia had conjured for her under the bed, she shuffles further out of the bed so that she can reach down and take it. "I want to."

Aveve makes a sound that's a cross between a squirrel squeak and a hiccup. "That's wonderful! If you're ready, follow me to the first floor where we'll have more room to work with." She turns and flies down the stairs in a flurry of her extravagant dress.

Maia takes a moment to stand up, using the staff as support. Then, using it as a cane, she makes her way slowly down the steps. Aveve is waiting at the center of the floor, arms crossed and mouth curled in thought.

"Ah, you're here," she says. "The staff will marginally help focus where you'll be conjuring items, specifically at either end of the staff. The real difference is students conjure things in their hands. So, you're not required to swirl that thing around or do any crazy motions, just point it at a space and let the magic happen."

Maia awkwardly holds the staff in both hands, resting one end of it on the ground. She nods.

"Well then, you may begin when ready."

Freaking out, Maia looks at her. "How am I supposed to conjure anything?"

"Oh, magic works the same way no matter what you're doing," Aveve says. "The basis for all magic is your will. Think about what you do with Elemental magic. What do you think when you're doing it?"

"I picture what I want to happen in my mind."

"Picturing it is a start, though anyone can do that."

"I... cause it to happen?"

"How do you cause it to happen?"

Maia is struggling. She hasn't ever thought this deeply into how she does it, much less put it into words. "What I picture and what I want... when I start to want what I picture to happen, it feels like a part of me thickens."

Aveve nods. "What part of you thickens first?"

"My head. Then it's as if whatever part of my body I'm using to direct my magic also thickens."

"Have you ever felt your entire body feel as if it were, as you say, 'thicker'?"

"I... don't know."

"It would be extraordinary for someone as young as you to experience it," Aveve says. "It happens when the magician is tapped completely into their will."

Maia remembers the feeling she had after she had fed the tree. "Does it feel like your body is larger than itself?"

Aveve looks at her thoughtfully. "That is one way to describe it. But I digress. What you've already said, picturing and then wanting it to happen, those things are the same for Conjuring. The big difference is you have nothing physical to manipulate since you're creating something from nothing. Now, give it a try."

Maia looks at the top of her staff a solid foot above her head. "What should I conjure?"

"Surprise me," Aveve says with a giggle.

Something from nothing, Maia repeats in her head, concentrating on the tip of the staff. What do I want? Food is the immediate thing that comes into her mind. A plate full of food: mashed potatoes, chicken breast… and apple slices, she adds to the image when hearing Aveve take another bite from her apple.

When she has the image firmly in her mind, she begins to feel her will spark to life. It's strange not directing it to move something or change something physical. Yet now the difference Aveve described, in that it's making something that was previously nonphysical, doesn't seem like much of a difference anymore. Tightening her grip on the staff, Maia feels her will ebb through her chest and reach down her arms.

Still focusing on the tip of the staff, she waits for the tingling sensation in her fingers that will signal her to conjure. Seconds tick by, and her fingers are buzzing, though nothing is happening. She realizes that she is relying on her experiences in Elemental magic. Throwing her mind back, she recalls the experience of feeding the tree; how her nonphysical will felt like it brushed with something else, and how that something else reacted when she let go of all the salt filling the water.

Experimentally, she focuses on the skin of her fingers gripping the staff and tries to feel with her will again. Sure enough, after another few seconds of distinguishing what her fingers felt and what her will felt, she senses there is an almost imperceptible lump between her hands that isn't wooden exactly. It's reacting to her will, though not at all like the tree— the tree had felt immovable like a wall, but this felt like the buzzing in her fingers is being mimicked. She is surprised she hadn't noticed it before, but the staff is buzzing all the way up and down, just as her will is doing within her. All she needs is…

Pop! A pure white plate topped with mashed potatoes, chicken breast, and apple slices arranged exactly how she pictures it appears balanced at the top of the staff.

Aveve claps her hands, laughing. "Spectacular! That's better Conjuring than most first-year students can pull off! Oh, let me help you with that." She whisks the plate off the end of the staff before it can fall off.

Maia lets out a deep breath and smiles.

"Of course, I should've expected as much from a student of Kellen's," Aveve continues. "Here, I have a feeling you conjured this for a reason. Eat up and then you can try again. Though, perhaps something a bit simpler?" She offers the plate for Maia to take and gestures to a wooden table near the edge of the room.

Maia takes the plate and brings it over to the table, resting it on the cracked surface as she sits. Placing the staff gently on the stone floor, she notices she has nothing to eat with. "Um, Aveve?"

"Yes Maia?"

"Would you mind conjuring some silverware?"

Aveve's face morphs into an apologetic frown. "Oh dear, I'm so sorry!" Three pops and Maia feels the table reverberate as a knife, fork, and spoon appear.

"Whoa. I didn't know you could conjure things from afar."

"With enough practice you can," Aveve says with a sly smile.

The tower door opens outward with a bang and the boy that was rude to Maia yesterday walks in. He eyes her, clearly annoyed she's there.

"Mark, you're here early," Aveve says. "Like usual. Want to show me what you can do?"

Mark, still watching Maia, steps near the center of the floor then closes his eyes. Holding his hands out, palms up, an apple appears in them. Opening his eyes again, he offers it to Aveve with an ingratiating smile.

"Why thank you Mark!" Aveve exclaims, taking it and throwing her mostly eaten apple away to the side.

Glancing over, Maia catches sight of the apple disappearing in midair. She wasn't aware Conjuring could... destroy? That didn't seem like the right word. Maybe dissipate, like Greg used to say about water.

Mark, still smiling smugly, looks over at Maia. Maia no longer watches them, turning her attention to her food.

Aveve takes a loud bite from her new apple. "Keep up your practice, Mark. I'll be down here helping Maia until she gets the hang of Conjuring, although she already may have gotten it."

Maia continues to eat, though suspects Mark is watching her. Minutes go by as Maia hears intermittent pops every time Mark conjures something new, followed by Aveve's soft coos of encouragement. Finally, she finishes her food. She stands up, picking her staff up off the floor, and walks back toward Aveve, who is standing to the side with a distant expression on her face.

Aveve's face clears when Maia nears her. "All right, ready for another go? Try to conjure… a single apple, like Mark did."

Maia feels her face flush and hopes neither Aveve nor Mark notices. She lifts her staff from the ground and angles it, using her shoulder as a rest for the top. This time she'll conjure from the bottom end. Once again, she extends her focus and feels the staff buzzing with her. The apple pops into existence two seconds after she concentrates, bright red and standing upright on the floor.

"Wonderful!" Aveve says. "Do it again."

Maia obliges, moving the end of her staff an inch away from the apple, and another identical apple appears beside it.

"Now, create two more in succession."

Pop. Pop.

"Very good. Actually, I don't think I'm even needed anymore, you picked it up so fast!" Aveve giggles, then moves to scoop up all four apples aligned in a row on the floor. "If you don't mind, I'm going to eat these as well. You can continue to practice with Mark, and once the other students arrive, you can begin exercises with the rest." Aveve begins racing toward the stairway, dress flying behind her.

Slightly startled by the abruptness of it, Maia calls out for her to wait. Aveve stops and turns, eyebrows raised. Mark is also looking at her, and Maia walks the length of the floor to question Aveve in a hushed voice. "Can you teach me to, uh, make things disappear?"

Aveve's eyes twinkle in the burning candlelight. "I'm afraid that's strictly taught to second-year students and above. Prevents the troublemakers from playing tricks on others, you see. Besides, you can only make objects that have been conjured disappear."

"Oh. Okay."

Aveve's mouth quirks upward. "I know your situation is unique, though I want to keep some allure to Conjuring.

After all, you aren't quite decided about what field of magic you want to choose yet, are you?"

Slightly perturbed by the woman's insight, Maia nods. "I'm actually most interested in Enchanting," she confesses. She then rushes to say, "But, that's not to say Conjuring isn't amazing!"

Aveve's smile grows wider. "You don't have to say which magic you enjoy the most. Everyone has different tastes. But, you say you're interested in Enchantment? That's very interesting. Sadly, I don't know any Enchanters. They seem to be very reclusive types."

Maia nods once more. She decides to ask one more question. "What's the largest thing you can conjure?"

Aveve throws her head back and bursts into laughter, then immediately stifles it. "You're the first person to ask me that, and I'm not being sarcastic. Well, I haven't created anything too big in a while, since it would cause disruptions in nature and other areas. Let's just say I conjured this tower."

Maia's eyes widen, looking around her as if seeing the tower for the first time. "You made all of this? I thought the Tower of Vern was named after a famous Conjuror?"

"It is, the tower just changes creators every couple decades."

"How does that work?"

"The former Tower Master destroys their tower to allow the next to create their own. It's considered a welcoming ceremony for the new Tower Master, and a farewell to the old one."

"That sounds kind of sad. And a little unnecessary. How does the new Tower Master reconstruct the old tower the exact same way?"

"The tower changes its structure every time, actually. It gives each tower a unique style so that students aren't confused about a new Tower Master."

"I imagine it's still confusing," Maia says.

Aveve giggles. "Indeed, it is. The Tower of Bel works much the same way, at least if what Darren tells me is correct. It is still made out of sand, right?"

"Yeah," Maia says, thinking it over. She supposes it does make sense a new tower would have to be created by a new Tower Master since the old one's Elemental magic would stop working once they left. "So wait, do conjured items disappear after they are left alone?"

"No, the items remain, even after the Conjuror's death."

That must mean the difference is Elemental magic doesn't persist because the thing being manipulated isn't natural to its original form, while conjured items are naturally its original form, which makes sense. Sort of.

"Do you have any more questions?" Aveve asks.

"No, no more. Thanks!"

Aveve beams at her once more, then turns and flies up the stairs. Maia looks back at Mark, who is still watching her curiously. He looks away when Maia meets his eyes.

She doesn't like the idea of being alone with him, though Aveve is already gone. Thinking for a second, she realizes she's already managed to conjure things. And Aveve is already impressed with her. That wasn't as hard as Elementalism, Maia thinks. Then again, Aveve said all magics were based on will, so already knowing how to perform one type of magic probably makes another easier.

"Are you going to stand there all day?" Mark asks.

She considers it, since it would annoy him, though walks toward him.

"That wasn't you actually conjuring those apples, was it?"

Maia stops fast, anger boiling inside her. "What are you talking about?"

"You may have been trying, but Master Aveve actually conjured them."

Furious, she lifts her staff and points it before Mark's feet. Another apple appears with a pop. "Did she conjure that?" Maia asks.

His face flushes and he kicks the apple away. It rolls several yards before bumping up against a bookshelf alongside the wall. "How did you do that?"

"Were you not listening when Aveve was instructing me?" Maia says, her voice pinched from trying to control herself.

"You just got here. There's no way you managed to begin Conjuring in a day, unless you've had experience before."

Maia considers whether or not to tell him and decides that it wouldn't matter either way if it caused the other students to scoff at her for being an Elementalist. She already proved she could conjure just as easily, if not more easily, than Mark. "I also know Elemental magic," she says.

Mark, who had just crossed his arms to strike another of his snooty poses, freezes. "You're an Elementalist," Mark states, his tone no longer superior. "I knew you must've had previous experience."

Confused now, Maia asks, "Don't you and students here think poorly of Elementalists?"

"Other students," Mark snaps. "I don't care what they think. My parents are Elementalists, but obviously I won't tell anyone that here, knowing what they say about them." He pauses, appraising Maia with his eyes. "You probably shouldn't either."

"Are you defending me now?"

"Or you could go ahead and tell everyone," Mark continues, uncrossing his arms and sticking his hands in his front pockets. "You won't change anyone's minds, though, even if you can conjure a few things. They're devout in their beliefs about Elementalists."

"Why did you act so arrogantly before, then? Are people here just snobby toward everyone?"

"Yes," Mark says instantly, causing Maia to raise her eyebrows in surprise. "And I did it to fit in, obviously. I don't know if you know many magicians, but they generally put themselves on pedestals."

Maia crosses her own arms. "And you don't?"

He looks at her for a short period of silence. "What I think hardly matters, since people are people and they're going to want to form ranks in some way or another. But no, I don't."

For a moment Maia wonders if he's fooling her, though his sudden change in attitude would be near impossible to fake. "What made you so doubtful I conjured those apples before, then? No one was here to put on a show."

"Like I said, conjuring something so easily wouldn't be possible. And I was jealous. Obviously."

Jealous?

The tower's door bursting open interrupts them, causing Maia to sense a pattern that the door always flies open dramatically. A mob of students rushes in. The flow of

251

students disperses, the majority turning to trickle up the stairs, while a few move to occupy spaces on the first floor. Among them are Tricia and Lin, who both spot Maia.

"Maia!" Tricia says unnecessarily loudly. "How was sleeping here? Was it spooky?" The two girls slow when they see she's standing next to Mark. "Is he bothering you?" she asks, standing next to Maia and folding her arms.

"He was," Maia says, earning a sigh from Mark. "Although he seems fine."

"Fine?" Mark repeats.

"Do you want to practice with us?" Maia asks. "I assume there are student guides or something here that overlook practice sessions, right?"

"It's actually very laid back," Tricia says. "There are guides, though they aren't assigned to anyone in particular. Our assignment this week is to conjure multiple objects at once."

"So we can practice on our own?"

"Yeah, pretty much."

Maia looks at Mark, Lin, and Tricia in turn. "Want to go practice outside?"

Mark looks at the three girls thoughtfully. Maia is sure he's about to object, since he has no reason to, and he surprises her when he says, "Why not?"

"There are no rules against it," Lin says.

"All right," Tricia agrees. They all walk to the door, pushing past several students still coming in, and exit the tower.

Outside the sky is a clear cyan, and the amber grass rolls pleasantly across the countryside. There is a trampled path through the grass, and more students are walking along it toward the tower. The group of four moves out of the way. Mark gestures for them to follow him toward the back of the tower, near the line of trees marking the edge of the forest.

They climb the low hill the tower rests against and stop at a nice secluded spot where other students wouldn't bother them.

"All right, you're trying to conjure several objects at once, right?" Maia asks.

Tricia and Lin nod. Lin holds out her hand (her long nails are now trimmed to the length of short daggers) and conjures a single leaf. "Darn," she says. "I still haven't gotten it at all."

"Let me try." Tricia places a hand out, conjuring a single blue marble. "Ugh."

Tricia and Lin both turn to Mark, who looks back at both of them innocently. "What?" he asks.

"Go ahead," Tricia says. "Try conjuring two or more things."

For the first time Maia sees Mark embarrassed, his cheeks reddening. "Fine." He lifts both his hands up, and two seconds later he's conjured a perfectly smooth pebble in each hand.

"Oooh," Tricia and Lin say approvingly, then Tricia says, "That's pretty good." She turns to look at Maia as if noticing her for the first time. "I forgot to ask you, have you conjured anything yet? You obviously don't have to be able to since you just got here."

Maia is nervous telling them, for fear they'll become jealous. Her eyes meet Mark's, who gives her a nod. "I've conjured several apples," Maia starts.

"That's awesome!" Tricia squeals and Lin smiles broadly. "Can you show us?"

Awkward, and a little tired of conjuring the same thing, she takes her staff and points it toward Tricia. "Hold out your hand," Maia says softly. When the other girl does, she allows the apple in her mind to pop into reality.

"Awesome!" Tricia says again, taking a bite out of it. "It's good!"

"Did Master Aveve teach you?" Lin asks.

"She did." Maia pauses, not sure what else to say.

"How much did she teach you?" Tricia asks slowly.

Maia doesn't hold their gazes for too long. "She told me Conjuring was basically the same as Elementalism: that all I needed to do was focus my will."

"Apparently she picked it up quick," Mark says. "She conjured several apples really fast, as Master Aveve instructed."

"I follow instructions well," Maia puts in before the others can mumble their awe.

"You seemed to have it down fast," Mark continues. "It made me think she had conjured things before. But she's an Elementalist, which somewhat explains it."

"Was that all Master Aveve had you do?" Lin asks.

"Were apples the first thing you conjured?" Tricia asks.

Maia looks at Mark, who is just as interested as the two girls. "The first thing I conjured was food."

Mark asks, "What kind of food?"

"The food you saw me eating earlier. Chicken, potatoes, and apple slices."

"You conjured that? What, with the plate?" Maia nods and Mark lets out a sharp laugh. "You know, if you hadn't been so quick to prove me wrong earlier I'd still be doubting you right now."

"Hold on, you're saying she conjured a whole plate of different kinds of food?" Tricia asks. "I don't think I believe that. You're gonna have to prove yourself to us."

"I don't want to conjure anything that we can't dispose of." Maia also doesn't want to show off.

"We'll eat it," Lin says amiably. "The food you just described sounds delicious."

"And the plate?"

"We can give it to one of the second-year students," Tricia says with a wave of her hand. "They're always looking for practice in disappearing objects."

"Actually, I am a second-year student," Mark says. "I can do it." Tricia and Lin both gawk at him. "What?"

"Really?" Lin asks.

"I guess that explains why we never spoke with you before," Tricia says.

While they're distracted, Maia concentrates once again and aims her staff at the ground. The sound of the pop grabs the others' attention, and they all look down at the plate on the grass with fresh apple slices, mashed potatoes, and chicken breast. Both the chicken and the potatoes have attractive steam rising from them in the crisp morning air.

"Great Dunlon, she did it," Tricia says, falling onto her bottom and conjuring a spoon for the potatoes.

"Hey, save me some!" Lin says, joining the other girl.

"That's impressive." Maia looks at Mark, who adds, "You may have to teach me a thing or two."

"Only if you teach me how to disappear things." Mark smiles at that, and Maia can't help but smile too.

Chapter 20: **Not**

Up until entering Telnas, I had all too brazenly drifted within towns pretending to be like any other average traveler. Now that I'm inside the grand city where I once lived, I am left with few other options than to flit between modestly shaded alleyways like some rapscallion. Though, with the red cloak, I'm more like some royal rapscallion which, while somewhat more dignified, makes me all the more conspicuous. I don't need to worry about the commoners, but I should avoid the attention of the Guard.

I halt myself just within the shadow of an alley's corner before a thoroughfare, eyeing the trickling of people passing by. It is neither crowded enough nor barren enough to walk across with the assurance I won't be caught. It's mid-to-late afternoon, getting toward the time streets should be bustling. Several decrepit market stalls are vacant; the space where wares normally would be displayed are covered by thin fleece blankets. Other stalls are open with peddlers pacing back and forth in front of them on the cobblestone street, though each seems to be selling the same thing: nondescript masses of hair.

"Luscious flax-dyed beards! The smoothest you'll find in Telnas!"

"Beards of corn silk here!"

"Twice-washed wool beards, now with multiple colors!"

I question whether the appeal of fake beards is increased by the number of times they've been washed. Still, I have to take a moment to gape at the dedication the people have to the beard shaving contest.

"Hey. Psst."

I turn and look at the ground several feet down the alley from where I stand. A dirty mass I mistook for a drab blanket shifts slightly. A hand reaches around from beneath the dirt-colored thing and pulls it off, revealing the scraggly head of a man. Two dark eyes peer at me from beneath his balding head and above pronounced cheekbones.

"Can you spare some change?"

The voice is gruff coming from such a thin figure, likely the result of living on the edge of his life. I feel a pang.

Crouching low and carefully adjusting the hood of my cloak over my head, its bright hem sweeping the dusty ground, I look at him closer. He has to be in his late forties. "Tell me, how did you end up like this?" I ask softly.

The man shifts some more, setting himself in an upright position against the alley wall. "It's easy to lose your way without friends," the man says. "I originally lived in the north. My family alienated everyone, including me. Soon enough I found myself alone, so I made my way here thinking I could scrape together a living. Didn't think I'd be doing that literally."

I nod. In my heart I know I'm just like him.

"That's a fine cloak," the man comments, stretching his skimpy arms over his head.

"I'd part with it in a heartbeat if it weren't for the trouble it'd bring you," I say, glancing back out at the thoroughfare. My eyes light upon a group of people walking by the market stall closest to the narrow alley, noting each of their dubious beards. "Maybe there's a way we can help each other out."

I lift my hands and pull the hood off my head, uncovering my light grey hair. The man reacts to my hair with a start. "Where do you come from?" he asks, pushing himself up some more so that he sits cross-legged. "I've only seen natural hair like that from my homeland."

"A similar situation to yours," I say. "Right now I need to focus on where I'm going. Do you have any experience with swords?"

"None at all."

Drat. Still, I think I can make this work. "What do you say about having a little street performance?" I tap the hilts of Halette's short sword and my own sword resting in the sheath on my back. I had managed to stuff both swords in there due to the sheath's maker doing a terrible job getting the volume right..

The man's eyes glint as he cocks his head. "What do you have in mind?"

"For you, it'll be simple," I say, pulling my hood back over my head and standing. "I'll give you one of my swords and all you have to do is stand still and hold your sword out. I'll do the rest."

"You're not going to skewer me, eh?" The man gets to his feet, his full height coming up to just above my shoulders. The clothes he wears aren't any less drab than his blanket.

"If I do, I'll have the Royal Guard on me faster than Dunlon could bend space." The man's eyes narrow. "I know what I'm doing."

The man thinks for a good second before nodding. "I'm Lief." Before I can reply he says, "I know there's a reason you're here and not out there," pointing at the thoroughfare. "There's no need to tell me who you are."

I nod once. "Thanks, Lief." Without another word, I turn and pace out of the shadows and into the thoroughfare. Pedestrians walking toward me from both ways slow their pace, though my hood obscures their expressions. I walk straight to a spot in the center of the thoroughfare and turn, watching as Lief follows my path to stand next to me.

With lightning speed I draw the short sword from my sheath, the steel singing as it scrapes against my sheath's brass. If anyone wasn't paying attention, they are now. I slowly hand the sword over to Lief, only letting go once his hands are wrapped around its hilt.

Slowly, but not any less dramatically, I unsheathe my own sword, its metal emanating a quiet hiss. I hold it vertically in front of my face, its sharp sides parallel to my body. "Hold your sword like this," I whisper so only Lief can hear. "Make sure the sharp ends aren't facing you."

Lief obeys my instruction, taking a moment to find a comfortable grip on the sword's hilt with both his hands. I take a step back and get into a casual fencing stance, my back foot perpendicular to my right foot which points directly at Lief. I tap my sword against the one Lief holds, letting the blades rest together for a moment. Then I begin.

My movements are fluid as I perform basic techniques any of the lower-rank guards of Lanmar can perform, though I'm just warming up. I perform each technique in succession, then switch the pattern up and begin again, mentally noting every move before I perform it: forward-step, right horizontal slice, backstep, parry, forward-step, backstep, parry, forward-step, right horizontal slice... Steadily I perform more complicated sequences of movements.

Each of my swings blends with the next, the sharp ends of my sword coming within inches of Lief's own sword and body but never touching. I can tell he's nervous, though he remains as steady as any good fighting dummy. When I get the chance between my swings, I check his expression; his eyes follow my movements, widening every time my sword gets close to him.

In my narrowed field of vision, I see a small crowd forming. Blurred faces standing just beyond Lief are still and facing me, though I don't bother looking at them.

My cloak dances with my body as I rapidly spin my sword around in a twirl, creating a 360-degree horizontal slice. The blade stops just short of Lief's neck. The speed and force of the movement causes enough of a disturbance in the air to tousle the remaining strands of his hair.

This impresses a few people and I hear several claps before I begin a new pattern of techniques from foreign lands that would assuredly impress even those accustomed to the Royal Guard's drills. Instructor only ever taught me the moves, never their origin.

I switch stances, holding my sword with both hands now. The stance I use now is typical of longswords, though it is fitting, since my own sword's length more than outreaches the one Lief holds. I create opposite forces with either hand; my right superior hand pushes while my left inferior hand pulls on the hilt, causing a basic vertical slice that I swing parallel beside where Lief holds his sword.

He flinches at how close my sword comes to where he grips his own, so I carry on my lightning-fast slices and parries while leaving more distance.

"You're not even fighting."

My blade freezes in the air, and I tilt my head toward the man who spoke. My hood obscures the upper part of his face, though I can see a chiseled smirk beneath a good deal of stubble.

"Why don't you have a real fight?"

I glance at Lief, who has lowered his sword finally. The small circle of people standing around us nod their heads, agreeing with the man. I lower my sword and say, "Would you like to duel?"

Lief's eyes widen in fear before he realizes I am not speaking to him.

"Now we're talking," the man says, his smirk turning into a grin. I see that he, too, has a sword, though it is sheathed in a buckle at his side. He grips its hilt and pulls it out. It's the same length as mine, though its width qualifies it as a broadsword. He has the upper-body strength to wield it easily enough, and the stance he gets in indicates he knows what he's doing.

I turn and pace over to Lief, holding out my hand so that he can return the short sword. He does with shaky hands before stepping out to join the ring of people in watching.

"Why don't you take that hood off?" the man asks, walking sideways around the circle's perimeter. "I want this to be a fair fight."

I begin walking counterclockwise so that I keep him at a distance while I size him up some more. "It'll be fair," is all I say without removing the hood. I can see he favors his right foot when he steps down with it, the barely perceptible shifting of his weight greater than when he uses his left. It matches the favoring of his right hand as well, its grip on his sword's hilt tightening and untightening above his left hand.

"If you insist," the man says, abruptly stopping his pacing to face me. I stop and face him as well.

Together we raise our swords, each pointed at the other, in a sort of mimicry. The idea is to engage the crowd further, and what better way than to give the appearance of not only being equals but facsimiles? Only, it is unknown to them who is mimicking whom.

The other man begins and I follow not a millisecond later, our swords swinging in diagonal cuts. They clash together, the metallic sound ringing in the otherwise quiet air. I realize even the peddlers are no longer calling out their wares.

We draw our swords back and swing them together again. He's testing my strength, I realize. The next moment he and I once again release and clash swords. The swings are coming quicker.

The next clash I move my arm and leg ever so slightly after my sword collides with his. He feels my sword shift, and draws his sword back. I wait for him to make a move, hoping he takes my feigned break in stance as a sign he has the greater strength.

I watch him draw his sword back farther than before in a strike meant to overpower my own in the next clash. My lips quirk upward.

Fast, so fast that the man doesn't even reach the apogee of his swing, I leap within his guard and lay the blunt end of my sword against both his arms.

In that moment, I pause to look him straight in the eyes. His are dark brown and wide with surprise. The next moment I'm two paces away again, sword lowered. I'm satisfied to see his smirk is gone.

"What was that?" a man in the crowd whispers to my right.

"He won," I hear Lief say.

"That was… kind of lame," another man says.

"Are you kidding? Did you see how fast he was?"

"That's what I'm saying, it ended too fast."

A harsh laugh silences the crowd. It came from my opponent. "You think real fights are meant to be fancy, minute-long ordeals?"

I tilt my head to get another peek of his full face. He is eyeing me with respect, though he has the same smirk plastered on his face.

"Watch again," the man says, raising his sword again at me in challenge. I mimic him once more.

This time his swing is conservative and he uses a vertical slice. I parry it with a flick of my own sword and follow the motion through so that my back is to him. The crowd gasps when they realize I had stopped a backward plunge of my sword just before piercing his stomach, my sword half-hidden beneath the folds of my cloak.

I step forward and away from the man, turning to face him once more.

"See?" he says breathily. "A real fight is over in seconds." He sheaths his sword and offers a hand.

I sheath my own sword and grasp his hand, shaking it. The crowd emits several claps until there is a weak applause that dies down the next moment. Just as quickly as the circle formed it disperses.

I hear a metal chink bounce several times off the ground and look down to see a single gold piece lying there.

Letting go of the man's hand, I stoop down and pick it up. "Not very charitable," I mutter, rising.

"That was fun," the man says. "What's your name?"

"Bellwether."

"Seriously, I'd like to know. You were wonderful, and I was clearly outclassed."

I don't reply. Lief steps beside me and pats my back enthusiastically.

The man lets out a breath. "All right. Bellwether. Well, thank you for indulging me. You should consider joining the Royal Guard. We could use someone with your skill."

"You're a member of the Royal Guard?" I ask.

"Not me, no. Though with your skill you'd be a member in no more than a week."

I nod and bid him farewell. He walks off toward where a growing stream of people are heading for the main festival, only looking back once to take a second and study me.

"You got us a whole gold piece!" Lief says.

"It's not that—" I cut myself short, realizing he is genuinely thrilled. Not wanting to lower his spirits, I tell him, "Could you do me a favor? Take this money and buy a beard as close to the color of my hair as possible."

"I—could, but why waste it on a beard?" he asks.

"The purpose of our little performance wasn't to get money," I say, eyeing the meandering people who no longer are interested in us. "I have my own money to give you, but only after you get me a beard. Please."

Lief smiles and nods. "I've trusted you this far." He steps away and moves along the thoroughfare to browse the stalls. I step to the side and lean against a building's wall, watching people walk by.

Several people glance twice at me and mutter among themselves before someone tells them I am only a performer and their attention shifts. A short man in familiar fancy blue dresswear catches my eye.

Looking both ways, I move toward the man. He notices me approaching and stops. I flick my hood up just enough for him to get a good look at my face.

"Ah! Ja—"

"Not," I say over the man's nasally voice, putting on a jovial smile and laughing. "Good to see you again!" Surprising even myself, I find that I more than halfway mean it.

The carriage driver beams at me. "It is lovely to see you too! What are you doing here?"

"Watching the festivities, of course. Where's your carriage?"

"Several streets over that way," he says, pointing. I silently thank Dunlon that it is not the same way the majority of people are going.

"I could use a ride to the palace."

"Of course! I just came from there, in fact. Jean and Halette will be pleased to see you tonight. I'll prepare it immediately!"

"Just a moment." I turn around to see Lief returning with a light grey beard. "Thank you very much for finding this," I tell him. From within my cloak, I pull the sack of money I had stolen from Jasmine and trade it for the beard.

Lief opens the sack and peers in. "This... is a lot..." he says. His breathing heavy, he looks back up at me.

"You did me a good service," I tell Lief, patting his shoulder.

The next moment the man is hugging me tightly, taking me by surprise. I swipe my hood down to keep it over my face, though return the hug. "Thank you," Lief says softly. He shakes the bag once my way for emphasis. "You are a miracle."

Unsure of what to say, I don't say anything. Lief nods several times, his eyes slightly teary, then walks off.

"You're truly a great ruler," the carriage driver says, stifling a sniffle. "I don't know how you do it."

"Easy," I mutter. "I don't rule." I tie the fake beard around my head. Once it is firmly fitted on my face, I remove my hood and let out a bright laugh. "How do I look?"

"Like you're ready for a shave!" the carriage driver says happily.

"Terrific. Now, take me to the carriage."

"Took you bloody long enough," I hear Idrid mumble when I burst in through the front door. "What's that on your face?"

"A fake beard," I say, crossing the entryway and standing in front of her. "Can't have people recognizing me for someone I'm not."

"Ah, Not!" Earl, the man who is the caretaker of the house and who took in Idrid when she was a little girl years before I ever met her, shambles down a flight of wooden stairs set against a wall. Its faded yellow wallpaper curls at the seams. "Welcome back!"

"Hello, Earl," I say, glaring at Idrid. "I've come to collect my Giant." Idrid narrows her gaze at me, and I narrow mine in return.

"That wasn't very nice." She rises from the small circular table. Luckily Earl had bought a bigger chair for future use once he found out what Idrid was, though Idrid left before she could grow into it. It's nice of him to have kept it.

"It wasn't very nice leaving me alone, either." I turn around and beckon her toward the door.

"Won't you stay for a bit?" Earl asks, his old legs wobbling a bit as he leans against the banister. "I can get you some tea!"

"I'm sorry, but we've got a palace to storm."

"We're doing that today?" Idrid asks.

271

I sigh dramatically. "What else are we going to do, enter the beard shaving contest?"

"Well, excuse me," Idrid huffs. "Wait, is that a thing? Why haven't I heard of this?" She turns to look at Earl, who has made it down the stairs.

"You were too young for me to expose you to such things," he says.

Idrid and I share a look. "I was too young to be exposed to beards?" she asks.

Earl's gaze deepens. "You don't know what it was like… to be young with a beard. The things we did." He continues to look on as if he is staring at the eternity of time. "The things we did," he repeats, drooping to rest himself in a chair by the stairs.

Moments pass before I sigh again, this time genuinely.

"Never mind," Idrid says. "So you got a crappy beard for a disguise. That'll help out here, but not once we're in the palace. And we still need a way in."

"Already covered." I move back across the entryway and hold the door wider so that she can see the very same carriage we came across by the Talwood. The nasally driver watches us with anticipation. "Now, are you coming?"

Without another word, though I catch her rolling her eyes, Idrid sidles through the doorway so that she doesn't hit the frame and moves to the carriage.

"See you, Earl," I say to the old man. He's still in the chair, stroking the air beneath his chin. My body involuntarily shivers, from what I'm not sure, and I shut the door and follow Idrid to the carriage.

"Heading to the palace, sir?" the driver asks.

"If you would, Darius," I say in a slightly deeper, authoritative voice that could loosely fit an elder nobleman's. Idrid gives me a withering look before climbing into the carriage. "Trust me," I tell her, "this is way better than wandering through the city."

"First you want to use the carriage to reach the palace, then you decide on foot would be faster, and now you're back to using the carriage. How did you get the carriage back, anyway?" Idrid asks as we take our seats.

I knock on the front of the carriage to signal to the driver we are ready to move. I pull off my fake beard and drop it onto the seat beside me. "A little after you left me I had to run because another magician came around, in addition to the Teleporter. I found the carriage while running along the road."

"Interesting," Idrid says with a hint of sarcasm. "I suppose that other magician was after that." She points at my cloak. "You shouldn't have messed with a high-level magician."

"Fine, yes," I relent. I should have known Idrid would recognize a distinguished magician's royal red wear, having read so many books. "But Jasmine stole it first."

"So her name's Jasmine."

"Yes. I met her at The Bludgeoned Boar while you were asleep. Figured you'd be too weirded out if I mentioned her, since you dislike magicians a whole lot more than I do. By the way, I didn't appreciate you ditching me back there."

"Sorry."

I'm about to go on a rant, though I freeze when I hear her apologize. I sigh, and let it go.

"What about the people originally using this carriage?" she asks, shifting in her seat uncomfortably despite having more than enough room.

"Oh, they were back in this carriage as well. Though I couldn't take riding with those two foreigners who still thought I was James so I jumped out."

Idrid's eyes open marginally wider at this. "And where are they now?"

"Well, I found the driver perusing the streets and asked him to drive us to the palace. He's already taken the others there, so we're unfortunately going to see them again. You know," I say, leaning forward and propping my head on my arms, "there are undoubtedly going to be magicians in the palace."

"You don't think I already know that?"

"Well, gee, the way you've behaved gave me the impression you're going to run off and leave me to fend for myself again!"

Her eyes flash, though she says nothing. She runs a hand through her oaken hair. I sit back, forcing myself to be gentler.

"I don't like magicians either," I say, looking out the shaded windows at the streets passing by outside. I know I should not push it, but I have to ask. "Why don't you like them, other than the obvious?"

"They're arrogant."

We both know she's stalling. I see several people pass by outside, all of them with enormous beards. One of them I swear is a woman, which is impressive since she wears it well, fake or not. The carriage wheels clunk along the street.

Finally she breaks the silence. "Magicians killed my parents. My village."

I look back at her. Her face is stony as she watches a nondescript spot on the floor. I figured something must've happened for her to be by herself, though I imagined her past to be similar to mine in that I left my family because they were bad people. I suppose that was wishful thinking.

"They didn't burn it all down. I'm not sure if I would've preferred that. They gathered us up, and we watched as our houses were swallowed by the earth. In seconds."

Elementalists. It makes sense. The Royal Guard and Magic Guild use them for their dirty work. Somehow her telling me this jogs my memory and I recall talk in the palace about how Giants posed problems for the kingdom. At the time, they were living in the Dagger Hills. Considering Idrid is younger than me by a few years, despite her size, the order was given just after I ran away and well before James inherited the throne.

"I escaped, obviously," Idrid says, her voice deeper than usual. "But when I looked back, I saw a chunk of earth— it fell over everyone. They didn't even get a chance to cry out."

I force my breathing to be steady, though my heart beats faster. It's a dumb thought, though I still think it. If I had stayed in Telnas, could I have prevented it?

She sighs, turning away to look out the other window.

I stay silent for a while to let her control her emotions. "You want revenge."

The look she gives me is annoyed, telling me she's back to her regular self.

"I want revenge too," I admit, now my turn to look away out the window. "Though you may have more reason for hating my family than me. Really, my own case seems more pathetic now that I think about it."

A man with a big bushy black beard distracts me for a moment. His beard reaches around his face like a huge mask, but there's something strange on his head. "Is that guy wearing a duck on his head?"

"What?" Idrid says, sliding across her seat to press her face against the window. "Huh. He is."

"Sorry," I say. "What was I talking about?"

"Your family," Idrid says, moving away from the window.

"Oh. Well, I don't need to get into specifics. My father never talked to me. From what I remember my brother was adversarial whenever our parents had us together, though sometimes we got along. My mother was the worst. She made it very clear that I didn't matter at all and didn't waste an opportunity to tell me in some way. Eventually when she was done treating me like dirt, she treated me like less than that. I was altogether ignored by everyone except my brother. After a while I think my father convinced my brother of something, since he became outright hostile. All of it, I'm sure, was because of the throne. So I ran away."

After a few seconds, Idrid lets out a breath. "Wow."

"Now you know my story."

"What happened after you ran away?" Idrid asks.

I laugh, remembering Instructor's glowing face from my dream. "That's another story for another time."

Chapter 21: **Not**

The driver knocks on the carriage roof, alerting us that we've arrived at the palace. I had not noticed; the dance of lights adorning the buildings outside as we travelled through Telnas had whisked me back into my memories.

The noise brings me to the present and I see Idrid gazing out at the royal palace. Instead of reaching upwards, the building spans a sizable chunk of the city. I picture the city, running through its dimensions in my mind. It is at least fifty square kilometers, and the palace is estimated to be taking up an eighth of it, which, roughly converted, would be around four square miles, including the grounds.

Looking out on the palace now, it has a more or less flat roof, only disrupted by two short towers built symmetrically on either side, north to south. The front of the palace was built first and was then later extended westward so that the sunrise could ignite the glittering metal of the front gate and light up the long steps leading up to the grandiose front door. Personally, I liked the architecture, and how it let the early morning sunlight stream in through the large windows spread at intervals across the front wall. I stop my thoughts, smiling to myself. Here I am, reminiscing over windows.

"Here," I say, removing my cloak and gathering it up to hand to Idrid. "Put it in your satchel. I won't be needing it here." I glance at the fake beard resting on the seat beside me. "We can leave that." Stepping out of the carriage, I look back at the massive gate, faint memories tickling my brain. "We'll need a way out," I tell Idrid when she joins me. "This place is surrounded by walls, and I don't fancy finding a way to get the gate open. Even then, it'll take too long for us to get the gate open if we're making a quick escape."

"I could throw you over the wall," Idrid suggests.

"No, there's a complex system of rooms making up a large basement under the palace. At least one way should connect outside, getting us under and away from here."

"How do you know that?"

"Gossip," I joke without missing a beat. "I lived here long enough to discover things, amidst being tormented by my family. Come on, let's get inside. Thanks!" I call back to the driver, who nods his head enthusiastically.

Not one person stood on guard outside in the courtyard, nor on the steps of the palace. "Looks like the Woodlanders were telling the truth about James sending the majority of his guards out to look for me."

"You didn't believe them?" Idrid asks, keeping pace with me up the steps.

"Well, it's not that wise to wholly believe anything some people living in trees tell you." At the door, I take the gold-colored handle and turn it. Without a sound it swings open, and the both of us steal inside, much like bandits in the night. Thinking over it, we pretty much are exactly that, though with a more murderous goal.

Is this the only way? I've been asking myself the same question ever since leaving the Talwood, and the answer hasn't changed. It's either be hunted until I'm killed or I die by some other cause, or end the bad blood once and for all. Death for either one of us is the most likely outcome, so I might as well choose who it is on my own terms.

I close the door and get a bearing on my surroundings; green and white floral patterns decorate the fully carpeted floor; chandeliers are hung at different heights, the chain links stretching up and up, connecting the glittering lights to the high ceiling; narrow halls stretch off to the right and left, and one wider hallway continues forward directly ahead from the boxy entrance that we stand in. It is vaguely how I remember it being. Several people now come toward me, calling me by the king's title.

Clamping down on my urge to tell them I was Not, I assume the role of James. "Uh—" I begin, raising my arms in welcome. The people walking toward me flit off in different directions as if brushed away by my hands. In the next few seconds they're gone. "Servants," I tell myself, letting my arms fall to my sides. Probably ran off to find me a plate of fancy cheeses. "Let's go."

"Go where?" Idrid asks.

"Exploring." I choose the left hall, where the fewest servants went, and follow it past the grand windows overlooking the courtyard out front. "We can make this a business opportunity as well as a... Well, whatever the heck else this is. Oooh, look-y here."

We come across a smooth mahogany door. I push the handle and let it open inwards. Inside is a small study, consisting of two desks pushed together in the middle of the room surrounded by shelves of books lining each wall.

"Oh. Never mind, nothing here of interest," I say, closing the door and continuing on.

"I like books," Idrid says.

"Okay, let's check out this one." I open the next door, identical to the other, and there is another study styled exactly the same way. Idrid pushes past me and clomps over to a shelf and begins reading the bindings of the books.

My eyes stray to something else, however. I spot a chest lying in the corner of the room. Stopping beside it, I kneel down and unlatch the gold clasp binding the lid shut. The wood creaks as I pull it open, and the contents of the chest are less than satisfactory: only pamphlets of sketches piled on top of each other.

Closing the chest, I walk back to the door where Idrid has in her hands a thick copy of Argris's Lanmar: A Traveler's Guide Pt. 3. "At least you found something," I mumble before continuing down the hall that extends a far ways off. I remember the hall travels all the way around the entire palace, forming a sort of square perimeter.

"Hey, wait a minute," Idrid calls, her footsteps thumping on the floor, the book still in her hand. "This doesn't have any mention of anything in the Talwood. What'd the Woodlander call it, Fwalinder?"

"Flwihhndg," comes a female voice. I only have time to see Idrid's gaze look over my shoulder and her eyes widen before a blow to the back of my head knocks me forward on the floor. I brace my fall with my palms though my mind and vision are fuzzy. I hear Idrid cry out and her lumbering steps advance. Shaking my head, I clear a bit of the muddled feeling to have the sense to roll to the side before Idrid charges over me.

The side of my abs knock into the wall roughly. A grunt and heavy footsteps halting tell me Idrid had run into something. Not much can stop a charging Giant. Leveraging my weight against the wall and lamenting the two bruises I'll be sure to have later, I focus on Idrid's fist suspended in the air. Her knuckles are a foot away from Jasmine's face, which wears a taunting smile.

"You may've drugged me before, though you won't get the best of me again, king's brother. Now, I'd like my cloak back, please."

My hand that had been instinctively gripping the hilt of my sword on my back loosens and moves to cup the aching spot on my head. "Oh, thank Dunlon it's just you."

"Just me!?"

Idrid rears her arm back and punches Jasmine. Her fist is stopped short in the same spot against an invisible barrier.

"You'll have to try harder than that," Jasmine snarls.

Roaring, Idrid twists her whole upper body to attempt another swing.

"Idrid, don't—!" I start to call out.

"NO MAGIC WILL STOP ME!" Her fist flies, connecting with the wall of air. A resounding whump catches her hand for less than an instant.

Jasmine flinches, then steps back as Idrid's knuckles break through, slamming into her cheek. Though softened, the blow is enough to cause her to fall onto her backside. Idrid moves to stand over her.

"Can you both stop?" I say, regaining my balance without the wall's support. I glance both ways to make sure the hall is still empty. The way we came from isn't. Four guards in Lanmarian chainmail swiftly approach. I jerk my head toward Jasmine when a torrential wind erupts from her body and levitates her off the floor. The wind forces Idrid to shield her eyes. "JUST STOP!" my voice cuts through the sound-wrenching gusts. "Guards are coming!"

Forcing my way against the current, I grab onto Idrid's forearm. I rip open her satchel and feel around. Finding the survivalist kit, I thrust it at Jasmine. "Just take the cloak and go!"

The wind coursing around Jasmine relents and she snatches the bag, peering in quickly at the resplendent red fabric within. "You're giving it to me?"

"I've no more use for it."

Idrid growls, "Why do you trust her?"

"She's a thief," I say simply.

"Who isn't a thief?" Jasmine retorts while glaring at me.

"Them." I point at the guards getting closer.

"No, they are too," Idrid says, reluctantly turning to ready herself for the guards.

I step close to Jasmine to whisper quickly in her ear. "The best way out is through the labyrinth below. Get through these guards and find a stairwell leading down along this perimeter hall. There you'll find a prison, which is the wrong way. Go the other way, and keep going."

Jasmine jerks her head away. "I know. They jailed me here, thanks to you."

I raise my hands in appeal. "I assume your business here is done, then?"

Clutching the bag, she humphs. She then sprints forward, propelled faster by another sudden gust of wind. She skirts between the guards like a leaf pirouetting in a breeze, then continues straight away. The guards let out confused shouts and begin chasing after her.

"That was fortuitous," I comment, turning and walking the other way.

Idrid moves quickly to match my pace. "She hit you in the head. And you gave away the cloak."

"Yeah, well. Don't worry about the cloak. She'll be a useful distraction for the remaining guards." A faint odor itches my nose. It smells old, like aged wood. The smell itself isn't unpleasant, though its effect is as if I had breathed in a clump of fuzz.

The wall to our right falls away, stretching down another smallish hallway toward the heart of the palace. I stop, tilting my head. The smell is stronger here. I glance from the floor to the ceiling of the new hallway, rubbing my nose furiously to get rid of the itch.

"What are you looking at?" Idrid asks, closing the book finally and watching me.

"I smell something," I say, lifting up a hand to wave it in the air in front of me.

"There's nothing—whoa, where'd that hallway come from?"

My hand passes through some sort of threshold of magic, and all at once the odor dissipates. "You couldn't see it?" I ask, pulling my hand back and giving it a sniff. Remnants of the smell linger on my fingers.

"No. It just appeared when you put your hand through the wall." She experimentally steps over the threshold as if testing whether the hallway was really there. "I haven't encountered magic like this either," Idrid says. "But I have read about illusion magic as a form of Mind Control."

"No, this isn't Mind Control. What I smelled grew stronger, not the usual rush of magic being cast. Like it was here all along."

"You can smell magic? That's news to me." I avoid her gaze and she sighs. "This seems like something that could've helped us plan before coming here."

"Plans—"

"Can fail and be restrictive, I know. Still." She scuffs her feet along the carpet while I wait for her to pry more. Thankfully, she decides to drop it. "It could be latent magic. Wait, it could be that the wall was conjured," she suggests.

"If it was conjured then I would've interacted with it with either sight or touch."

"Your nose interacted with it."

"Whatever," I say, looking up and down the larger hallway. "Let's check it out before someone else comes along."

I go down the formerly concealed hallway, closely followed by Idrid. We are met with an abrupt left turn and then a door marking the end of the hall. The door is a deep red, like a strawberry. Or like a Magic Guild cloak.

"Are you worried about servants finding us wandering around?" Idrid asks.

I open the door and go inside. "I'm James, kiddy. I do what I want."

"James or Not, you always do what you want."

I ignore her and walk further into the room. The interior is much larger than those of the studies, though it is filled with less furniture. It is a bedroom, given that there's a massive bed against the opposite wall. Between me and the bed is a round carpet, which I find unnecessarily excessive since the floors are already carpeted.

I stride up to the bed and press my hands deep into the folds of the sheets, feeling their softness. "How'd you like a bed like this?" I ask Idrid, who is still standing in the doorway. "You could actually fit in it, too."

I hear her make a noise similar to a growl and step away from the bed, moving to the dresser. Sitting on top of the dresser is a lamp with a curved neck, a quill in a pot of ink, and a lit candlestick.

"This doesn't seem safe, not to mention excessive," I say, blowing the candle out. Fingering the first drawer, I slide it open and gasp. "Oh—"

"What?" Idrid is beside me in seconds, peering over my shoulder. "Oh…"

I yank the crown out of the drawer and twist the bulb in the lamp to turn it on. "What the hell is a crown doing in a drawer?"

"Do I know?" she retorts.

"Look at it! Does this look like something you just leave lying alone?"

"Well, to be fair, we kind of aren't meant to be here. Whatever, why are you so worked up about this?"

"It's just HERE! I mean, come on, I wanted some sort of challenge for something of this value at least!" Gripping the crown, I shake it around, testing to see how sturdy it is. It is covered in jewels that sparkle magically in the faint lamplight, none of them shifting in the slightest. Turning it over in my hand, one gem in particular catches my eye.

Neither the largest nor smallest gem on the crown, it is the color of fire. Every glint it gives off is a lick of flame, seeming to emanate from the stone. Deep down there is a desire inside of me for this multi-colored rock. Calling it a rock doesn't do it justice either; it looks so alive.

Reaching over my shoulder I wriggle the short sword I had taken from Halette free of my sheath. "Hold this steady," I tell Idrid, handing her the crown.

She holds it firmly on the desk and waits for me to do something. I carefully stick the wicked point of the sword in the crown, adjacent to the fiery stone. Using the sword as a lever, I push it further in so that it sticks between the metal and the gem and pry it off with sudden force.

The gem pops free and rolls onto the carpet, coming to a stop on a leaf design. I bend down and scoop it up. Pulling my right sock open, I drop the fiery stone in so that it rests comfortably in the curve of my foot.

"Okay, we can go now," I say as I stand and walk to the door.

"We're not taking the crown?"

"Nah. This'll be more than enough to get me out of my debt. Plus, it'll be funny if they notice a gem missing. It'll also be funny if they don't. Come on."

Idrid drops the crown back in the drawer, shutting it, then follows me out. "Are you happy now?" she asks.

"Surprisingly, yes." Where my skin touches the stone I feel it heat up, as if it really is on fire. After the period of time walking back to the entrance hall, I am sure that it's just my foot feeling warm from the sensation of touching something stolen.

"Let's get this over with," I tell Idrid. We walk briskly down the main hall that leads to the dining room, unless my memory deceives me. There are servants walking by us now, though they try to avoid making eye contact. Some of them I catch looking at me in confusion, though they quickly look away.

We round a corner and find a group of people not wearing the common servant attire standing in a circle near the two doors that should lead into a passage toward the dining room. They're talking in low voices, and it isn't long until their attention turns toward us. From their more practical tunics and legwear they seem to be guards not in all their gear.

Idrid nudges me with her elbow. "Do something kingly," she mutters.

The four people watch me as I jut one of my legs out in a broad, imperious stance. With a swift motion I sweep back my hair and let it fall majestically around my face. I extend my right hand, forming a cup. Looking at each of them in turn with what I hope to be an authoritative squint, I bring it to my mouth and let out a single pathetic cough.

Some of the guards glance at the others, blank-faced.

I snap my fingers, extending my hand. "Handkerchief," I demand.

"You're not James," one says.

"Blast," I say, stepping out of the ridiculous stance and dropping my hand. "What gave it away?"

"It was a good try," Idrid says softly.

"No it wasn't," another one, a woman, says.

The first one, a man, steps closer to the wall where a sconce holds a sputtering fire. He dips his hand in and draws it back wreathed in flames.

So they aren't just guards but Elementalists. The man points his arm at us, extending his index finger and a bar of fire shoots directly at Idrid's chest.

In an instant my own hand extends out in front of Idrid and catches the fire. It sizzles in my grasp, burning me slightly, though the bar wanes and dissipates.

Idrid, who hadn't reacted in time, steps back in shock. "Not... you're hurt."

"It'll heal." It is only my left hand and the burns would heal soon enough without any treatment. I unsheathe my sword with my right and get ready for another attack. On cue, the man lets loose another bar of fire from his flaming hand, this time aiming at my face. I move my sword parallel to the floor so that it is pointed directly in line with the approaching flames. This time, rather than dissipating, the fire sinks into the metal.

A confused look crosses the man's face and he cuts off the stream by extinguishing his hand. "How are you doing that?"

The spot where the last of the flames wash into the sword glows warmly for a moment before fading. I swing it and extend it towards them. "How does your magic work?" I retort. I pull my sword back and run my left hand along the side of my blade. A faint sizzling sound emits between my skin and the metal.

I watch the Elementalists' reactions when I withdraw my hand, which no longer has burn marks. Their looks are what I expect: horror.

Extending the sword out again, fire bursts forth from the tip and races towards the woman. It is extinguished with a rush of air that she must be manipulating, since she raises her own hands as if moving an invisible force.

"Better stand back," I advise Idrid, who is already several paces behind me. The other Elementalists follow the woman's lead and push at the air, sending four separate waves of intense wind at me.

I hold my sword out in front of me, angled slightly upward toward the ceiling, and swipe it in several arcs, cutting through each wave of air. All at once, the cacophonous wind vanishes.

Gritting his teeth, the first man asks, "What is happening?"

Instead of answering or waiting for another attack, I spring forward. The distance is still too far for me to land an attack first, but anything they can do won't have any effect.

I go for the first man while every one of the other guards blasts me with compressed air. None of it fazes me, and I deftly smack the side of my sword against the side of his head before he can block.

He collapses to the floor, unconscious. The other two run towards Idrid while the woman sends a continuous stream of air at me. All of it washes off me harmlessly. Ignoring her, I race after the other two and catch up to them before they can do anything.

In the same way, I touch the side of my sword to their cheeks and each of them crashes to the floor, out cold. I turn to look at the woman who has since ceased the stream of air. "How loyal are you to James?" I ask.

She breathes in and out fast, thinking. "Not very," she says.

"Why don't you step out for a bit, then?" I say, gesturing with my sword away from the double doors and down the hall.

The woman makes several slow paces, then retreats with the occasional glance back. She gives a wide berth while passing Idrid, who walks toward me.

"What in the spanses was that?" Idrid breathes. "I didn't know you could use magic."

"I can't," I correct her, sheathing my sword.

"Then what, I ask again, was that?"

I sigh, though look up at her with a wry smile. "It's complicated, but my sword has magical properties. It can invoke magic."

Idrid, on the verge of another question, stops and thinks for a bit. "Then your hand… Magic doesn't affect you, unless your guard is down like with the Woodlanders? You let yourself get burned and then transferred the residual magic to your sword?"

"More or less, yeah. You caught on fast."

Idrid whaps the back of my head, sending a wave of pain along my skull. "You never told me you had some special power!"

I grimace and cradle the spot Jasmine had hit me. "We've had no business with magicians, so it's never really been useful or relevant for anything until now."

"So you smell and absorb magic? What're you, like some magic detector-slash-sponge?"

"I also didn't want to tell you since I know you dislike magicians."

Idrid blows out a raspberry. "Are you serious? Aren't you more like an anti-magician?"

I shake my head. "Not exactly."

She sees the sour face I'm making and a smile lights up her face. "Well. Thanks for saving me."

I stare at her, taken aback by her sudden warmth. When was the last time she smiled? The next moment it's gone, and I'm reminded of what we're doing. I wave a hand dismissively. "You could've taken them."

"Yeah, sure."

We step up to the luxurious double doors, though behind them isn't the dining room from what I can recall. "This isn't the dining room, from what I can recall," I tell Idrid. I pause to scour my memories. "It should be through here at the other end of a hall." Grasping the elegantly curved wooden handle, I step back to let the door swing open. My eyes meet James's. He's sitting on the opposite end of a long table. "Actually, this is the dining room," I whisper.

Chapter 22: **Jasmine**

Curses, she thinks as she rushes through dark hall after dark hall. She doesn't know how much time has passed since she pulled the stunt with her enchanted ring, and then the encounter with Not. Now she is lost running around somewhere beneath the palace, undoubtedly being pursued by most of the Royal Guard. Having doubted Not's information, she questioned a servant at the top of the stairway that brought her down here and, with mild prompting (maybe just a little suffocation), he told her it led outside the palace. Since then she forgot where the stairway was, and has passed several identical stairways leading back up.

Oh, there goes one now, she notes, passing another. Her breathing is ragged, since she's been running for ages. At the least she now has the cloak back, tucked away in the bag slung over one shoulder like a purse. Finally she stops, leaning hard against a smooth stone wall. Her shoulders hitch as she draws in air. She hasn't seen another servant since the one at the top of the stairs, so he must have been telling the truth. None of the rooms down here are food stores or servants' quarters, and most of the floors are barren stonework. These halls must've been earlier used as a prison network. What's with that guy, anyway? Couldn't he have told her something more specific?

Letting herself slowly slide to sit on the floor, she sighs. Whatever the king is up to, he has it out for his brother. She has little reason to trust Not, though not being on the side of brainwashers is enough.

After several moments, her breathing slows. She feels subtle vibrations through the wall. Placing a hand against the cool stone, she holds her breath and listens. There is no sound, but she is sure she can feel something large causing the walls to quiver.

She stands and steps away, going to the opposite wall to put her hand against it. The same vibrations meet her touch.

Stooping down, she kneels and puts her hand on the ground. It also quivers. Jasmine tries to sense what it is exactly, but no matter where her will probes, all she finds is stone.

She stands back up, muttering, "Feels like I'm by the Sundering Sea." She pauses, thinking about it for a moment, then laughs at the thought. There's no way Telnas's underground spanned all the way there.

Jasmine continues down the hall. Some ways ahead, the hall turns sharply to the right. Getting a sneaking suspicion she may be going in a loop, she turns the corner and finds a door built into the wall under an empty sconce. She walks up to it and senses the vibrations more severely, sending quivers beneath her feet.

She places a hand on the lock on the door and wills it to unlatch. The lock breaks and falls to the floor with a clatter. Pulling the door open with a hand, she's met with a gust of dank air and the roaring sound of water. Her hair lifts slightly around her shoulders. Her eyes widen as she steps over the moist stone floor, not bothering to close the door behind her. A railing lines a space where the floor suddenly drops down on either side, forming a crevice. Stepping over to the railing with her hands held out to balance herself, she peers down and gasps. Far below is a stream of rushing crystal blue water. Not even the water of the Sterling Sea looked as blue.

She glances around and notices a metal bridge crossing the gap in the floor. The other side of the room has a set of stone stairs rising up and to the right, the same direction the water is coming from.

There aren't any springs in Telnas, Jasmine thinks, taking the bridge and then the steps, eager to get away from the room with heights. At the top of the steps is a door. Another hall, though this one compact, allowing only enough room for one person to walk through, travels ahead of her at a slight incline. The walls, ceiling, and floor around her visibly shake with the heavy water pouring around it.

Jasmine notices the hall has no light sources. With a finger, she rubs her ruby ring again. Its last remaining fire sputters to life, the illumination within the gem brightening the grey hall around her. Breathing in the strange spray that hangs in the air, she marches ahead.

Almost imperceptibly the hall, still rising at a steady incline, begins curving to the left. The sound of rushing water echoes faintly behind her, starting to diminish. The walls curve more sharply, and the incline rises even more until it suddenly becomes stairs leading up in a spiral. Jasmine trudges up. The vibrations grow fainter, somehow giving her a greater sense of trepidation.

The stairs end in the ceiling with a wood trapdoor. Gripping a metal clasp hanging from it, she pushes up. The trapdoor swings away easily. Jasmine holds onto it to prevent it from slamming onto the upper room's floor. Several boots pacing along the floor step away from the trapdoor.

Jasmine pushes the trapdoor all the way open and lifts herself up into the room, attempting to brush her dress free of wrinkles and clinging moisture. The people, magicians wearing Royal Court uniforms (green tunics with Lanmar's crest embossed in yellow across the breast) appraise her before continuing about their business.

Somewhat put off by their disinterest, Jasmine pushes the trapdoor shut with her foot, causing it to bang.

"Shhhh!" a magician breathes, giving her a glare.

Jasmine blinks. She looks around, trying to get her bearings. The walls circle around her, various tables occupied by various vials containing various liquids attended to by various magicians who inspect the vials closely. The walls rise up far above. It's a tower, she realizes. The magicians are measuring the liquids before adding them to vials via droppers. The vials then disappear and reappear in another magician's hand at a different table in a very efficient and organized routine. Vale Tower she notes given the Spatial magic.

"What are you waiting for? Did you come to take up the next shift?"

Jasmine looks to a woman in her mid-thirties beckoning to her.

"Well, come on, then," the woman says, waving Jasmine over to yet another flight of stairs spiraling up.

Sighing, Jasmine begins to follow but is interrupted by a loud knock on the other side of a single mahogany door at the far wall. She turns to see a magician who was previously tampering with steaming vials move from his table to the door and pull on its gold inlaid handle.

It opens in slow motion, and Jasmine's eyes meet the frowning face of the woman whose cloak she stole. Faye's eyes narrow, her mouth opening, about to shout.

Jasmine raises her hand swiftly. Extending out from her palm, a torrential wind spirals toward the door. The wind hits the back of the door, yanking the handle out of the male magician's hand, and slams it closed on Faye.

The woman Jasmine was about to follow reels around at the disturbance, only to be barraged with another wave of air. She is sent flying to the side, her body smashing against the side of a table. All the vials are knocked over, and their contents begin pouring over and down the side of the table to intermingle on the floor.

Jasmine rushes to the spiraling stairs, hitting their banister with a clang before taking them up. The first magicians, who've by now figured out what's going on, begin shouting at her. Out of the corner of her eye, she sees one throw a vial with bright red liquid at her.

A second before it would have hit her, she ducks. The vial whizzes over the top of her head. Several trickles of the liquid splatter her hair, and she smells burning.

In an instant she extinguishes the flame with a rush of air while rocketing up and up in circles. Below her Faye is now shouting orders to stop her. Jasmine wonders for a second why Faye isn't attempting to stop her herself, but then Jasmine's vision blurs.

A tremor ripples through her brain as if each individual cell is vibrating of its own accord. The sensation causes her to lose her ability to focus and she drops into a crouch on the metal stair, clutching the sides of her head.

Blinking furiously, she watches as the world appears to shift when she moves her eyes. The grim realization dawns on her that the tower wasn't filled only with Spatial magicians but Mind-Controllers. The Concilium are here.

She is forced to lie down on the stairs, though she still grips the banister fiercely, attempting to force some semblance of control into her mind. Each of her thoughts moves sideways, much like her vision. It's too much to hold onto one for longer than a few seconds.

The sounds of calmer voices emanate from below her, along with several pairs of feet ascending the stairs. This won't do, Jasmine thinks, clenching her teeth. Not only are her thoughts spinning wildly, it's like there is a growing pressure within her brain itself.

One thought, she tells herself silently. What do I need? Leave.

As soon as she thinks it, she reinforces it by pulling herself an inch further up the stairs. The incremental motion builds into a bigger one, and she's climbed up a single step.

Leave.

Her hand rams into the next support on the banister, clenching it. She pulls some more, her other arm working to hold herself up so she doesn't rake her body against the edge of the next step.

Leave.

She mouths the word, getting into a crouch. The footsteps resounding below her are approaching, almost on top of her. Fortunately, she now has the single purpose implemented in her mind.

Her vision clears, just enough for her to speak a single word aloud, expending enough of her will to lace it with magic. "Liquify."

The metal step beneath her feet turns soft instantly, and the metal around her begins to melt. Forcing herself up from her crouch, she stumbles forward and catches herself on the next set of steps. Still, her vision is all but useless.

Grimacing, she shuts her eyes, runs her hand along the banister, and begins feeling her way up the stairs. Each step is elevated at equal heights, and she begins to get a rhythm of taking the next step up and up.

Leave, she repeats again and again, the single thought warding off the pressure in her brain. Suddenly the footsteps on the stairs below her are cut off, and seconds later she hears what's left of the un-liquified portion of the stairs collide with the floor with a loud crash.

Whether it's the sound or the damage the stairs caused that disrupts the Mind magic, Jasmine's thoughts are free. She opens her eyes and circles up the stairs twice more before she has ascended to the second floor where the stairs end.

Concentrating her will to her hands, she plants each of her fingers at the top of the metal stairway. The rest of the stairs melt under her touch and drip to the floor below. Still, that won't stop Spatial magic. She has to find a way to seal off the hole.

Searching frantically on this floor for anything, thankful no one else appears to be here, she finds a medium rectangular table that is just about the perfect size. With a swift flick of her hand, the table upends itself and lands on its back before sliding to cover the hole left by the stairs.

Jasmine appraises the room more carefully, noting that while there aren't stairs, the tower still ascends upward to a third floor. Far above she can see a landing, obviously meant for Spatial magicians to teleport to.

Over the clamoring of people below is a continuous crashing coming from above. Since there aren't any doors or windows on this floor, the only way to go is up.

Jasmine raises her hands as if she is lifting two platters of food. She feels herself elevated off the floor. The bubble of air she creates beneath her feet grows larger, raising her further up. She causes the bubble to thin and disperse so that she lands lightly on the wood landing jutting out that leads to the third floor. The crashing sound is louder here, undoubtedly emanating from this floor. She takes the few steps up from the landing and freezes on the third floor. Five magicians wearing the same Lanmar-crested outfits as the magicians below all monitor a thick, rapid stream of water extending from the ceiling and falling to the floor.

Jasmine's eyes follow the stream, bewildered at the impossibility of the waterfall. It's originating from nowhere and disappearing nowhere. Stooping down, she levels her eyes with the floorboards and sees the water is falling onto the floor, yet does not collide. It's like the floor isn't even there.

She takes a step back onto the landing below and peers under the floorboards to make sure the water is in fact not falling straight through. Indeed, it isn't. That must mean the magicians are using some kind of magic. It would require a powerful magician to continuously conjure water only to then disappear it once it hit the floor. No, that isn't it. The water isn't even touching the floor despite the stream rushing straight downward to meet it. She can't feel the floorboards vibrating from any impact either. This had to be some form of Spatial magic. But how?

Eyeing the second floor, noting that the table covering the way down is shifting slightly, she moves back onto the third floor and appraises the five magicians. One has both her hands raised toward the beginning of the stream at the ceiling, both thumbs and index fingers pressed together in o-shapes. A second has her hands lowered toward the end of the stream at the floor, her fingers identically matching the other female magician's. The three other magicians, all male, hold spray bottles from which they are spraying some sort of liquid into the stream. The sight of it all would have been comical in another situation, though Jasmine doesn't have time to question them.

A loud bang erupts from below, indicating that the table had either been obliterated or thrown aside. Without thinking, Jasmine rushes toward the five magicians. The three with spray bottles turn their heads, their eyes widening as Jasmine passes by. With a leap, taking in a large breath, Jasmine plunges into the stream and is sucked away.

The current pulls her downward past the floor and into darkness. She blinks rapidly, trying to get some bearing as she falls. Her body collides with something hard, almost knocking the air out of her. The water twists around her, turning into a sharp downward slope that Jasmine slides along beneath the surface. Still, there is no light.

Jasmine claws forward in an attempt to break the surface only for her hand to scrape roughly against hard concrete. She's being pulled along a tunnel. Semi-consciously she remembers the rapid stream of bright blue water in the underground tunnels beneath the tower. Almost as if her thought kindled it into being, the water around her begins to illuminate.

The light in the water doesn't come from any visible source. Twisting around, Jasmine makes out the walls of the tunnel she is being pulled down. Her back scrapes harder against the bottom of the tunnel as it begins to level out somewhat, though the water does not let up in the least. Around her, the water appears to brighten and turn a translucent, bright blue. The wall above her recedes, giving way to a ceiling far above.

In an instant Jasmine pushes herself to the surface, sucking in a new breath of air. The walls on either side extend upward toward the ceiling, but don't quite reach it. Is this the room she was previously in with the chasm? She splashes around, failing to stop her forward progress. Ahead is another tunnel coming up fast.

Knowing she can't stop herself, she takes another deep breath and plunges her head back beneath the surface. The water around her is a warm blue, sparkling in her vision as she tumbles forward.

Just as she's about to suck in another breath, the tunnel ends. She's plunged into broad daylight. She gasps fresh air, spluttering as she bobs above the water. On either side of the expanding stream are stretches of land. She begins to swim to the right side.

Her hands meet coarse sand, and she drags herself up the shore and collapses on a dry patch that is far enough from the rushing stream. Pushing herself over onto her back, she gasps in air for a full minute before her breath steadies.

Staring up into the cloudless sky, her worries turn away from survival to the question of her whereabouts. Pushing herself up into a sitting position, she gazes along the waterline. The torrential stream continues on into the distance toward the horizon and the Sterling Sea. That places her somewhere west of Telnas, which means she is close to the home where she began her accursed journey. A part of her wishes she never left Picaroon Port, though the thrill of conning unwary men and women of their money was too good to pass up. Come to think of it, winding up back near her hometown is fortuitous. The people who live there come from all walks of life and know all there is to know about the goings on of the land even as they happen. It's uncanny how much they know, probably thanks to the pawnbrokers that frequent the streets.

Jasmine stands up and brushes off the clumps of sand that stick to her wet clothes, then scrapes off the remains from her hands and fingernails. Whatever the magicians in that Occult Tower are doing can wait. For now she can relax.

She unlatches the bag at her side and withdraws the lovely, albeit muted from wetness, red cloak. She runs her fingers along the hem and stops. Turning the fabric over she sees a ragged edge where it was cleanly torn. Turning it over again, she searches for the inside. There is none.

"Curtains!?" She yells, throwing them onto the sandy floor. She glares back up the canal where the water tunnels out of an opening in the cliff. Even if she went back there's next to no chance he'd still be there. Forget the Concilium. She turns and storms up the incline. Forget the king and his blasted nobles. She has to find someone who knows where the man who calls himself Not will be.

Chapter 23: **Not**

Guests in fancy attire all turn their heads to look at me, then look back at James.

"Grab that imposter!" I shout, pointing a long arm at James. Most of the guests leap out of their seats and back away toward the respective walls on either side of the table. A beefy man with a unique mustache leans over in his chair and murmurs something to James. They make no move to stand up as servants pile into the room on the opposite end of the hall, going for James.

"Stop, you fools, he's the imposter," the mustache man says hotly, waving a hand at me.

"That's absurd!" I cry, taking several long steps to the table and slamming my fist down on it. "He's been impersonating me all this time! Why do you think Lanmar has been going to the dumps?"

The servants stand around James while several of the guests still seated murmur to themselves. I overhear one saying, "He's got a point." Another says, "He's a bit petulant. Must be James." The others don't look as sure.

I look over all the guests and notice familiar faces. "Halette, Jean, back me up here."

The two foreigners glance at each other. "All right," Halette says, standing up. "Only the real James will know why I'm really here."

I pause, my eyes falling down to his freshly trimmed beard. "Oh! You're here for the beard shaving contest!"

"He's right," Halette says, pounding the table for emphasis. "He's the imposter!" He points at James sitting calmly in his seat. The other guests murmur at the revelation.

"Yeah!" I point as well. "Also," I begin but pause to think. It would be a gamble; I don't know more than the average commoner about my parents, only that they died naturally. But Darren's question from our brief confrontation surfaces from the back of my mind. What happened to the former king and queen? Why would a Guild magician ask such a question? It may very well be every royal here knew and were present during their decline. But, even if James chose a lie, it could plant enough suspicion. "Also, only the real James would know what happened to the late King and Queen." Gasps emanate around the room at the vague implication, and I tilt my head at James whose face creases minutely. That, I think, is definitely a tell.

"Oh, shut up everyone," James finally speaks, rising from the table and throwing his napkin down. "Age claims us all, as it did with my parents. He's not James, because I am. Put him in the dungeon, the dinner is over."

At this the man with a mustache claps his hands and immediately the servants' bodies shudder all as one and start toward me.

"Is that how this'll go, eh? Fine." I draw both swords out of my sheath and hold them on either side of me, feeling their weight and testing my balance with both. The first few servants closest to me begin picking up silverware and chucking them with incredible accuracy.

I bring both swords up, letting the forks and knives bounce off them and clatter to the floor. "Look, the coward is running away!" I call to anyone listening as I cut down several servants in nonvital areas. Blood sprays across the tablecloth, causing the remaining few sitting guests to jump up shrieking and exit with the already standing guests.

None of the servants are dissuaded by my swinging blades. The smell of phosphorous or garlic fills my nostrils, alerting me that magic is being used.

"Idrid!" I yell, avoiding killing them by leaping onto the table and sprinting along it, "Knock them out!" Hands sweep out to grab my legs but I leap over them. James has left sometime during the chaos. The only other one staying there is the beefy man with the mustache.

He is gripping the tablecloth, preparing to rip it out from under me, which would be a surprising feat given the length of the table. I leave the table, letting the forks and knives fly past my head and weave through the multitudes of servants. Several arms grab me but I shake them off as I run.

A knife sticks into my back beside the right shoulder blade, but I ignore it, focusing on the man with a mustache. I am closing the distance between us when he claps his hands a second time.

The knives and forks flying through the air cease. I come to a halt a few paces out of his reach.

"Can we be a little more civilized?" he asks with arms spread wide.

"Uh, yeah, but that doesn't mean I will be," I say, yanking the knife out of my back with a wince and tossing it on the table. My body is buzzing with excitement, the anticipation of facing a worthy opponent increasing.

Shouts of surprise erupt behind me, from what I take to be Idrid pummeling the rest of the conscious servants, who are now no doubt free from whatever magic was used on them.

"Smart, to come here when all the guards are away," the man says, surprising me by stepping closer to my outstretched swords.

"Stupid to send them all away," I reply. "But I suspect that's the king's fault."

The man jumps in between my swords with incredible speed and presses his hands around my skull. At first I'm surprised, turning my blades around to slice into the man's back, but then I stop in bewilderment.

I feel a gentle electric shock zap my skull, followed by warmth emanating between the man's hands and my head. My eyes flick between his bushy mustache and pale green eyes. "Ahem. What are you doing?"

His eyes blink, refocus, then fill with confusion. "How are you still conscious?"

Taking a step back, the man's hands fall limply to his side. I am once again shielded by my swords. I shrug. "Magic and I don't get along?"

The man shakes his head, taking quick, terrified steps back, and leans against a chair.

"Hey, look, I only came to tell James to leave me alone. Maybe even kill him. Probably kill him. Anyway, do you want to help out?"

The man looks at me unsteadily for a moment. The next, he is fleeing out one of the doors in the back of the dining room.

"So much for that," Idrid says behind me. I turn and see the bodies of servants lying on the floor. They all seem to be breathing.

"No way, I'm going to chase them." I pull a nearby napkin off the table and dab at my back, the small cut stinging slightly. I observe the little flecks of red. Not too bad. I throw the napkin on a plate and look at Idrid.

"Watch out for anyone else following!" Turning, I sprint out the way the man left. The door slams against the wall as I shove by, and I hear the heavy footfalls of the man escaping. I find it exhilarating, running with my weapons out.

"Hold on a moment!" I call. "What's your name?"

I turn a corner and spot the man's foot disappearing around another. Putting on a burst of speed, I bound around the corner and find myself racing to catch up to the man and James himself hurrying down a set of stairs.

The dungeons. Running out of breath, I fling my short sword in their general direction. I watch it fly through the air and clatter against the curving wall just behind James's head. The sound causes him to pause and turn, giving me the time to reach him and swing my other blade down.

James reacts quickly, picking up the short sword and blocking my swing.

"Hello, brother," I pant, using my weight and height advantage to press the swords down.

James doesn't say anything, exerting all he can on keeping my sword from piercing his body.

"Ha, get it? It's a joke. You know, because we hate each other and all that?" I release the pressure, sliding my blade back along his, creating a shrill metal sound.

James stumbles away and down several steps, his back bumping the wall. He pushes off, bringing the short sword up, ready to fight.

"James!" The man with the mustache is back and gives James a longer, larger sword to replace the short one.

"Two on one?" I ask, tossing my own sword between my hands like I would a ball, testing whether or not I feel like being right-handed or left-handed for this fight. The slight wound in my right shoulder stings. I decide to use my left. "Pretty unfair. You should get at least three more people to help you."

James's cloudy eyes flash, and I instinctively parry the weapon so that the momentum of his strike causes him to lose balance. I don't take the opening, instead taking a step back. That was good, because the man with the mustache now has a sword of his own that he uses to lash out and defend James.

I make a pouting face. "You know I was kidding about that whole 'you need more people' thing, right?"

The man with a mustache feints right and left several times. I stand a couple steps above them in amusement.

"Hey, mustache man. Make up your mind, this isn't a dance."

"Oh, but it is," the man snarls, plunging his sword toward my stomach. I easily dodge right, letting my own blade serve as a barrier, the metal singing as the swords scrape together, so that he can't build his own momentum to gain an advantage.

James goes for my vulnerable side, rearing his broad sword back to get the most velocity. The sword rushes toward me. I don't move, letting them think they have the best of me for as long as possible.

Too fast for either of them to follow, I flick the mustache man's sword away with my own as I bring it around to meet the large sword.

CLANG!

We all stand motionless, observing the two swords clashed together. My sword is perfectly fine, not broken or dented in the least from the sheer weight and speed of the other sword. Instead, my sword has cut into the other slightly.

I bring myself closer to James, peering carefully at the entwined blades. "Huh." I rake my blade out of the other sword and plunge it between James's ribs. At least, that is what would've happened, had he not let go of his sword and backed away. The mustached man moves in between the both of us.

"I know you're not a swordfighter," I tell the man. "You're some type of magician. I could smell it back in the dining room. Who are you?"

"Filento," Filento says.

I lower my sword slightly, surprised he actually answered. "Oh."

"James," James says suddenly, conversationally, as he shifts down a few steps.

I move down to follow, feinting under Filento's sword to get him to step back as well. "I know your name. Or are you talking to yourself?"

"I'm sure you've gone by that name quite a bit," James sneers. He begins to step back slowly, taking his time while looking up at me. The sickly sweet smile hanging on James's face urges me to cut down Filento, but I restrain myself and prod his sword away, causing Filento to back up even further.

"Have I?"

"All this time your actions have indicated an unhealthy obsession with me," James says. "What do you call yourself?"

"Not," I say. The mustached man slices an arc toward my right shoulder, and I flick the strike away.

"Not...?"

"Not James," I finish, getting impatient.

"Not me," James says. "Part of your name is my own, and don't pretend I haven't heard the rumors about a second me prevalent across Lanmar. They ripple shortly after you do some sort of stunt or another. You seem to have built your life around me."

"Not around you. Opposite you, in fact."

James huffs out a laugh. "You know that idiom, something about those who protest something enough are often guilty of it?"

"I do. In fact, I had it in mind when I first devised calling myself Not James." Filento tries to take advantage of me talking, though I sidestep and turn my body so his sword just misses my arm. Instead of moving back, he follows through with the momentum of the strike and shifts behind me onto one of the upper steps.

Sighing, I bring my sword down toward his head hard. He blocks it, as I knew he would. I repeat the strike, harder. Our swords clang. I do it again. The metal shrieks. Again. Clang! I hammer his sword relentlessly, until finally his sword breaks and he's left with a stub.

I hear James move behind me and feel the back of my knees being kicked. My legs buckle. Before I fall, I swing once more and cut the front of Filento's chest. A line of red follows my sword as I go down, and he falls backward with a curse.

Before James can get an advantage on me, I bring my sword back around and he jumps away. I no longer have to worry about Filento since he retreats back up the stairs, apparently abandoning the king. "You know that other saying," I continue, rising to my feet slowly as James backs further down the stairs. He doesn't look as confident now that Filento's footsteps can be heard retreating back up the stairs.

320

"The simplest case is often the case? I thought calling myself Not James to be very simple, and with how much I need to explain who I really am, it seemed the easiest way to drill it into people's minds. Though they have yet to fully catch on," I add, remembering the two foreigners Halette and Jean, who probably still believe me to be the king.

James is approaching the bottom of the stairway. He turns his head, spotting a pair of decorative swords hanging on the wall above the last few steps. He leaps up, grabbing both, and brings them up to defend himself. "Either way, you've certainly benefitted from my existence. Even you can't deny you've used me as a cover for whatever it is you do."

"I've used you as much as I've used the ground."

James cocks his head, confused. "Is that an admission?"

I sigh. "Would you say you use the ground?"

"To walk on, sure, but that's inevita—" He cuts himself off and his face furrows as the point sinks in.

I spread my arms. "Exactly. Now shut up and fight me."

Idrid hears the clatter of metal far down the curving stairs, though she doesn't move to investigate. She knows Not can hold his own in a sword fight. What she's more interested in is the man with a mustache holding a wound on his chest as he

321

hurries up the steps. He stops fast when his eyes look up and meet hers.

She recognizes him. Despite staying away from magicians, she's not a stranger to his magic. He's the one who tried mind-tapping Not. He caused all the servants to go berserk and hurl silverware at them in the dining hall. And he's one of the ones who was there when her village was destroyed by Elementalists.

"Who are you?" he asks.

"Idrid." The images of the upstairs servants' vacant eyes as they were manipulated flash in her mind, forcing her memory back to the time her life was ruined. The Elementalists shared the same expression, like they didn't know what they were doing nor cared. Figures that magicians would use each other like servants.

"Get out of my way," the man says, walking briskly toward her.

Idrid feels a tugging on her mind that is telling her to move out of his way. She clamps down on the urge. The man, who is roughly the same build as her, walks into her, though she doesn't move. He bounces back, just barely shifting a leg out so he doesn't fall back down the steps.

"Move," he insists.

The pressure on her brain doubles, causing Idrid's vision to blur. Forcing her eyes shut, she concentrates on the image of her parents disappearing beneath an immovable hunk of rock. Anger swells within her, burning away the force. When she opens her eyes again her vision is clear. "Your magic will not work on me," she says.

Snarling, he lashes an arm out at her stomach. The blow knocks Idrid back, though she stays on her feet and catches her breath. Looking down at him sneering up at her, she can see a similar fury burning in his eyes. How a man could hate so much after doing so much wrong... it enrages her further.

Stepping forward, she kicks the man's chest hard. He flies back and bounces off the curving wall. She steps forward some more, reaching him before he can stand.

With a cry of fury, she kicks the man's side. He rolls away, sliding down the steps before hitting the wall again and coming to a stop. His chest is bleeding in several steady streams now.

Coming to his side once more, she pauses. "What's your name?"

He breathes hoarsely, coughing several times. He tilts his head to look up at her for a moment, then spits on her feet.

She doesn't move.

He looks up at her again and opens his mouth.

Before he says anything, Idrid brings her foot down on his head. His head is caught between the bottom of her shoe and the edge of a step. There's a loud crunch, and Idrid looks away. Putting her foot on the step itself, she breathes in several times.

Stooping down, she sits beside the man's unmoving body, her gaze distant. Still the sound of swords clashing reverberates up the steps of the stairs. She finally looks at the man's compressed head, his lifeless eyes somehow meeting hers.

"I hope your death was as swift as my parents'," Idrid says. She looks away, wiping the back of her hand across her face. She pulls her hand back, surprised to find it to be perfectly dry.

James moves with the speed and precision of a trained guard, thrusting one sword toward my chest and the other out to prevent my blade from stopping it. My years of being taught by Instructor prepared me for all sorts of attacks, and he often brought another student to team up and fight me at the same time.

I tilt my entire body to the side, just enough to let the blade harmlessly tickle my chest momentarily, then spin inward behind James's guard. Without even using my sword I am now free to cut him anywhere.

I flick my sword to make a shallow cut along his left arm. The cut may be shallow, though the particular area I cut will lose a lot of blood fast without closing anytime soon. He hisses and moves fast enough to block my next flick that would have sliced his abdomen.

His speed matches mine, making the fight somewhat equal. My goal, other than dispatching him, is to get him down to one sword.

He glances down at his arm, the hole in his sleeve turning red from the thin line that I sliced. "I see you've been taught well despite running off," James growls, extending his right sword out while keeping his left sword close in a hybrid stance.

I take up a fencing stance, clanging my sword against his outstretched one and we begin trading blows. I expect him to try another full attack, though he keeps his left sword in a tight guard as he gracefully moves his body to counter and attack.

One of my strikes he pushes away with hidden strength that throws me off balance. I leap away from his blade milliseconds before it cuts the air where I stood. Catching me off guard again, he follows through with his other blade and manages to cut into my left shoulder.

Wrenching my shoulder back before the cut gets too deep, I bring my sword up to block his next swing.

"I always knew you'd be back to take the throne," James sneers as we trade blows once more.

"You forced me back when you made me a wanted man," I retort. My shoulder aches, though it's minimal compared to the new wound in my left shoulder. I ignore the pain as I switch my sword to my right. At least it isn't my main sword arm that is badly wounded.

"But you're a thief," he says, our swords gleaming in the torchlight as they dance between us in clangs and hisses. "A king's job is to protect his country."

"I'm sure your motives were benign," I say, "and not at all an effort to remove another potential heir. Such a waste."

"What is it you really do?" James asks.

"You said it yourself. I'm a thief." Our swords clatter together in a standstill, both of us forcing our own blade to try and overpower the other.

"And you never thought about stealing the throne?" His eyes glint, and I catch a hint of the same anger I saw reflected in them when we were kids. A jealous yet fearful anger.

"Did I not make it clear when I was still around?" I ask, throwing his blade to the side with my own and stepping inward to thrust at his chest. His left sword blocks it, and I step back again before he can bring his other sword in to slice me. "Or when I ran away, surely? I have no interest in becoming the king. I never did."

"What does it matter? You came here to kill me all the same."

"And you weren't trying to kill me?" I ask.

James's left arm droops slightly. A red stain has been spreading along his shirt sleeve. "I—" His voice catches when a sickening crunch echoes down the stairway.

I glance backward at the noise. Thinking nothing more of it, I turn back and freeze when I see James's face. His mouth is twisted and trembling in the same fury, but his eyes are affixed and growing wider. "I... I..."

Slightly shaken, I lower my sword for a moment and stare. "What's wrong?"

"I... It—all of it... Right? I did it."

I feel my blood chill. "What are you talking about?"

"I did it all!" he shouts. The flickering light emanating from the stone sconces along the outer wall reflects off his glistening eyes.

His voice dissipates across the stone, and only then do I recognize what's different. His eyes are clear and the faint smell of phosphorous no longer tinges the air. I hadn't realized the magic was there until it left.

"I wanted to," James says a fraction more calmly. "So I did it."

"James," I say. "When did you first meet Filento?"

He shakes his head. "What does it matter?" he says again. "I wanted to, therefore I did it."

"It matters."

Finally the cut I made on his arm has gotten bad enough for him to drop his left sword and take up a sturdier fighting stance. He doesn't say anything, though his expression speaks for itself. He's through talking. Grunting, he begins the real fight.

It isn't nearly as long, though it is twice as intense. We both attack, parry, counter, and recounter, every time our swords meeting together to resound spectacularly. Simultaneously, as if we both know it useless since our strength with one arm is equally matched, we shift our hold on our swords so that we swing with both arms.

My left shoulder spikes with pain every time I swing, though I still ignore it. I know it will fatigue faster than the cut on James's arm, so I have to find an opening. Just as I think it, I notice the metal of our blades.

The sheen of mine is perfect, untarnished, while his is very battered and dented. Instructor's blade will carry me through this fight.

I stop looking for an opening and begin targeting the dented spots of James's blade. I find a promising one toward the bottom-middle section, and begin swinging to hit it. Our blades collide, ringing in the hall.

I push against the pain in my shoulder and swing harder, bringing my sword again and again against the spot on James's sword. The telltale clang cutting off unusually faster than the others signals my opportunity.

We both pause, staring at our entwined blades. My blade is embedded within his, and I don't wait a second more. Following through, I twist, yanking his sword out of his hand, and bring my sword straight down between James's neck and left shoulder.

The other sword sticks to mine, awkwardly unbalancing my swing, and I quickly right my aim. My sword stops midway in James's chest. A grotesque, clean cut travels from the top of his shoulder down to where his heart is. I glance down at the knife James now has in his hand, pointed midway at my chest. If I had acted a moment later the concealed knife would have gotten me.

It isn't more than a second before James collapses, the knife clattering down several steps. In that second I see the anger leave his eyes, replaced with surprise. "I… see it now… it was all my doing… D-do… not… forgive me… Not…"

My hand clenches my sword hard, the tension making it quiver. I kick off the sword still stuck on mine. I stand silently for a second, fighting to close the hole that had opened in my own chest. I turn and walk unsteadily back up the steps. For a second I turn back, looking at James's body. It is shuddering, though the shudders are easing out.

I sheathe my sword and walk back. Kneeling down, I place a hand on the side of his head that is slick with blood. "I'm sorry."

With that, I turn around and sprint up the steps. Near the top I find Filento lying on his stomach, his head unnaturally caved in. Seeing him lifeless all but confirms my reeling thoughts. I look up and see Idrid standing at the top of the steps. I debate telling her what I learned, but my mind runs into a nefarious question. Who else, if anyone, knew what Filento had been doing with James?

"Is it done?" she asks.

"Yes," I say, deciding to think over it more before jumping to conclusions. I walk up the last of the steps and stop in front of her. "We can go home now."

For the first time since I've known her, Idrid laughs genuinely. "And where might that be?"

Chapter 24: **Maia**

Lin, Maia, Mark, and Tricia all shuffle back into the tower's entrance, the door opening with its usual loud slam. "Seriously," Maia remarks, "what's with that door?"

"Why're you hanging around with the new kids, Mark?" one of the other students asks suddenly and paces toward them when the door closes. "Feeling generous?" The other students stop their activities and begin listening.

Mark glances at Maia, though winks at her. "Uh. No, actually," he says. "They're doing fine without me."

"Really?" the student says. "I bet they still can't—"

"Conjure multiple items!" Master Aveve's voice booms as she rushes down the stairs, taking everyone by surprise. "Come now, everyone line up! This is what non-magic folk call a surprise exam! A pop quiz!" Her dress flourishes around her as she makes her way near the center of the room beside the student who was about to make some sort of negative comment. "Ah, Leslie, since you're here you can go first. Then you four," she adds, flicking a hand at Maia and her friends.

Leslie, who seems to be shrinking in place, stands up straight and holds out his hand. In it two gold pieces appear, chinking together.

"Ah, you have an eye for the monetary things," Aveve says. "This can work as a lesson for everyone else, too. Can anyone tell me why conjuring money won't make you richer?"

Maia's mind goes blank. She doesn't have the faintest clue. Mark raises his hand slowly. Aveve makes a full turn before her eyes find Mark's hand.

"Yes, Mark!" she calls on him.

"Increasing the market's total currency only serves to cause inflation?"

"A very economic answer, Mark, though not quite the answer I was looking for."

"Civil rights activists commonly frequent our houses," Mark whispers only to Maia. "My family has to explain the detriments to the market if we simply conjured gold for everyone. They don't seem to hear us, even when my parents tell them they aren't Conjurors like I am."

Maia nods, though is more interested in what answer Aveve wants.

Aveve looks back at Leslie, who awkwardly fingers the gold pieces in his hand. "Well, I guess it isn't common knowledge, though I had hoped someone would've read about it in one of the many books provided around the tower," she says. "Conjured currency, despite having virtually the same properties as actual currency, can be detected as fake. The founding magicians crafted inventions that can detect what is magic-made for the non-magicians to use, though any magician can determine what's real and what's fake on their own. Maia."

Maia jumps at being addressed. "Uh, yes?" she stammers.

"The staff you're holding, tell me how it feels."

Maia grips the staff tighter, feeling the familiar currents running through it echoing her will. That is just a natural property of the staff, though. She concentrates harder, her mind returning to what the tree's will in the Tower of Bel felt like. It was hard, firm, much like the staff she holds now, though the staff she is holding she wouldn't describe as having a will. Her eyes widen as she realizes the staff does, in fact, not have a will. It is will.

"I'm not sure how to describe it concisely," Maia says softly, placing one end of the staff on the floor to prop herself up. "But if I were to try, I'd say it's not real, though it's also not not real. It... just is."

"You really do have a way with words," Aveve says, beaming at her. The other students take it as sarcasm and begin to laugh to themselves. They cease when Aveve glares at them. "I know what you mean," she continues, looking back to Maia, "And I know that you know what the difference is. I challenge the rest of you to figure it out on your own."

The other students gape at Aveve, realizing that the new student, according to their tower's master, knew something they didn't about their own magic.

"Nice one," Mark murmurs, tapping her arm with his elbow. "Even I don't know what you mean."

"Now then, let's get the rest of this over with. Maia, you can go ahead and conjure two of something." Aveve waves her hand and the gold coins in Leslie's hand disappear. He lets out a shocked yelp then retreats to the side of the tower to stand with everyone else.

Why me? she thinks, slowly stepping towards Aveve. She doesn't want to earn the envy of everyone in the tower by showing she could do so much already in just a day. Before Maia can step to the center of the floor, the tower's door slams open and Darren walks in, his regal red cloak bouncing fervently with each step.

"Aveve," Darren says seriously, glancing around at the students lining the walls quickly. "I have to talk with you. Now." His eyes find Maia's and he nods at her almost imperceptibly before turning back to Aveve.

Aveve's face turns bitter. "Now? Ugh, can't this wait?"

"No. Please tell your students to wait on this floor." Darren waits for Aveve to do something, though the tower master simply folds her arms and, impressing everyone, pouts further. "It involves Master Kellen," Darren says with a sigh.

Aveve's face lights up instantly. "EVERYONE DOWNSTAIRS NOW!" she bellows, her voice echoing up the walls of the tower. She grabs Darren's arm and drags him up the steps, her pace only slightly deterred by his extra weight.

Maia tries to catch Darren's eye again, though he is too busy trying to stay on his feet. If something involving Kellen happened, she needs to know what it is. Spinning in place, she moves to the door fast and pushes it open.

"DOWNSTAIRS!" Aveve's voice bellows from above just in time to muffle the door slamming once more against the outer wall of the tower.

"Where are you going?" Mark asks, following her.

"I want to hear what they're going to talk about," Maia says, circling around the side of the tower to the spot they had been practicing magic earlier.

"We want to know too," Tricia and Lin say in unison, also having followed her.

"I don't think I can get us all up there," Maia says, eyeing the uppermost windows on the tower.

"You don't have to," Mark says, surprising her. "Just tell us once they're done."

Maia nods, then focuses on the substance of the tower. Thanks to Aveve's serendipitous—yes, that was the word she knew Greg had used to describe something lucky—lesson she isn't surprised by the tower being totally concentrated will. She places a hand on its stone and presses her fingers into it.

The stone recedes under her fingers, forming a shallow niche for her to grip. She puts her other hand further up the wall and makes another handhold with her will. Kicking a foot into the tower, a foothold forms around it, and she begins climbing.

"Elementalists are really resourceful," she hears Tricia murmur below.

Her thoughts wander to what Mark thinks and once again she is thankful she is wearing her close-fitted outfit and not a dress. The pace is slow, though it is much less draining than something Kellen might have done, like causing the ground to erupt into a tall pillar or just levitating himself up using the air.

Several moments later, she passes the second floor's windows, and soon after she is clinging to the wall just beside a window on the top floor. She tilts her head to look inside and quickly moves away when she sees Darren and Aveve standing directly on the opposite side of the wall where she clings.

Now she has to figure out how to actually hear them. She eyes the window, though knows moving it would cause too much noise.

Instead, she grips the wall with one hand hard while with the other she pinches her index finger and thumb around a space in the stone at her eye-level, as if she is drawing a straw. Pulling at the stone, a tube-like piece of the tower comes away, and she pushes her ear against the circular hole about the size of a dilated pupil.

"So what you're saying is this doesn't involve Master Kellen?" Aveve seethes.

Maia breathes out in relief. Thank Dunlon, I can hear them!

"It does!" Darren says. "Because we were right, Aveve. The Concilium were here under our noses, and they're working with James. Time is short, but thankfully we have someone else on our side."

"How do you know this?" Aveve asks, still angry. "And what about Kellen, why didn't you bring him?"

"He has… his reasons," Darren says. "The point is, we have to be prepared. Every tower has a risk of its students being their children. We don't know how many there are. But luckily, we have someone on our side."

There is a pause in which Maia gets worried they may have spotted the hole in the wall.

"Tell me already!" Aveve blusters, the sudden loudness causing Maia to recoil.

"I'm sure you've already heard the rumors about the king having a brother."

"What, you're telling me they're real?" Aveve laughs. "Wait, you've met him?" It's not a question but a statement. There's another short silence.

Aveve's voice returns. "You think some vagabond is help? Why does he matter?"

"Because," Darren says, "if James is corrupt, which I can now confirm he is, literally anyone else would be a better ruler."

"What can you confirm?"

"Long story short, I brought a rogue Elementalist to the capital. She escaped, but during her escape I caught one of James's advisors using Mind Control on a servant to kill her."

"What's the advisor's name?"

"Filento."

Another pause. Maia hears Aveve sigh, followed by, "That's not good. He's from Oala. That means at least one other nation is involved."

"It also means the Concilium are confident enough to be practicing their magic in front of others within the Magic Guild. Something big may be about to happen, but their overconfidence may be our opportunity to do something before it does."

"And that vagabond you mentioned before, you think he'll help?"

"I know he'll help."

"How?"

"When I ran into him while transporting your new student here, he mentioned heading for Telnas and... well, doing something heroic."

"How do you know he wasn't lying?"

"He was forthcoming about stealing one of these."

Maia wonders what he is referring to, then remembers Darren interrogating the person on the hill by the town with the strange tavern called The Bludgeoned Boar. Darren accused the man of stealing a cloak, the same type he wears.

"He stole one of the Magic Guild's cloaks?" Aveve asks. "There's no way he could've—wait, if this is true then did you arrest him?"

Darren lets out a breath, and there's the sound of shuffling footsteps, as if he is pacing. "I did try to arrest him, but he got away."

"How the hell did he get away? You're a Teleporter for crying out loud!"

The footsteps stop. "To be fair, I let him get away. He is... different. Unlike any magician I've ever seen. Unlike any magician ever seen."

"What does that mean?"

"I don't know. All I know is that when I tried to teleport him, it didn't work. My magic was totally useless on him. I didn't stick around to find out what else he could do."

Silence.

"Okay," Aveve says more quietly. "So a vagabond with some unknown type of magic that negates other magic who also allegedly happens to be the king's brother is heading for the palace to do 'something heroic' by himself. What do we do when he does?"

"What I proposed, and what Master Kellen agrees with, is dialyze the Magic Guild. We can't have another corrupt monarchy."

"Can we do it just by ourselves?"

"Maybe. Maybe. I don't know." Darren pauses. "We have to try, though."

"Well, I'm sorry to hear that." There's a light popping sound, and Darren utters a gasp of surprise.

"What are you doing!? Take this off me!"

Maia's aching muscles tighten. She couldn't be. Aveve couldn't be...

"I can't have you ruining our plan." Something thuds against a table. "Tell me, who else other than Kellen knows?"

Come on, Darren, what are you doing? Teleport! Maia realizes Aveve must have blinded him in some way.

"I—I don't know," Darren mumbles as if it's difficult to speak. Another thud.

"Are you lying?" Aveve's voice has become dangerously hushed.

"…yes," Darren replies. "But I won't tell you who."

Aveve breathes in loudly. "Well, that's good to know."

Maia pulls her head away from the wall, fearful of what is about to happen next. Instinctively, she punches the wall hard.

A massive chunk of the wall flies forward under her fist, connecting with the opposite end of the tower's inside. Maia peers in, and Aveve's surprised face rises to peer back. "Maia?"

Maia reels her right foot back and kicks in another bit of the wall. The piece of stone connects with Aveve's chest and she stumbles backward, losing her breath. "Darren!" Maia cries. "Are you all right?"

She tries to peel away more of the wall so she can squeeze inside, though Aveve is already holding her hands up.

Maia braces for something terrible to happen, but nothing does. She watches as Aveve doesn't move, her hands still raised. Maia sees it isn't an attack, but a surrender. "Darren, where are you?" Maia calls, pulling away enough of the wall to finally get in.

Darren rises from a table, pulling a blindfold from his head. "What are you doing here Maia?"

"She attacked you!" Maia says, raising a piece of the wall still in her hand above her head as if to throw it at a moment's notice if Aveve does anything.

"So you heard everything," Aveve says, laughing now. "I wish you'd brought her to me sooner, Darren, she's a treasure."

"Why are you laughing?" Darren asks.

"Because I had to know you weren't part of the Concilium trying to oust me," Aveve says.

"Blast it," Darren mutters, arching his back. "Did you really have to slam me into a table?"

"Wait, so you're not evil?" Maia asks, lowering her hand and dropping the stone on the floor.

"No one's just evil, Maia," Aveve says. "They just have different agendas. That's another lesson for you. Of course, it's also good to know you aren't part of the Concilium, since you came to Darren's aid."

"This is all so confusing," Maia says.

"Of course it is," Darren replies. "I'm a bit confused myself. But you're still very young and shouldn't be involved with any of this. It's already a disaster since you now know the name of a corrupt organization."

"I'll make sure she doesn't tell anybody," Aveve says.

Maia's eyes widen and she raises her hands in fists to fight.

"Hey," Aveve laughs, raising her hands again. "Remember. Not evil."

"You won't tell anybody, right?" Darren asks Maia, eyeing Aveve.

Sensing it to be in her best interest, Maia says, "I won't."

"Good."

Maia squints her eyes at him. "So I wasn't far off calling it the 'Magician' Guild."

Darren shakes his head and walks over to the hole in the tower's wall, gazing into the distance. "Make sure to continue practicing magic. You may need to use it soon." He looks over his shoulder at Aveve. "I suggest you get some practice, too. You just got outmatched by a young Elementalist."

Before Aveve can respond, Darren turns and disappears. Maia watches Aveve carefully.

"He didn't mean that last part in a bad way," Aveve says, smiling at her. "Elementalists really are some of the best when it comes to combat."

Maia looks back at the broken tower wall. "Sorry about your tower."

"Don't worry about that." Aveve waves her hand. The hole is instantly sealed with an identical wall. The remaining broken pieces on the floor and the opposite wall disappear. "Now, let's get back to that surprise exam, shall we?"

Chapter 25: **Not**

Despite my worry about escaping the palace, it had been much easier than I thought. All I had to do was flash a couple servants a devilish smile, and they let us back out through the front gates with no questions asked. During the hours-long trek through Telnas to the city's outskirts, in which I had reapplied my fake beard and found a large-brimmed hat to cover my conspicuously grey hair and eyes, Idrid disclosed that Filento was the one who orchestrated the murdering of her village. More evidence that fit my theory that James was being manipulated. The only confound was James's final moments. I'm sure he truly wanted to kill me, otherwise he wouldn't have attacked, but that didn't change the ever-increasing likelihood he was manipulated for some time. Was it while my parents were still around? I never had gotten a straight answer from James about my parents. Or perhaps age really was all it was. And then there were his last words that echoed in my mind…

Luckily by the time we reached the outskirts of Telnas, news already had gotten out that James was dead, which posed a much simpler dilemma to occupy my mind.

"And I'm sure everyone suspects you did it," Idrid remarks, flinging a flier about the beard shaving contest back onto the dirt road. Halette and Jean had won.

"That would make having to explain who I am less hard," I say, fingering my sword. We are beside a stable awaiting the owner to bring out a pair of horses to carry us across the country and out of Lanmar. I sit on the grass while Idrid paces back and forth.

"Did you say the thing before you killed him?" Idrid asks, stopping in front of me.

I frown, glancing up at her. "What?"

"You know. 'I have a sword.' That's the thing you say."

"Oh. The opportunity didn't present itself."

Idrid sighs before continuing to pace, though I know it's only to be dramatic. "That's a pity." Her face darkens and she stares at me.

"What?"

"Last night I met a man."

"Wait, I think I've heard this one!"

"Shut up." Idrid blushes but goes on and says, "He gave me his name. Tang."

I stop playing with my sword, my gaze unmoving from a spot on the ground.

"He said he wanted to kill you." My eyes slowly move and meet hers, though I stay quiet. She crosses her arms, huffs, then uncrosses her arms. "What are you thinking?"

"Well, I was going through words that rhyme with Tang and came up with fang, rang, and gang."

"Seriously."

"Did he say anything else?"

"He lives in a guardhouse on the border of Lanmar and Lynnor."

I hum in thought. "You know, I'd normally avoid threats of death—"

"No you wouldn't."

"My brother was an exception. But it's awfully kind of him to give me directions on where to go to get killed."

"Who is he?"

"He's a friend."

Idrid scoffs. "Why is it your family and friends want to kill you?"

"You don't want to kill me."

"Depends on the time of day."

A laugh escapes my lips and I sit back.

"Excuse me, sir, are you a swordsman?"

I find the source of the high-pitched voice quickly, lifting my head up and narrowing my gaze at a young boy resting on his stomach on the roof of the stable. Nonchalantly,

I look back at my sword and continue gliding my fingers across its flat surface. "Why? Because I have a sword?"

The boy doesn't answer, though I can feel his eyes still on me. Idrid continues pacing, pretending not to care.

"Do you call a man who rides a horse a horseman?" I ask, looking up at the kid.

"Yeah."

I shake my head. "No, I mean—what about a man who herds sheep, you don't call him a sheepman, do you?"

"They're called shepherds," the boy says.

"Look, the point is the man and the thing are separate entities. I wouldn't call myself a swordsman because it does a disservice to us both. I'd call me… a man… with a sword."

"Us?" the boy asks.

"My sword and me," I say quickly, putting it back in its sheath. "It's precious to me."

"You do have a strange attachment to it," Idrid murmurs, and I glare at her. "As well as a strange proclivity to randomly play with words."

"Here you are, travelers," the stablemaster says, returning with a pure brown and grey horse on either side of him. "Hanma and Idrid will carry you well on your journey."

"The horse's name is Idrid?" I say, gasping and trying to hide my glee.

347

"It's a name from the west," the man says. "A good, strong name for a female."

"Indeed," Idrid, the woman, says. "I'm riding Idrid."

"Where are you two off to?" the man asks as Idrid and I climb onto the horses' backs.

I look at Idrid. We both shrug. "South," I say. "I've a longing to visit the desert again."

"May your journey be safe," the man says with a nod, stepping away from the horses.

I wave to the boy still lying atop the stable and then the man, and we urge our horses forward and down our path. I feel the gemstone I still have in my sock pressing warmly against my foot. I begin calculating what its worth could be and what market would pay the most for it. Suddenly a man in familiar red appears on our path. I curse under my breath, reining in my horse. "You again?"

I can see Idrid stiffen beside me, though I focus on the Teleporter ahead.

"Where are you going?" Darren asks.

I look at Idrid. "South," I repeat. "I've a longing to visit the desert again."

"I thought you were heading to the palace," Darren says, walking closer so that he stands directly in front of my horse. Darren raises a hand and I half expect the horse to bite it, though my horse instead lowers his head and allows himself to be stroked.

"I did go to the palace, now I'm leaving."

Darren's face pales. "You've already been to the palace? That means…"

He didn't know. That is good. His reaction will be a good gauge for whether he is James's friend, James's enemy, or somehow otherwise involved in James's Mind Control. "Yes," I say, "I killed the king. Now no one's in power."

"Just like that?" Darren asks.

"Just like that. Are you here to apprehend me?"

"Stop talking like you did it yourself," Idrid mutters.

"No," Darren says slowly, then repeats, "No. Let me introduce myself again: I'm Darren, and as you probably know I'm part of the Magic Guild."

"Why weren't you in the palace, and why wasn't the rest of your little guild there too?" I ask him.

Darren's face pales further. "None of the Guild was there?"

"Well, there was one magician named Filento, though Idrid killed him," I say.

"Dunlon," Darren breathes, color returning to his skin. "You two are more capable than I originally thought. Who are you?"

Apparently the news of both James's and Filento's death is relieving which is a good sign, and yet a question remains: where, if with neither James nor Filento, does his loyalty lie? "You already know who I am," I say. "And this is my Giant."

Idrid growls, "I'm going to break your shins at the next inn."

"Giant?" Darren asks. "She's pretty normal looking."

"I like this magician," Idrid comments.

"Half-Giant," I amend.

Darren looks between us. "Why is she traveling with you?"

"Look, Darren, I don't mean to be rude, but we don't really know you and I'd rather not go over our life stories. Judging by your complexion, you probably have some work cut out for you back at the palace that you're not looking forward to." I glance over at Idrid and chuckle. "Haha. Cut."

"That's putting it mildly," Darren says softly. "You did say none of the Guild was there, right?"

"Yes."

"It's worse than I thought. You two should stay and help since there's bound to be an uprising."

"What if we refuse?" I ask.

Darren folds his arms. "Well, I know I can't stop you even if I tried. But I will appeal to your sense of duty, being of royal blood and all. And it also should be your responsibility to at least prevent something worse from happening."

I look at Idrid again, considering it.

"He has a point," she says.

"Ugh. Tell you what," I say before my guilt overcomes me to agree to something worse, "I go back and make an announcement. I don't know what it'll be since you're the one who is going to come up with the specifics," I pointedly tell Darren. "It'll be something along the lines of 'Your king is dead, and now there's a new ruler.' The people won't care who it is and will probably rejoice since they already hated James."

"You really don't want to rule?" Darren asks.

"Not one bit. After the announcement, I'm gone."

"Deal," Darren says, walking around to the side of my horse and offering a hand. I take it and give it a shake. His eyes move to look over my shoulder. "Your sword is strange," he says. "What kind of metal is it?"

"Pure," I say, noting that he hasn't let go of my hand.

"That's not a type of metal," Idrid comments.

I feel a light tingle, signifying Darren is trying to perform a teleport and fails. He smiles, letting go. "You both are strange, you and that sword. Anyway, since I can't move you myself I'll meet you at the palace."

He steps back and the next moment is gone.

"That guy referred to you and your sword as both, the same way you did not a few minutes earlier," Idrid says. "Now I'm intrigued."

"Maybe I'll tell you about it someday. But now we have to go break the news to the people that their king is officially dead." I pull on my horse's reins. It turns in place and begins pacing back toward Telnas.

"Oh, so now it's 'we.'"

I don't reply.

We trot in silence for a bit, waving casually at the stablemaster and his boy, who look back at us, confused that we're going the other way. "What happens if the people revolt?" Idrid asks finally.

I look at her and grin wickedly. "I have a sword."

Acknowledgements

This book would not exist without paper (or digital technology as the case may be).

Some people I want to thank: Rosemary Sease, for providing the cover art; Pat Oey, for many necessary edits; and Padfoot and Tessa, for being the bestest dogs that helped me through to the end of this project while my previous dogs could not.

I'd be remiss not to extend further thanks to readers for also existing. Without you, this book would not have been read.

About the Author

Torion holds a BA in psychology and creative writing, and an MS in psychology. He has written every year for National Novel Writing Month since 2014 and self-published the mystery novel *Loco Motive* on Amazon in 2019. Torion is an SFWA member and a Galaxy's Edge Mike Resnick Memorial Award finalist and he has had works featured in Expanded Field Journal, Terror House Magazine, and NonBinary Review.

CPSIA information can be obtained
at www.ICGtesting.com
Printed in the USA
LVHW040523141222
735196LV00009B/438